WEDDING BELLS

Ulterior motives turn into everlasting love for three couples who enter a Valentine's Day contest. Get lost in the glamour of ballroom events and experience the power of Valentine's Day with three novellas from Arabesque's most renowned authors in this unforgettable collection, where everyone is longing to say . . .

I DO!

I DO!

Pinnacle Books
Kensington Publishing Corp.

http://www.arabesquebooks.com

PINNACLE BOOKS are published by

Kensington Publishing Corp.
850 Third Avenue
New York, NY 10022

First Printing: February, 1998
10 9 8 7 6 5 4 3 2 1

Printed in the United States of America

CONTENTS

AFTER MIDNIGHT

Robyn Amos

Chapter One

"Tracy! Tracy, come on. Open up!"

The impatient shouts finally filtered through Tracy Fields flu-induced coma. Her eyelids creaked open, and she waited for the colorful blurs before her to shift into focus. The door rattled again. She fought to lift her head from the couch where she'd collapsed earlier that day . . . or week . . . or month. At this point, Tracy couldn't be sure.

She aimed her gaze at the door that shook with another round of forceful knocks. It looked so far away.

She would have felt better if someone hadn't mistaken her for an aspirin bottle and stuffed her head with cotton. She tried to suck in a deep breath and released a weak moan instead. Where had the elephant come from, and why was he standing on her chest?

The pounding grew louder.

"I'mb cumbing!" she shouted, but with her throat dry and sore, the sound was barely louder than a whisper.

Her legs nearly gave out twice, but Tracy managed to make it to the door. It took all her strength to pull it open.

"What took you so long?" John Fitzgerald strolled right past her, already shrugging out of his jacket. "I'm having a crisis here. I just got dropped."

"Valerie dropped you?" she croaked, collapsing against the door.

"Valerie? No. Actually, we broke up two months ago. I'm talking about the newspaper. Good. You still have it." John grabbed the remains of her three-day-old Sunday paper and sank down on the sofa, spreading it open. "They're dropping my column. This is the last edition of 'Consumer Watch' by John Fitzgerald."

Tracy felt herself slowly sliding to the floor, but she lacked the power to stop herself. "Dat's terrible, John."

"Hey, what's wrong with your voice?" He looked over his shoulder, really seeing her for the first time. "Oh, my God!"

She leaned her head back as she finally slumped to the floor in a sitting position. "I have a duffy dose. It cumbs with the flu. The sinus pressure and chest congestion was a bonus."

He tossed the newspaper aside. "Aw, honey, I'm sorry. I had no idea you were sick." He scooped her up into his arms. "And here I was going on about my problems."

Tracy let her head roll into the warm comfort of John's chest as he carried her to the couch. He'd been her best friend since they were eight years old. Of course, it had been three months since she'd seen him. But that's the way things were now that they were adults, struggling with their careers.

Nevertheless, whenever something came up, one showed up on the other's doorstep, and it was as though no time had passed between them. Good news or bad, they were always there for each other.

John eased her onto the sofa. "What are you taking?"

She pointed to the assortment of pharmaceuticals on the end table.

"What? No Fitzgerald miracle broth? I guess I'll have to make you some."

Two hours later, Tracy was sitting up, wrapped in a comforter John had pulled from her bed. She sipped the last of John's miracle broth and sighed. "It feels good to be able to breathe again. This stuff is wonderful."

"I told you." He took her empty bowl and tucked the blanket tighter around her shoulders.

"Thanks, John. I'm actually starting to feel better, but I hope you don't catch this from me."

Returning from the kitchen, he nudged aside the edge of her blanket and sat beside her. "Don't worry. I had my flu shot. I couldn't afford to be sick this year."

"Oh, John, your column. What happened?"

He pinched the bridge of his nose, shaking his head. "They're actually replacing 'Consumer Watch' with another one of those horoscopy advice columns. After three years, I'm losing my primary source of income."

"That's outrageous." Tracy poked a hand outside her cocoon to squeeze his shoulder. "When did you find out?"

"Yesterday afternoon." He widened his dark rum-colored eyes like a cocker spaniel. "Just before I found Shaq belly up in the fish tank. I couldn't even give him a decent flushing. Jordan and Rodman ate everything but his tail."

She shook her head, sharing his frustration. As much as John loved his pets, she knew losing a fish didn't compare to losing his column. "What are you going to do? Anything happening at Spotlight?" she asked, referring to the comedy club where he occasionally sold jokes to some of the comedians.

"No. Things are slow right now. Hopefully, my material will be hot again in a few months."

She made a sympathetic murmur. "And for a while, I was sure you would make your first million selling jokes. Remember how you used to treat us to pizza and movies with the money you made selling momma jokes in high school?"

"That's right." John snapped his fingers at the memory. "But you carried us through the summer selling hand-painted T-shirts and homemade comic books."

"Yeah. I painted your momma jokes on some of the T-shirts."

He put an arm around her bundled shoulders. "We had our own little enterprise going back then, didn't we?"

She smiled. "It beat the heck out of a lemonade stand."

He tucked his hands behind his head and stared up at the ceiling. "How come we can't make easy money like that anymore?"

"We can," Tracy said, grabbing a tissue just as she sneezed. "But remember, back then thirty-six dollars for a day's work was big money. Now it wouldn't put a dent in my car note."

"I know. I just feel like I'm wasting my time." He stretched his arms, trying to alleviate the tension Tracy could see knotting his shoulders. "I want to write what *I* want to write. My screenplay is a hundred pages from the end, but I just can't get through it because little things like heat, water, and food keep getting in the way."

Tracy burrowed deeper into the comforter. "You probably don't want to hear this, but my temp agency is always looking for people."

He twisted his lips into a smirk. "Yeah. I got your E-mail about that chili pepper suit."

"I know dressing up as a chili pepper for Pepper's Bar & Grill wasn't a high point in my career, but, most of the time they work really hard to give me jobs that let me exercise my creativity."

John gave her a knowing look. "And I'm sure that was your father's priority when he hooked you up with them."

"My father's priority was making sure his only daughter didn't make the phrase 'starving artist' literal." Tracy's father, who had always been militant on the issue of supporting Black-owned businesses, had been thrilled to connect her with a temp agency that had built its client base on that principle.

"Unfortunately, temping was supposed to *supplement* the income from my artwork, not substitute for it. In the past three months, I've spent more time grooming dogs, answering phones, and waiting tables than I've spent sketching."

John shoved a stack of folders aside so he could prop his feet on the coffee table. "Thanks for the offer, Trace, but I'm not that desperate yet. I have some freelance articles out that will hopefully turn into sales."

"It's really not that bad. My latest assignment is with a wedding coordinator. I was hired to help her prepare for a local bridal fair, but she asked me to help her with some marketing ideas, too. She's just starting out and she needs to attract clients. I think it will be fun."

John ran his hands over his face, shaking his head. "Yeah, but you just said yourself, you haven't been sketching. It's been at least three months since I've touched my screenplay. What are we really accomplishing? I'll probably have to dip into my L.A. fund again just to eat next month."

Tracy stared at the floor. John had been living on hot dogs and tuna fish for years, so he could afford to move to California and make contacts for his screenplay. It hurt him any time he had to borrow from his savings. She knew he'd taken out more money lately than he'd been putting in.

She sighed heavily. "John, we have this conversation at least once a month. We knew it wasn't going to be easy. Either we go out and get 'real' jobs, or we wait for our big shot."

He answered with a weary nod, and she decided to change the subject.

"So, what's this about you and Valerie breaking up two months ago?" She swatted him on the shoulder. "How come you didn't mention it?"

"Whoops." He grinned, giving her a sheepish look. "Really, it wasn't a big deal. It just didn't work out."

"Translation: she wanted more than you were willing to give her."

"Look, I tried to be honest with her right up front. I told her what my plans were. She kept dropping hints about our future together. Did I like kids? Would she like California? I couldn't take it."

He turned to her, searching with his eyes. "Trace, why do women insist on getting their hearts broken?"

Tracy bit her lip. Why indeed? She could have made a quip about John being too irresistible for his own good, but she knew he was serious. He didn't want to hurt anyone. Eventually, he was leaving. Period. He tried to be open about that, but some women couldn't help falling in love with him anyway.

"I know you don't want to get into anything serious because you're leaving, but it sounds like Valerie wanted to go with you."

"No, I need to do this on my own. I can't have someone tying me down, making demands on my time." He slumped against the back of the couch, playing with a corner of her comforter. "Besides, I can't think about a relationship right now. I have nothing to offer a woman except a bowl of grits and a tuna sandwich."

Tracy laughed.

John raised his brows, pinning her with a heavy look. "And what about you, Ms. Fields? What ever happened to Abubakar, Shaka Zulu, or whatever his name was?"

"His name is Shakir, and I stopped seeing him a long time ago. He was the one I met in that Egyptian art class last fall." She reached out to trace the colorful patterns on her comforter with her index finger. "He had no respect for my pencil drawings. He kept telling me that if I wanted to be a *serious* artist I should focus on painting."

He waved that off. "Nah, he sounds like a jerk. You're better off without him."

She nodded. "I think so, too."

Tracy looked over at John, slouched in his favorite position at the other end of the sofa, and a funny thought hit her. This was probably the first time in years that neither of them was in a relationship.

She winced, chiding herself for letting her thoughts flow in that direction. Maybe she was still running a fever or the congestion was building up in her head again.

She hated it when people would insist that a man and woman couldn't be friends without sexual attraction interfering. She always argued, holding up her relationship with John as an example. But if the truth were told, she'd have to admit . . . on more than one occasion there had been sparks.

"Maybe we should—oops!" John moved his foot on the coffee table, knocking over the manila folder that had been lying on top of the stack. "What's this? Ribbon-in-the-Sky Wedding Consultants?"

"Lisa, the wedding coordinator I told you about, sent that over for ideas. She needs a thebe or a gibbick to draw in dew clients."

He quirked his head. "What?"

Tracy reached for a tissue, then tried again. "She needs a theme or gimmick to draw in new clients."

"Oh." With a mischievous grin, John began flipping through the folder. "I'll give her some ideas."

"Oh, no." She pressed her fingers to her temple. She was going to need more Tylenol to get through this.

"Okay, for this one," he said, passing her the brochure for a honeymoon suite. "Tell her to give away a bottle of Pepto-Bismol with each honeymoon package."

Tracy giggled. The photos showed a room decorated in early Liberace, complete with a heart-shaped hot tub and a red velvet bed with gold cherubs frolicking on the headboard.

John continued picking out items and making silly comments as he flipped through the folder. "Oh, give me a break," he said pulling out a pink flier. "Did you know the Rainbow Room in New York was having a contest?"

"Really? My uncle took my family to the Rainbow Room to celebrate my parents' anniversary a few years ago. It was so beautiful, and it had the most incredible view of the city."

"Well, get this, they're sponsoring an essay contest. 'I've always dreamed of a wedding in the Rainbow Room because . . .' in a hundred words or less. The prize is a wedding and fifty thousand dollars in cash and prizes. Wedding rings, a honeymoon, etc." He dropped the folder back onto the table. "Why is it that all the easy contests always give away prizes I have no use for?"

"Well they—wait a minute, *easy*? What makes you think winning an essay contest is easy?"

He waved a hand. "Shoot. You remember when we were kids? I used to win essay contests all the time."

"Yeah," she said, wrapping the comforter around her more closely. "That's because back then they were impressed with any eight-year-olds who had the patience to string a few sentences together. They wanted to encourage you."

He sat forward. "Are you saying I only won those contests because I was a kid?"

"I won just as many art competitions at that age, and it doesn't mean a thing. In fact, you only entered that first contest because I won a prize for the giant sunflower I drew on the class mural. You hated watching me get all that attention."

He rolled his eyes, tucking a throw pillow under his head. "I can't believe you're back on that again."

"I'm just making a point. You made sure the plaques and medals on our shelves stayed equal because you couldn't stand to have it any other way. You entered contests to keep up with me, not because of any great desire to write."

"Give me a break." He shook his head and closed his eyes, pretending to nap.

"No, it's true. If I entered this Rainbow Room contest, you'd enter it just to prove you're a better writer than me."

"I am. I don't need to prove that." He sank into the sofa, shielding his face with a pillow, waiting for her to slug him.

She would have, but she couldn't untangle from the comforter quick enough. "Excuse me? I can write. I wrote all the text for those comic books I made. Sometimes I write poetry and short stories."

"Shoot." When she didn't attack, he tucked the pillow behind his head again. "I can draw a decent stick figure, too, but I don't go around trying to call that art."

Tracy knew he was baiting her, but she still couldn't resist it. "What are you trying to say? Are you saying I can't write?"

"I'm saying it's not your specialty. I'm the writer, you're the artist."

"See. That's your problem. You think just because you can't draw—"

"Come on. Admit it. If we both entered this contest, I would have the advantage."

"I don't think so. You may know all about grammar and punctuation, but I have soul and emotion. That's what really reaches people in contests like these." When he rolled his eyes comically, she said, "Okay, Mr. Fitzgerald. You don't believe me? Would you care to prove me wrong?"

"It would be my pleasure, Ms. Fields. What do you have in mind?"

She picked up the pink flier. "The contest. We both write essays. If you're so sure this is an easy win, then, you should have no problem."

"You're serious?"

She nodded.

"Okay . . . but if we're going to do this, why not do it

right? Writers' magazines are full of essay contests, I bet we could find one that—''

"No way. It's this contest or no contest. Neither of us wants a wedding at the Rainbow Room, and there's no added prestige to winning, so it's fair."

"Fine, but to write this thing, I'm actually going to have to pretend that I want to"—he shuddered in mock horror—"*marry* you."

She jerked the pillow from behind his head and bounced it off his crown like a Washington Redskin spiking a football. "Imagining a marriage to you doesn't exactly float my boat either, buddy."

He laughed, taking back the flier. "I don't know. I bet I could celebrate our divorce in style, fly to L.A. first class with this prize money."

"And I could celebrate on some exotic island resort with the free trip," she joked.

"Fair enough. We have a deal?" He held out his hand.

She clasped his large hand with her smaller one. "It's a deal."

Chapter Two

"I've always dreamed of a wedding in the Rainbow Room because . . ." Tracy added a flourish to the three-tier wedding cake she was drawing. "Because the prize money could pay off my mortgage and cover the down payment on a Jaguar."

She pulled her hair away from her face and began to draw in the cake's tiny bride and groom. "Because John Fitzgerald is an overconfident know-it-all, and I want to put him in his place."

The up-tempo Bob Marley song Lisa had pumping throughout the shop started getting to her. Tracy's pencil stroked over the pad on the down beat. "Because . . . because . . . we're jammin'," she sang. Lisa joined in, her ample hips swaying in her long brown knit dress as she carried in a box full of lacy white hearts and other odds and ends.

"I just love the island music, don't you?" Lisa asked in her throaty Jamaican accent. She put down the box to move along with the rhythm. She reached up to twirl the gold and blue silk scarf knotted around her neck. She'd used a similar scarf to hold back the large copper curls swirling down her back, which she tossed boldly.

Tracy looked down at her gray wool sweater and leggings, feeling as dull as the lead in her pencil next to the lively full-figured woman. She turned over her sketch. "I can definitely say this is my kind of work environment."

"Oh, you know I wouldn't be playing this music if business wasn't so slow. But since I don't have any customers, we may as well enjoy ourselves, eh?"

"I'm sure business will pick up soon."

Despite the reggae music, Lisa's warm little town house shop would be soothing to any jittery future bride. Several white overstuffed sofas accented with colorful pillows were arranged around the room and the wall covering was woven from a variety of pastel ribbons. Displayed around the room were various bridal mementos, from fluted crystal and ivory spiraling candles to pearl-encrusted veils and sample bouquets.

As a sketch artist, Tracy lived the phrase, "A picture is worth a thousand words," so naturally, the high-gloss poster-size photographs on the walls spoke volumes.

One showed a close-up of a woman's hand, delicately splayed as a large male hand slipped a glittering diamond on her finger.

Another showed the faces of a bride and groom poised inches apart after the minister announced them as man and wife.

But Tracy's favorite was the photograph of a child, no more than four, proudly offering a pink rose in full bloom to a smiling bride.

Tracy frowned down at the pencil in her hand. She'd think with all this inspiration, she could at least come up with one line to open her essay with. For a split second, she'd considered asking Lisa for suggestions, but she couldn't imagine explaining the situation without sounding crazy. It didn't even make sense to her.

How did she and John keep getting into these situations?

Once they got a bet rolling, they were both too stubborn to let it go. In high school, she let him goad her into selling candy bars to raise money for the school paper. They bet on who would get rid of their candy bars first. They each, rather than lose to the other, ate most of their stock in one night. They'd been sick for days, but even a chocolate-induced stupor hadn't taught them any lessons.

Here they were, at it again, and she wasn't any closer to starting her essay. "I've always dreamed of a wedding in the Rainbow Room because . . . I'm mentally unbalanced and prone to crazy impulses," she muttered.

"What is it, Tracy-girl? Are you talking to yourself?"

She smiled into Lisa's round, cherubic face. "Don't mind me. It's a bad habit."

"Okay, just don't be going crazy on me now. I'm counting on you." She shifted the box to the floor and sat across from Tracy at the dining table.

"Don't worry, I'm not there yet."

"Well, the bridal fair is coming up. I'm running the fashion show, but I want something special for my booth. Something to set me apart from all the other wedding planners there. Valentine's Day is next month. Couples will be getting engaged and planning Valentine's Day weddings for 1999."

"The fair isn't for two more weeks. You'll come up with something."

Lisa flipped over Tracy's sketch. "You're quite an artist."

"Sorry." Tracy flipped it back over. "Another bad habit."

"Don't be silly. I need your creativity. Did that folder I sent over give you any ideas?"

It had given her ideas all right, but nothing that was going to help Lisa. "It sparked a few things, but nothing I'm ready to discuss yet." She glanced down at her watch. "I'm meeting a friend for lunch in a few minutes. I think better on a full stomach."

Lisa stood to walk her to the door. She laid a hand over

her hip. "If that were true for me, I'd be a millionaire by now."

Tracy pulled on her winter coat and stepped outside, hoping the crisp air would clear her mind. It had been three days since she and John had come up with this crazy plan, and she hadn't written a word. January twenty-third was two weeks away.

With a defeated sigh, she reached for the door handle of the fifties-style diner Lisa had recommended. "I've always dreamed of a wedding in the Rainbow Room because . . . if I don't beat John at his own game, I'll never hear the end of it."

John whistled as he entered the diner, late as usual. He saw Tracy in a booth in the corner, her head bent as her pencil skimmed across her pad.

He strolled over and slid across pale blue vinyl. "Hey, Trace."

She didn't glance up from her sketch pad. "John, late as usual."

"What can I say?" He smoothed his fingers over the fake inscriptions etched in the table. Joey loves Donna, heart and arrow. "I was job hunting."

"Any luck?" Her voice was flat as she focused on her drawing.

His feelings weren't hurt. She'd once told him that if he could show up any time he felt like it, then she could take her time acknowledging his presence.

"Actually, I stumbled across something very interesting. Possibly a new career."

She looked up briefly. "Really? Doing what?"

"I don't want to talk about it until I've checked out all the angles."

She shrugged. "Okay."

He looked around, taking in the tacky peach and blue decor, completed with wall-to-wall forty-five-inch records and a tiny stage with a huge jukebox in the background. "This is an interesting place."

"Lisa said the food is wonderful. She likes to come here for karaoke on the weekends."

John stared at the crown of Tracy's head, then shifted his gaze to her hands as she worked on a sketch of the waitress behind the counter. She had such tiny hands. Short, square-cut nails. No polish.

Same as always. Everything about Trace was familiar . . . yet new. He recognized her short, pert bob, similar to the style she wore in high school, but when had she gotten those cherry highlights that made it shine like polished wood?

Her lips were pressed tightly together. He knew that expression. She wore it whenever she tried to perfect a specific detail in a drawing, but when had she started wearing lipstick? It made her lips look soft and moist. . . .

John reached across the table for a menu, trying to concentrate on the lunch specials, but he found his gaze rising over the stiff plastic until he was focused on Tracy again.

She flicked her gaze at him impishly, before looking back to her pad. He knew those light caramel-colored eyes, but when . . .

John shook his head. When was he going to get a grip? Up until high school, he'd had no trouble seeing Tracy as just one of the guys. Toward the end, he'd become all too aware that she wasn't. After that revelation, he'd done his best not to treat her differently, but he'd never really mastered that act in his head.

He blinked. Why were his thoughts going in this direction? When he wrote, he submerged himself in his work, and the mood often carried over into real life. Knowing he'd be meeting Tracy, he'd sat down this morning to knock off his contest entry. Wait till she saw how soulful and emotional he could be. Tapping into all that sentiment must have put him in this weird mood.

Tracy used her fingers to smudge shadows into the waitress's frizzy red bouffant, before leaning back. Her drawing was complete.

"Let me see." He slid the sketch across the table. "Very nice. You put a lot of time into this one."

She winked at him. "Well, not only did I *have* a lot of time, but the way things are going lately, I may have to go back to leaving sketches instead of tips."

John laughed. He and Tracy had gone to different colleges, but whenever they'd gotten together over a break, both had had just enough money to pay for their meals. In those days, there were a lot of waitresses receiving sketches and poetry instead of tips.

"What's wrong? I thought you had that huge commission for a mural at Buchman's Coffee Shop."

"While I was laid-up with the flu, I missed a crucial deadline. They took back their commission. Looks like I'm a full-time temp for a while." She cocked her head. "*Is* there such a thing?"

The waitress Tracy had drawn came to the table. She cracked her gum. "Hey, folks, I'm Patty, your waitress this afternoon."

John put down his menu. "I'll have a roast beef French dip sandwich, extra fries."

Tracy ordered her usual. "Let's see, I'd like the dinner-size chef salad, no tomatoes, carrots, or dressing. And, uh, let me have a turkey sandwich on the side, whole wheat lightly toasted, no mayonnaise." She closed her menu and handed it to the waitress.

Patty scribbled furiously and John grinned. Tracy was the fussiest eater he'd ever known. She always picked the pepperoni off her pizza but she refused to order plain cheese.

While they waited for their food, John brought up the subject he knew Tracy was avoiding. "Okay, hand it over."

"Hand what over?" Her carefully blank expression told him she knew exactly what he meant.

"Your essay. Hand it over. You may as well get the humiliation over with now."

"I'm not finished yet." Her brow wrinkled. "Are you?"

He pulled his notebook out of his jacket pocket. "Of course. We've had three days."

She widened her caramel eyes and blinked like Bambi. "But, I've been sick."

He grinned. "You've always been sick, so what does that have to do with your essay?"

"Fine, let's hear what you whipped up in three days, smarty-pants."

"Are you sure? Once you hear what great work I've done, you may not want to finish yours."

"Give me a break. Just read."

He flipped over the cardboard cover of his notebook. He'd really outdone himself this time. "I've always dreamed of a wedding in the Rainbow Room because of the words of my Grandmother Fitzgerald. She raised my brother and me on a small farm in Virginia, and she taught us—"

"Hold it right there. That's just out and out lying. You and Joe never set foot on a Virginia farm. You're from California, for goodness sake!"

"It's called creative writing."

She crossed her arms over her chest, staring at the ceiling. "It's ridiculous."

"Shh. I'm not finished." He couldn't wait for her to hear the part about adopting children with his new bride. Contest judges ate that stuff up.

John read his essay proudly and when he was done, he looked up, anxious to see her reaction.

Her face was solemn. A strangled noise erupted from her lips and, for one crazy moment, he thought he may have moved her to tears. Instead she threw back her head and cackled so loudly he longed to stuff his napkin in her mouth.

She finally calmed down enough to face him. "I should have known you weren't going to take this seriously."

"What are you talking about?"

"That was a joke, wasn't it?"

"Of course not. You can't tell me it isn't well written."

"Maybe I can't, but I *can* tell you it stinks. Do you honestly expect them to buy that junk about your dying grandmother's last wish? How trite can you be?"

"How can you say that? It was full of emotion."

"Yeah, it was full of something, all right. Look, John, you're a great writer, but when it comes to sincerity, believability, and integrity . . ." She pinched her nose.

"Wait a minute. Let me see what you came up with. You said you weren't even finished."

Her expression changed. "Well, I just have a few notes." She tore a sheet of paper off her pad, but held it so he couldn't see it.

"Let me see that." He pulled the page out of her hand. Instead of notes, he saw three panels of drawings. A rough sketch of the Rainbow Room. A half-finished wedding dress. And a faceless bride and groom standing atop a wedding cake.

"I thought you said these were notes."

She snatched the sheet back. "They are." When he gave her a skeptical look, she added, "Well . . . I think in pictures."

He threw his head back and laughed. "I'm sorry, but in this case, a picture is *not* worth a thousand words. Not even a hundred."

She folded her arms over her chest. "Leave me alone. I'm still in the planning stages."

"Yeah, at the rate you're going, I won't have to compete with you. By the time the deadline rolls around, you'll be lucky to have formed a complete sentence."

"You just threw yours together. How long did it take you, an hour?"

He looked down at his hands.

"Come on, when did you do this?"

He released an embarrassed laugh. "Okay, you got me. It took me forty-five minutes this morning."

She slapped the table. "See. I knew it."

Before they could continue Patty brought their meals. John reached for his sandwich and took a large bite. He'd finished most of the first half, before he noticed that Tracy had barely touched her food.

"What's wrong?"

She stopped pushing around her lettuce and dropped her fork. "While I was working in the shop today, I realized something. Even when I was surrounded by wedding memorabilia, I couldn't get inspired. I can't relate to it. It's not personal enough. So, I think you ought to . . . propose to me." She said the last three words so quickly they ran together.

John felt an onion lodge in his throat. He dropped the remainder of his sandwich, trying not to choke to death. "What did you say?"

Suddenly her appetite had picked up. She couldn't answer him because she was too busy eating her sandwich, drinking her lemonade, wiping her mouth. She loaded her fork with salad before she said, "You should propose to me."

John rolled his eyes. Why wasn't he used to her quirky ways by now? She was always getting him into these crazy situations. To this day, he couldn't stand chocolate, and it was all her fault.

"Why do you want me to propose?"

"Because . . . I'm not as good a liar as you are. I need motivation."

He sighed. "I still don't see what good it would do."

"The idea behind this contest is for people who are presumably already engaged to explain why they should have their wedding in the Rainbow Room. I'm not engaged. I've never been engaged. I'm nowhere near having someone propose to me. I think if I know what it feels like, it would help."

A wicked idea began to form in John's head. Tracy deserved to know exactly what it would feel like.

"Okay, you asked for it, you got it."

Tracy jerked to attention when he got up. "Where are you going?"

He just grinned. "You'll see."

John walked up to the counter, and after explaining his situation to Patty, she walked him over to the stage in front of the jukebox and set up the microphone.

"Good luck," she whispered with a giggle then flipped the switch on the karaoke machine.

Gripping the mike, John took a deep breath. "Good afternoon, ladies and gentlemen. Today is a special day for me and my girlfriend, and I'd like to share it with all of you."

He watched Tracy's eyes go wide, then she dropped her head to the table. *Oh, Tracy dear, the torture is just beginning.*

"Tracy Fields, will you please stand up." Her forehead remained hermetically sealed to the Formica table. "Let's give her some encouragement, folks. Join me. Tra-cy! Tra-cy!"

Finally, she surged to her feet, and he knew it was just to quiet the riotous cheers he'd incited. John grinned at his mischief-making. This was more than he'd hoped for from a lunch crowd.

He drew his index finger across his neck to halt the noise. "Thanks, everyone. This beautiful woman you see before you is the love of my life, and I'm standing here because I want to ask her to marry me."

Applause erupted from the audience. Someone shouted, "Get down on one knee!"

Not wanting to disappoint, John lowered himself to one knee. "What do you say, Tracy?"

She just stood there with her mouth slightly parted as though she couldn't believe this was happening to her.

"I think she needs some inspiration. Maybe some music will motivate her." He nodded toward the waitress, and the Temptations's "My Girl" began to play.

"I've got sunshine, on a cloudy day . . ." John sang at the top of his voice, watching Tracy with every note. Her hands were covering her face, and she shook her head, peeking at him through her fingers.

He hit the last note and the audience gave him a standing ovation. "Tracy, will you marry me?"

She nodded.

"I can't hear you."

He saw her lips move.

He cupped his hand to his ear. "What?"

"Yes! Yes! Okay? Yes!"

As they left the diner later, Tracy's face was still glowing with embarrassment. "We'll never be able to eat here again."

John chuckled. "Hey, look on the bright side, at least we got a free meal out of it."

Chapter Three

Tracy felt like breaking her pencil in half. She'd been trying to make herself write this stupid essay for over an hour.

Her mind kept wandering back to John's little farce at the diner. She couldn't believe he'd done that to her.

A smile crept across her lips. She'd deliberately put him on the spot, and he'd turned the tables on her. Tracy laughed out loud. She should have known John wouldn't let her off easy.

For all her embarrassment and protests it had actually been kind of fun. After John's spectacle aka proposal, well-wishers had stopped by their table. They were full of such genuine joy for the two of them that Tracy almost wished the whole thing weren't pretend.

Almost. The fantasy needed a few adjustments before she could step into it. First she had to find the right man and right now, she had an essay to write.

What would her perfect wedding be like? She could hear the music. See her dress. She picked up her pencil to write and found herself sketching. It was almost therapeutic to hear the lead scratching against the tablet. Writing didn't come naturally, but watching images flow from her pencil tip did.

Then, suddenly, the image shifted. Instead of a lace hem, the border came out smooth. Instead of billowing skirts, the line was straight. In her minds eye, her dress was blue taffeta instead of white satin. The music was Luther Vandross instead of soft violins. She was no longer in the Rainbow Room . . . now she was at *the prom*.

Tracy swallowed hard, trying to push away the memories, but the floodgates were open. She was wading knee-deep in nostalgia. Unable to help herself, she got up from the sofa and went into her bedroom. She pulled one of her mother's old hat boxes down from her closet shelf. If anyone asked, she'd deny it, but she had every keepsake from her night at the prom. That had been the most perfect night of her life.

Feeling like Pandora, she lifted the lid on the box, freeing the spirit of prom ten years past. She pulled out a long silver prom ticket, the thin white ribbon from her corsage, a tasseled program, a souvenir glass in the shape of a slipper, and a picture in a cardboard frame.

Setting the rest aside, Tracy studied the photograph. She remembered feeling like Cinderella in her blue taffeta gown, and John had looked more like Prince Charming than she could have imagined.

She would never forget that night. She was supposed to go to the dance with Kevin Miles, but he'd had to cancel at the last minute because he broke his ankle playing basketball that afternoon. Not to worry, he'd told her over the phone from the pay phone in the emergency room, he'd lined up a replacement. John.

Tracy had rolled her eyes, partly out of frustration and partly to hold back her tears. How much fun could she have with a guy who never liked dances and preferred watching the fight on Pay Per View with his father.

She hung up the phone, knowing she was on the verge

of hysteria. She paced the living room unable to believe what was happening to her. Tracy couldn't miss her senior prom, but the thought of John showing up at the door wearing his "I'd rather be watching Tyson" attitude, could be worse than not going at all.

Her mother had pinned up her hair, leaving a few curls around her neck and ears. Her blue strapless sheath floated around her ankles, making her feel sophisticated, and she'd finally mastered walking in high heels.

For once in her life, Tracy truly felt beautiful, and now no one would know. All the time she'd spent getting ready had been wasted. No one would ever see her.

She'd been on the brink of tears when the doorbell rang. She wanted to run up to her room so she wouldn't have to face John, but her mother insisted she answer the door.

Taking a deep breath, Tracy prepared herself for the worst. John in a neon tie and tails? John in Chuck Taylor's and a tuxedo T-shirt? She pulled open the door, and her lips parted in shock. He wore a traditional tuxedo and held a corsage of white rosebuds. His dark curls were freshly cut. She looked down at his shoes. Shiny black wingtips.

"John?"

"Your fairy godmother told me you need a date for the prom. So here I am."

They indulged her parents by posing for the obligatory pre-prom snapshots, then he took her arm and led her to the car. John's father let him borrow his sports car. Tracy felt unusually shy sitting across from him in the tiny car. John looked like a completely different person. She glimpsed her upswept hair and shining eyes in the side mirror and didn't recognize herself either.

The prom theme that year was *After Midnight.* The prom committee mixed up their dates with the hotel, so they could only have the ballroom until eleven forty-five. Come midnight, they all had to be out of there. It became Cinderella's ball with pumpkins, coaches, and a huge clock with the hands turned to midnight for decorations.

Once inside the dance, the awkwardness between them continued. She saw some of his friends waving to him from across the room. "I don't want you to feel like you're chained to my side all evening."

He took her hand, leaning close to her ear. "This is your night," he whispered, "and I'm not leaving you for a second."

And he didn't. She'd had no idea he could be such a gentleman and she wasn't sure how to react. He posed for pictures with her, brought her drinks from the punch bowl, and danced with her whenever she wanted.

When the DJ played the first slow song, "Any Love," by Luther Vandross, John reached for her hand. "May I?"

He led her onto the floor and took her into his arms. Tracy's world was never the same again. She rested her head on his shoulder, taking in the smell of his aftershave. He rocked with her slowly, but Tracy had begun to feel dizzy from the overwhelming new emotions swirling inside her. She felt lighter than the balloons suspended from each table.

When the dance was over, they walked out to the parking lot together. They'd already made arrangements to meet several friends at the after-prom breakfast, but John hadn't been in any hurry to leave.

As he unlocked her car door, Tracy wanted to make sure he understood just how much that night meant to her.

"John, I know you never really wanted to come to the prom, and that's why I want to thank—"

He stopped her with a finger on her lips. "You don't have to thank me. Did you really think I'd let anything spoil this night for you?" He winked at her. "Did you think I'd pass up the opportunity to see you in this dress?"

She laughed, reaching out to touch his boutonniere.

"In case I haven't mentioned it, you look pretty sharp yourself."

He tugged on his lapels and posed for her. "Thanks."

She reached up to hug him as she'd done so many times before, but somewhere along the line things had changed.

He held her close, and she could feel his hands on her hips. His touch burned through the fabric of her dress. She was hit again with that swirly feeling she'd had while they were dancing. She pulled back from the hug, letting her arms slide down from his neck, but his hands only loosened on her waist.

She raised her gaze to his and their eyes locked. She knew what was going to happen next. Somewhere in the distance, she heard the hotel's clock tower striking twelve. His lips touched hers and then stilled, drawing out the softness of the contact. Then his lips began to move, brushing, parting over hers.

Instinctively, she opened her mouth and she felt his tongue gently stroke her upper lip. He pulled back.

"Tonight was my pleasure," he'd whispered.

What had followed, still made Tracy's heart ache when she thought about it. She closed the hatbox lid on those memories. Freezing a perfect moment, just as she wanted to remember it.

John slipped past her and headed straight for the kitchen, when Tracy opened the door for him that evening. He could feel her eyes boring into his back.

"John, what are you doing here?"

He returned with a bag of Tracy's weird baked potato chips. "My brother's home from Morgan State this weekend."

She still stood at the door with her hands on her hips. "So, I repeat, what are you doing here?"

He crunched on a chip before he answered her. "He

actually gave me fifty bucks to let him have the apartment tonight. I'm so broke, I took him up on it."

"So you plan to crash on my sofa?"

He gave her his famous cocker-spaniel eyes. "Please? I'll cook dinner for you."

Tracy cocked her head. "That's just your way of getting a free meal out of me, too."

He grinned, propping his feet on her coffee table. "Whatever works."

She sank down on the couch and snatched the bag of chips from him, burying her hand in the bag. "What if I don't want a roommate tonight? How do you know I don't have plans?"

John felt his spine straighten. It had never occurred to him that she might have a date, or be expecting company. "Do you?" he asked carefully.

She crunched on a chip, then smiled. "No." She handed him back the bag of chips. "So what's for dinner, roomie?"

He folded up the bag and started toward the kitchen. "Depends on what you've got."

"I went grocery shopping this morning. Make me something good."

While making dinner, another wicked idea struck John. He'd enjoyed getting a rise out of Tracy at the diner. And she was always a good sport. He decided to push her buttons a little more.

He came out of the kitchen an hour later with two plates of beef stroganoff.

"Mmm, this smells incredible," she murmured. She curled up on the sofa with the plate on her lap, and he sat across from her in the comfortable old easy chair his parents had given her.

He didn't eat, waiting for her to butter her biscuit. He watched her dip her knife in the low-fat margarine and part the fluffy buttermilk halves.

She squinted into her biscuit. "What's this?" She poked her finger inside.

He couldn't suppress his laughter. "It occurred to me that I didn't give you a ring when I proposed in the diner."

She pulled out the homemade ring fashioned of twisty garbage ties on the tip of her finger. "Oh, darling, you shouldn't have." She held it out to admire it as though it were flawless diamonds and fourteen-karat gold instead of white plastic and twisted wire. "Please do the honors."

He moved across the room to help her put it on. With little effort, he molded it around her ring finger.

She clutched her hand to her chest. "I'll cherish it always!"

John sat back down. He took a bite of his food and chewed somewhat absently. Tracy was wearing a large purple sweatshirt, baggy green boxers, and thick white socks. Her legs were curled under her, giving him a perfect view of one long slim honey-brown leg.

Tracy couldn't stand to be cold so she usually kept the thermostat jacked up to near eighty degrees, then ran around her apartment in shorts in the middle of winter.

"John?" She snapped her fingers. "What are you staring at?"

He blinked. "Oh, uh. Nothing. I was just thinking."

What was wrong with him? This was the second time he'd caught himself *noticing* Tracy. He knew better than to allow himself to think of her as a woman. He'd learned that lesson ten years ago. He watched her lick her lips before she praised his cooking skills again. Apparently he hadn't learned it well enough.

His eyes strayed back to her legs. He probably never would.

She took her plate into the kitchen and returned a minute later. "I can't believe it. I actually finished eating before you? What's wrong?"

He stared down at his plate, still half full. "I had a lot of junk before I came over here," he lied. He got up and took his plate into the kitchen. When he returned, Tracy was curled up on the couch again.

Lord! Why didn't she have the decency to put on some long pants?

"So what do you want to do tonight? I'm surprised you decided to spend the night over here. I don't have cable, and you're always raving about Carter's big-screen TV. Did he have plans, or what?"

John frowned. Why *had* he come over here? He hadn't even checked with Carter or any of his other buddies. For three months, his only contact with Tracy had been E-mail and the occasional phone call. Now, suddenly, she was the first person on his mind?

"Or what." He decided to change the subject before she could question what that meant. "So, did you finish your essay?"

She froze in the middle of a stretch. Her arms were arced over her head, her back was bowed, and her eyes darted around like those googly-eyed stickers she used to collect as a kid.

"I take that to mean no."

Tracy relaxed into her normal position. "We've still got a week left. Stop rushing me. True genius takes time."

He slumped in his chair. "Translation": he said, stealing her favorite phrase, "you don't have zippity-doo-da."

Her fingers instinctively reached for her sketch pad, or her security blanket, as he liked to call it.

"That's not true. I'm working on it."

"Oh yeah? Let me see." In an instant he was across the room, slipping the pad out of her grasp.

"Hey!" She fell, head first, off the sofa, trying to get it back from him. She gently somersaulted onto her back. "Wait. Don't—"

He threw his ankle over his knee and opened the pad. Most of the drawings he'd seen before. The Rainbow Room sketch. The wedding cake. He skipped past those to the newest drawing.

The moisture evaporated from his mouth. This wasn't a wedding sketch. It was a collage of memories. A clock tower with the hands frozen at midnight. A cluster of rose-buds. A couple dancing.

He looked closely at the two figures dominating the page. She'd drawn them in silhouette, but he knew instinctively who they were.

John swallowed. This wasn't an old sketch. It hadn't been in the book when he looked at it a few days ago. Why had she been thinking about their prom date? He felt his throat constrict. He worked very hard at not thinking about that night. Had it meant more to Tracy than he'd thought?

He raised his eyes to hers, searching for the answer. Her expression was unreadable.

Finally, she walked over and lifted the pad from his lap. He didn't try to stop her and neither of them spoke as she closed it and returned to the sofa.

"My mom and dad called from the Wisp, that ski resort in western Maryland. They told me to tell you hello."

"Really. Tell them the same from me." John took the hint. The topic wasn't open for discussion. Nevertheless, seeing those sketches raised a lot of questions in his mind.

They sat up talking for a while before they decided to go to sleep. Tracy pulled out the sofa bed and tossed John some extra blankets. "If you get cold during the night, I keep the blankets in the hall closet outside my bedroom."

He settled down in the covers and she pulled the blankets up to his chin, pretending to tuck him in. "Good night, John."

She leaned down to kiss him on the forehead, and her hair fell forward, grazing his cheek. He could smell her light flowery scent. When had she started wearing perfume?

Her lips brushed his head, soft and cool. He wondered what she would do if he reached up, grabbed her around the waist, and pinned her beneath him?

He was afraid he already knew the answer to that one, because he was the one who taught her how to handle nasty little boys who got too fresh.

"See you in the morning," she said, turning out the light and heading for her bedroom.

He could hear her moving around inside and his mind kept teasing him with images of her getting undressed. He had no idea what she wore to bed. Maybe she didn't wear anything.

John groaned and rolled over onto his stomach. Why was he torturing himself like this? Tracy was his *best* friend. His pal. His buddy.

A guy didn't have thoughts like this about his buddies. Right?

Chapter Four

Tracy woke up the next morning, craving a cup of coffee, but before she could even think about rolling out of bed to get some, she heard a tap at her door. "Come in."

John poked his head inside. "I forgot my toothpaste, Trace. You have some I can borrow?"

"Sure, sure." Sighing, she slipped out of bed and dashed into the bathroom, hopping around as her bare feet touched the cold tiles. She grabbed her tube of toothpaste. "Do you need mouthwash, too," she called.

"Yeah, thanks."

She was ready to take John his morning supplies, when she caught the rear view of her skimpy T-shirt in the mirror. It barely skimmed the tops of her thighs. She glanced around for a robe and didn't see one. Oh well, it was only John, she assured herself.

She walked back into her bedroom, but was unprepared for "only John" wearing only a pair of jeans. His muscular torso stopped her in her tracks. "Uh, spearmint mouthwash okay?"

He reached for the toothpaste, bringing her back to earth. "Is there any other kind?"

He started down the hall and she trotted after him. "Let me make sure I left enough towels in that bathroom."

While she set out fresh towels, John pulled out his toothbrush. "Aw, man, this is paste. Don't you have gel?"

She frowned at him. "You're kidding, right?"

He shook his head. "No. I like gel."

"Too bad, buddy. That's all I've got." She reached out to take it back. "If you don't want it—"

"No, I'll use it." He pulled the open tube away from her, accidentally squirting a big dollop of toothpaste onto his bare stomach. "Look what you made me do."

She giggled. "I didn't make you do that." She picked up the toothbrush. "But don't worry. It's still good." She got most of the paste back on the brush, but she also spread it around on his stomach.

He gave her a withering look. "You expect me to use that now? After you rubbed it all over me?"

She bit her lip. "That's a good point. We don't know where your stomach has been."

"That's it." He scraped the toothpaste from his navel and wiped it off on her T-shirt. "There. How do you like that?"

She looked down at her shirt and then back at John. "That was completely unnecessary." She picked up the toothpaste and started to squirt it at him.

He slipped behind her and his arms came around each side grabbing the tube of toothpaste from her. She bent at the waist, trying to get it back. The two of them ended up squirting it on the floor.

"No, no. You can't have it." She giggled.

He laughed, hoisting her off the floor. "Let go of your weapon."

When her feet left the ground, she wrapped her ankles around his jean-clad legs for support. They both laughed, and she dropped the toothpaste. During the tussle the back of her T-shirt had ridden up, allowing her pink panties to press squarely into his pelvis. She could feel his bare muscled chest rubbing over her back.

"No, oh!" she squealed, doubling over more.

They both had toothpaste on their hands. "Now I'm going to tickle you, but don't worry, at least you'll be minty fresh."

Tracy gasped as his fingers started wiggling over her skin. She lost her grip on her shirt and John's hand slipped under it.

His hand stilled on the curve of her bare stomach.

She sucked in her breath and held it. He was leaning over her, still supporting most of her weight on his other arm and her head was cocked to the side. Her short bob had fallen into her face, and when she tossed her head back, they were eye to eye.

For a moment neither of them moved.

Then she felt him slowly lowering her back down. When her feet hit the floor, she pulled down the T-shirt, backing up.

She jerked her thumb toward her bedroom. "I'm . . . going to go . . . change." Why did she sound like she'd been running a marathon?

He nodded, and she tried not to stare at his heaving chest.

"After I clean up in here, I'll . . . find us some breakfast."

Once she was safely behind her closed door, Tracy sank down on the edge of her bed. Her face was stinging with heat.

"Whew!" She shook her head to clear it.

She and John had wrestled dozens of times when they were kids. She'd just learned that it was a completely different sport as adults.

Her body still felt warm from where she'd rubbed against him. Clearly, it had been too long since she'd let herself get close to a man. John shouldn't be affecting her like this.

She'd gotten too caught up in her nostalgia from the prom. That's where this had come from.

John never had any problems attracting the ladies, so she was sure his old buddy Trace couldn't stir him up. He would probably be very uncomfortable if he knew just how breathless he'd made her. How her nipples tightened and her skin burned from his hands moving on her.

Tracy pulled a pair of jeans and a sweatshirt out of her closet. She'd get herself together and act like nothing happened.

Nothing *had* happened.

Besides, they'd been in this situation once before, and the last thing she wanted was to make John uncomfortable.

John was uncomfortable. He'd had to set Tracy away from him before she realized just how uncomfortable his jeans had become.

He'd thrown on a shirt and was trying to concentrate on scrambling eggs, but he was still remembering her legs wrapped around his and her little derriere pressed up against—

Damn! He jerked open the toaster oven and dumped two pieces of scorched bread in the garbage. That was the second time he'd burned the toast.

He was just setting two full plates of eggs, bacon, and toast on the coffee table when Tracy came out of the bedroom. She'd covered herself from head to foot in a turtleneck, a baggy sweatshirt and faded jeans. At least she'd covered her legs.

"Breakfast is ready."

She sat down in front of her plate. "Mmm, that smells great. I could get used to this. You're welcome to cook for me any time."

He started to reply when he noticed the wrapped gift she'd dropped on the end table. "Oh, you shouldn't have. What did you get me?"

She scooped up a forkful of eggs. "Nothing. That's for Carter. His surprise party is tonight."

John slapped his forehead with his palm. "That's right. I forgot all about it."

She put down her fork. "Here." She got up and crossed to the counter. "I didn't sign his card yet. We can just say the gift is from both of us. You can pay me back later."

She flattened out the card in front of him, signing her name with a graceful flourish, then she handed him the pen. He scrawled his name under hers.

One gift. From both of them. Like a couple.

Carter and all their friends knew he and Tracy were close. No one would think anything of it. But it still felt strange. Different somehow. He knew it was because his mind had taken a crazy track lately. Going places where it had no business.

"Shelly told us all to get there at seven thirty sharp. Do you want to go together?"

John shook his head. Showing up together with one gift from the two of them . . . it was more than he could handle at the moment. He had to put some distance between him and Tracy before he put his crazy thoughts into action.

"Don't forget this is a surprise party. You can't seem to get anywhere on time. Are you sure you don't want to ride with me?"

"I don't know how long I'll hang around. I should probably check out early to get some writing done. I need to finish my screenplay and head out to L.A. before I squander the rest of my savings. I've been wasting time."

He'd said it to remind himself that he wasn't staying. To bring it home that he shouldn't start anything he couldn't finish. Anything that would be complicated and hard to walk away from.

Tracy nodded, picking up their dishes. He watched her jeans mold to her behind as she went into the kitchen. If he gave in to these feelings he'd started having, Tracy would be impossible to walk away from.

* * *

John knew he couldn't make it by seven thirty, so he didn't even try. He showed up at eight thirty because he knew that would be safe.

The party was in full swing by that time. Toni Braxton played on the stereo and people were filling plates from a buffet table against the wall. Good, he wasn't too late for the food.

He walked over and began loading his plate with hot wings and potato salad, exchanging greetings with old friends. He couldn't help himself. He searched the room for Tracy. She stood across the room between Carter and a guy he'd never seen before.

Tracy and Carter exchanged a few more words, then Carter moved on. The other guy stuck close. And no wonder. Tracy wore a little black skirt and one of those fuzzy white sweaters that looked so soft you wanted to run your hands all over it. No doubt just what her new friend had in mind. He looked like a college boy fresh out of school. John recognized his stance. The way he leaned in toward Trace, his head lowered. He was putting the moves on her.

He was surprised how much that annoyed him. Throughout their friendship, one of them had always been in a relationship in one form or another. It hadn't ever bothered him before, right? So, why was he overcome by the need to stalk across the room and pop college boy in the mouth?

A couple of guys he worked out with at the gym came up to talk to him, but he wasn't feeling very social. After a minute of small talk, he moved off to a corner by himself where he could watch Tracy and her new friend. His scowl grew deeper.

He had no right to feel this way. Tracy could date whomever she wanted. There wasn't anything more than friendship between them. She wasn't his girlfriend. She wasn't

going to walk up to him and throw her arms around him.
She wouldn't kiss him hello with those soft, moist lips. . . .

He needed a drink. He went to the bar to refill his ginger
ale and when he returned to his seat, Tracy was gone. He
scanned the room. Had she left? College boy was nowhere
to be found either. Did she take him home with her?

"John?"

He nearly jumped when he heard Tracy's voice at his
shoulder. "Trace!"

She plopped herself on his lap, draping an arm around
his neck. "I saw you come in a while ago, but you never
came over to talk to me," she said, kissing his cheek with
her soft moist lips. "You're not mad at me are you, *honey?*"

Honey? Was he hallucinating? This wasn't the real Tracy
Fields. This Tracy had walked straight out of his fantasies.
He looked over her shoulder and saw that her *friend* had
followed her across the room like a puppy dog. His gaze
moved back to her face. "I didn't want to interrupt."

She gave his shoulder a squeeze, trying to convey something with her eyes. "Don't be ridiculous. I already told
Rick that I have a boyfriend." She winked at him. "I wanted
to introduce you two. John, this is Rick. Rick, this is my
boyfriend, John."

John blinked, finally catching on. He reached over Tracy
to shake Rick's hand briefly, then slid an arm around her
waist. "I thought you were trying to make me jealous." He
raised his eyes to Rick's and locked gazes with him. "Rick
has been awfully *attentive.*"

Rick took a step back immediately, spreading his hands
in innocence. "Who, me? Oh no, I was . . . just being
friendly. In fact, I'm going to go mingle."

When he left, Tracy released a huge sigh of relief,
slumping against him. "Thanks for playing along. I've been
trying to get rid of that guy all night. When I saw you come
in, I told him you and I are together. He didn't seem to
believe me, and it didn't help when you didn't come right
over like I thought you would."

"How was I to know that you didn't want the guy's company?"

"It worked out, though. When I saw you sulking over here by yourself, I told him you were probably jealous. I got a little nervous when he decided to walk over with me, but you covered. Thanks."

"Any time." He started to drop his arm from her waist so she could get up, but she stopped him.

"No, not yet." She leaned against his chest. "You have to stick close. That guy strikes me as the type who doesn't mind messing around with another man's girl. No matter what I said, I couldn't shake him until I brought him over here."

"Okay."

"So, why *are* you sulking?"

"I'm not sulking."

"Okay, then what would you call it? Normally, you're the life of the party."

"I guess I'm not feeling as social as I thought I would. I got three rejections in the mail this week."

She rested her hand on his chest, her eyes wide with sympathy. "Aw, why didn't you say something?"

"I didn't want to dwell on it, but I feel better now." How could he tell her that his mood had cleared the minute he realized she wasn't interested in her friend Rick?

"Do you want to leave? We could stop and get a cup of coffee and talk."

He grinned down at her. "I'm fine, but if you go over there and snag me a hunk of that cake, I'll feel even better."

She leaned over and gave his cheek a kiss. "You got it."

She returned with one slice of cake and sat down beside him.

"Where's mine?"

"Sorry, John. It's chocolate."

"And so you're just going to sit there and eat it in front of me?"

She licked the frosting off her fork and his eyes followed the movement of her tongue. "You can have a piece if you want. Your aversion to chocolate is all in your head."

He wrinkled his nose with distaste. "I'll pass." *But if she didn't stop wrapping her tongue around that fork . . .*

"Oh, good! Rick just left. Finally. I'm sorry I had to put you on the spot. Did I make you uncomfortable?"

If he'd had Tracy's firm little body in that short skirt sitting on his lap for much longer, he would have been more than uncomfortable, but she didn't have to know that. He had to get a rein on his thoughts. This was Trace, for goodness sake.

"It wasn't a problem." *Liar!*

"I guess we could consider it practice."

His eyes widened. "For what?"

"The contest. We did the proposal and the ring. Now, we're supposed to be engaged. You know, planning our Rainbow Room wedding."

"Forget practicing for the wedding, why don't we go right for the honeymoon?"

He saw her blush, but she just nudged his leg with her own. "Silly."

He needed to redirect his thoughts. "Did you finish your essay, yet?"

She smiled proudly. "As a matter of fact, I finished it this afternoon."

"Well, let's see it."

She went into the bedroom to retrieve her notepad, but walked back holding it against her chest, shyly. "Did you bring yours?"

He pulled his notebook out of his pocket and smacked it on his hand. "It's right here."

"Okay, let's trade," she said, passing her pad with one hand and reaching for his with the other.

He took her notepad and flipped it open. He scanned the first few lines quickly. He couldn't help himself, he pulled out his red pen and began to edit.

Tracy looked up immediately. "Hey! What are you doing?"

He sighed, putting down his pen. "It's too long."

"I know, but—"

"And you've used the word beautiful at least—"

"Whoa. I said you could read it, not rip it to shreds. I don't recall asking for your opinion."

"You can't expect to win without some revision."

"It's just a first draft and I didn't think it was that bad."

He saw the hurt in her eyes and realized he was being a bit harsh. "It wasn't bad. Actually, it was very good, but you leave out the entire focus of the contest."

"Well, I'm sure I can fix that. *Your* approach, on the other hand, is pretty mercenary. It's clear from every line you've written that you're just trying to win the prizes. What did I tell you about sincerity? They're going to take one look at this and laugh out loud."

Carter stepped between the two of them with his hands raised in surrender. "Hey, hey, this is a party, not a war zone. What is it this time, kids?"

John glanced up at their high school buddy, knowing Carter was all too familiar with his and Tracy's quirks. "Do you really want to know?"

Tracy sighed. "It's a bet, Carter."

Carter rolled his eyes. "I knew better than to ask. When are you two going to learn?"

She laughed. "Not any time soon. John is being very unfair."

John didn't even bother to defend himself. He just gave Carter a she's-out-of-her-mind look.

Carter grinned. "Okay, kids, I'm not going to let you two spoil the party, so I'm going to break my hard and fast rule to stay out of your witless schemes and help you out. Tell Uncle Carter what the deal is."

John wasn't going to touch that one, so he nodded to Tracy. He had to hand it to her, she almost made the story make sense. She skimmed past the part about them having to marry if they won the contest, reducing it to a simple disagreement over who could write a better essay.

Carter rubbed his chin, making a show of thinking the problem through. "I think the solution is simple. The two of you write the essay together. Apparently, Spencer's writing is too mechanical and Tracy's is too emotional. If you combine your efforts, you've got the perfect essay."

Tracy bit her lip. "Doesn't that defeat the whole purpose of the bet? How do we know who wins?"

John raised his brows, amused to see what Carter would come up with.

"Okay, okay. . . ." Carter rubbed his chin a bit longer. "From what you've told me, John thinks winning the essay contest is a snap and, Tracy, you disagree. Am I right?"

She nodded.

"Okay! If you enter the essay written with your combined efforts and it wins, John proves his point. If you lose, Tracy proves hers. Yes? How am I doing here?"

Tracy looked at John. "Do you think we could work together?"

"What have we got to lose?" He shrugged.

"The contest, and if we lose, I win, right?" She nodded, considering the prospect. "It will be a relief to share some of the misery. Writing is hard!"

John grinned. "Who are you telling?"

"How do we do this? Do we piece together what we've already got, or throw it all out and start from scratch?"

"We should start fresh."

"Sounds like you two have got it all worked out." Carter snapped his fingers. "Another satisfied customer."

John reached up and slapped Carter's hand. "Hey, thanks, man."

"No problem. Enjoy the evening, kids." He started to walk off. "Oh, and thanks for the tarot cards. Shelly's going to read them for me tonight."

John leaned toward Tracy. "We got him *tarot cards?*"

She shrugged. "Hey, you had your chance to pick out something of your own."

After the party, John walked Tracy to her car in the parking garage. "Why don't you come over tomorrow and we'll work on the essay? We could probably get it finished in one day, send it off, and forget about it."

She unlocked her car door. "Sounds like a plan."

John looked at Tracy, patiently waiting for a hug good-bye, and he decided to give in to an impulse. He leaned in and let his lips touch hers. He didn't linger, but held the contact just long enough to throw her off balance.

There. Let her see what it felt like for a change. "See you tomorrow, Trace."

She pressed her finger to her lips. "Good night, John."

Chapter Five

Tracy was so cold, she knew she was on the verge of hypothermia. Of all the lousy rotten days to snow. Her little Toyota was stubborn when it came to snow, so she'd taken the bus to the Metro station and then walked two blocks to John's apartment.

She raised her hand to knock and winced in agony. She'd lost her right glove last week—it was always the right one—and hadn't had time to replace it. Her poor little knuckles were frozen into position.

John's apartment door swung open and Tracy's first reaction was, thank God, heat. Then she noticed the way his T-shirt clung to his biceps and her second reaction was, oh God . . . *heat!*

"Trace, what's wrong? You look like a popsicle."

"Have you looked outside?"

He shut the door behind her. "No. Not yet."

"Well, it's snowing."

He jogged over to the window. "Wow. How about that." He turned to her. "Wait a minute, you're covered with snow. How did you get over here?"

She knew she was beginning to thaw by the stinging of her ears and the tip of her nose. "Bus. Metro. And . . . *walking*." She thought bitterly of the way the wind had batted her around like a piece of lint.

"Tracy! What were you thinking? Why didn't you call me to pick you up? Or we could have worked at your apartment."

She would have shrugged, but her shoulders were still too stiff. "I don't know, but I'm here now, and I think I'm losing the feeling in my right hand."

"All right, Trace, come here."

She walked over and he covered her right hand with his two larger ones. "Damn, girl, you weren't kidding. You feel like ice."

He rubbed his hands over hers and she began to warm up. Oh, was she warming up! But in all the wrong places. Quickly she pulled her hands from his.

"I'm fine now. What I really need is a huge cup of hot chocolate."

He folded his arms over his chest. "Now what would *I* be doing with hot chocolate?"

She bit her lip. "That's right, I forgot. Okay, coffee."

He shook his head.

"Tea?"

"Sorry, kiddo, I don't have any of that stuff."

She wrapped her arms around herself and shivered. "Great. I tramp all the way over here and you don't even have anything warm for me to drink? Why don't you go ahead and put my toes in the freezer with the rest of the ice cubes?"

"Okay, come in the kitchen. Let's see what I've got. We'll improvise."

Tracy had witnessed John's kitchen improvisations before. Banana and marshmallow cookies? Never again. But she knew better than to comment. John was Julia Child compared to her. She'd been known to burn water.

John pulled open the refrigerator. "Steamed milk?"

She shook her head. "Blech!"

He shut the refrigerator and started opening cabinets. "Don't have any soup . . . hot apple sauce? No. Okay, either we boil the orange juice or you go with this can of chili."

She sighed with relief. "The chili is fine."

An hour later, she and John were sprawled on his living room floor with two empty chili bowls beside them. He flipped open his laptop computer and turned it on. "Okay, time to get down to business."

Tracy flopped over on her back. "I don't feel like writing now, John. I'm sleepy."

"If you don't wake up, I'll have to tickle you."

She instantly drew herself upright, remembering how their last tickling session had gotten out of hand. "Oh, no that won't be necessary. I'm awake."

"Are you sure?" He winked. "I've been told that my fingers work magic."

Tracy raised her brows. She'd never heard John speak to her like this before. And there was the goodbye kiss he'd given her last night. What was happening between them?

She picked up her legal pad and leaned back against the sofa. "How do we begin?"

He stretched out on his side, facing her. "Let's start with some brainstorming. We can just toss out ideas until something sparks. They don't have to be good."

Unconsciously, Tracy began moving her pen, sketching a rough outline of John's body down one side of the pad. "Okay, you go first."

John mumbled under his breath for a few minutes, then Tracy took pity on him.

Reaching into her tote bag, she pulled out a stack of magazines. "I don't have any idea where to start either. That's why I brought these."

He spread out the stack between them. "*Modern Bride? Metropolitan Home? Today's Bride?* What are all these for?"

"Whenever I draw, I need to set the mood. I borrowed

some of Lisa's old magazines to help us get into the right frame of mind.''

He nodded. "I do the same thing when I write.'' He stretched out alongside her. "Let's see what you've got here.''

They opened the first magazine and began flipping pages. John stopped on a picture of a woman in a large square hat and veil. "She looks like she keeps bees in her spare time. Who would actually wear that?''

Tracy laughed, pointing to the next page. "That's not as bad as this one. She's got so many flowers in her hair, she's literally drawing bugs.'' The model in the photograph had two butterflies affixed to her headpiece.

He shook his head over a pale pink gown. "They never put realistic clothes that everyday women could actually wear in these magazines. Whatever happened to the traditional white wedding gown?''

"Not all of them are off the wall.'' Tracy looked wistfully at all the beautiful wedding gowns. "There are also a lot of beautiful looks. I don't know how I would ever choose.''

John shrugged, flipping to a page showing a bride wearing a very traditional gown, with a long train and a pearl-encrusted jacket. "This one is pretty.''

Tracy frowned. "No. That's too ordinary. It's got to be something a little different. Something with flare. Something a bit avant-garde.''

"I don't think it's ordinary. It's elegant. You're not going to be in a fashion show, it's a wedding. It should be traditional.''

She rolled her eyes. "Translation: boring. I'm not talking about a freak show. I just think it should be . . . special.'' She opened a magazine they had looked at before. "Look at this gown. It's silver. Very elegant. And this one, I think the gold overlay is a bit overdone, but it's a very classic style with a twist.''

He frowned. "Just because I don't think a wedding dress should be silver or gold or chartreuse doesn't mean my taste is boring. It just means that I have some. It's a good thing we're not really getting married, because we'd never be able to agree."

Tracy was surprisingly stung by John's words. Sure, they could be at opposite ends of the spectrum sometimes, but they usually found a happy medium. When he wanted to see sci-fi and she wanted to see comedy, they saw *Space Balls*. When she wanted to see a romance and he wanted to see action-adventure, they watched *Speed*.

Why did his words matter so much? Why did it feel so personal, as if he were rejecting her as marriage material?

"I didn't mean to say your taste is boring. I just meant that when I walk down the aisle in my wedding gown, I don't want to be like every bride that's come down that aisle before me. I want to be *spectacular.*"

He nudged her shoulder with his own. "Trace, don't you know that you would be spectacular in any gown. You could outshine a dress studded in diamonds."

Her breathing halted and she felt her face heat. "Do you mean that?"

He looked down at the magazine, clearly uncomfortable with the direction of the conversation. "I wouldn't have said it otherwise."

Tracy looked down at the magazine, too. *Idiot! Why did you have to press him like that?*

She pulled out *Dream House* magazine.

"Remember when we used to ride through Potomac on our bikes, looking at all the fancy houses, picking out the ones we would live in one day?"

When he nodded, she continued. "Well, I still do that when I read this magazine. In each issue, they show five dream houses, with floor plans and photos of every room."

He looked over her shoulder. When they'd flipped through the magazine once, John turned back a few pages, pointing to a beautiful country stone cottage. "I like this one the best. It's quiet and secluded."

She nodded, smiling at him. "That's my favorite, too."

"I don't like the way it's decorated, though. I'd want something like this." The room he pointed to was meagerly decorated in dusky browns.

Tracy frowned. "Don't you think that's a little sparse?"

He shrugged. "I like sparse."

She glanced around his living room. "I noticed." He had no real furniture to speak of, which was why they were spread out on the floor. He didn't have a sofa. He had one barstool in front of the narrow counter that separated the kitchen from the living room, a beanbag chair, and a tiny slatted coffee table that sat between two mismatched upholstered chairs. Everything was black, gray, and brown.

His living room said a lot about him. He wasn't committed to the apartment. He didn't want to set down roots. John could pick up and leave at a moment's notice. A very good reason for Tracy to keep her growing feelings for John in check.

She turned to a plainly furnished room with ivory sofas and chairs. "Well, at least perk up the room with brighter furniture. It's still a simple room, but the light furniture opens the place up."

He wrinkled his brow. "But I like dark furniture."

Tracy resisted the urge to roll her eyes as she flipped through the magazine. "Why not compromise? This room uses dark wood with light cushions."

John nodded. "I could live with that, but I'm surprised you like something so conservative. I could see you filling the room with those pink chairs that look like misshapen L's and cow-print sofas."

She giggled. "I wouldn't want the house to look tacky. Besides, I'd save the furniture that really expresses my personality for my studio." She turned to the floor plan of their dream house. "The veranda down the hall from the master suite would be perfect."

"Wait a minute, that room would work much better as an office. See, the computer would go next to the balcony, and there's enough wall space for bookcases."

"No, it's perfect for a studio because of the natural light from the veranda, and the attached bathroom could be used to wash out paint brushes. The basement room would make a better office."

He shook his head. "No, that's the lounge/video room. When I get tired of writing and you finish with your sketching for the day, we meet in here to talk and watch videos."

She sighed and he studied the floor plan. "Why use this room on the main level as a living room? *That* can be a studio. It has French doors that connect to the garden terrace, so it still gets plenty of natural sunlight."

"But there's no sink for washing brushes and mixing paints."

"You use charcoal and pencil more than you use paint. You keep saying you need to paint more, but let's face it, Trace, you don't really like it. Besides, the outer room that connects to the main hall could be a gallery for your work."

She raised her brows, nodding as she began to warm to the idea. "Wow, that actually sounds pretty good." Then she became aware of their proximity. They were lying side by side looking at the magazine. At some point John's hand had moved to her back where it was absently stroking up and down. Now that she was paying attention, the sensation took on a new dimension.

She laughed nervously, looking at him shyly out of the corner of her eye. "Listen to us. For a minute there, I was really starting to believe we were going to live in this house."

His hand stilled, then he rolled away from her onto his back, propping his hands behind his head. "Yeah, I guess we did get a little carried away. And stalling won't get us any closer to finishing this essay."

She sat up, closing the magazines and stuffing them back into her bag. "I guess it's time to get down to business. The entry has to be in by four o'clock next Friday. Less than a week."

John headed into the kitchen. "Okay, but first I have

to satisfy my craving for a double-decker peanut butter and jelly sandwich. You want one?"

"No! We've got to get this essay written."

"Come on," he called from the kitchen. "You love my peanut butter and jelly."

"That's true, but what about the essay? We can eat later."

"No, I think better when I'm full."

While John was busy in the kitchen, Tracy rolled her eyes, pretending to pull out her hair. She wanted to get this project behind them. Maybe then, her life would go back to normal. If he wasn't going to help, she'd just have to get started without him.

She turned his laptop to face her and started typing whatever came to mind. "I've always dreamed of a wedding in the Rainbow Room because . . . I've always believed in fairy tales. The reality of everyday life can dull the shine of our dreams and steal the magic from our fantasies, but, on the most important day of my life, I want my fairy tale to come true."

John finally ambled out of the kitchen, chewing on a thick layered sandwich. "What are you doing?"

"Shh," she whispered. Tracy wrote a few more sentences then went back to count up her words. After crossing out a few extras, she printed out her work. "There. It's still pretty rough, but it's a start."

She waited nervously for John to finish reading. He lifted his head. "I'm impressed. This has potential."

"Do you really think so?"

He nodded. "It just needs a little polishing, but the content is excellent. Here, if we just move up this sentence . . ."

For ninety minutes, she and John perfected her prose. Tracy expanded on her original ideas and John made her words sparkle.

She felt herself getting emotional as she read through the essay. They were a good team.

She put down the finished product. "We did it!"

John stood. "We sure did." He crossed to the window. "It's not snowing anymore. I think we ought to celebrate a job well done with a little fresh air. We've been cooped up in this apartment for too long. Let's go outside for a while."

"In the snow? It's too cold. That's not celebrating, that's punishment."

He got up and retrieved their coats. "Come on. I have an extra pair of gloves you can wear."

When he tossed a pair in her lap, she said, "They're too big. They'll fall off."

"I can fix that. Just put on your coat."

She reluctantly shrugged into her coat, and he returned with a handful of safety pins. She stood while he dutifully pinned the gloves to her sweater. "I feel like a five-year-old."

He put on his jacket and nudged her out the door. "Whenever I've been writing for a long stretch, I have to stop and do something physical for balance."

"And going for a walk in the snow is the best you could come up with?" Tracy grumbled.

She heard him laugh wickedly from behind her. "No. But it's the only thing that won't get me in trouble."

Was he implying what she thought he was implying? She looked over her shoulder to check. He winked at her.

The cold air was a welcome salve for her flaming cheeks.

When they were standing on the sidewalk outside his apartment building, she asked, "Now what?"

"There's a park across the street. Why don't we go over there?"

She tromped behind him, trying not to slide on the ice. Her hormones were raging. Why was John suddenly affecting her like this? Guilt stabbed at her heart. It wasn't sudden, was it? She may as well admit that she never fully recovered from the crush she'd developed for him at the senior prom.

He'd made her feel like Cinderella that night. But just

like Cinderella, she should have realized that the spell wouldn't last. He'd held her close when they were dancing, put his arm around her when they weren't and held her hand when they walked. All her friends had been jealous of her devoted Prince Charming. But after one incredible, magical kiss . . . the spell had been broken.

Her heart had been dancing on glass slippers and she couldn't wait for the end of the evening for him to kiss her again, but he had become distant after their first kiss. When he dropped her off that night, instead of kissing her again, he'd apologized for kissing her in the first place.

He'd made the most magical moment she'd ever experienced seem like a mistake. She'd instantly agreed, claiming she wanted to tell him the same thing. When she said they should keep it strictly friends, he'd looked so relieved. And apparently, he'd had no trouble acting as if nothing had ever happened.

For Tracy it had been torture. Thank goodness they'd gone to separate colleges the next year, so when they saw each other on breaks, though still painful, seeing him had gotten easier. Now she faced that same trauma all over again.

Her skin still prickled from being so close to him, and though it was less than twenty degrees outside, her body was hot. She wanted nothing more than to run over and throw herself on top of him, covering his lips with her own.

And there he was calmly dusting snow off the playground equipment. The jerk! How dare he get into her blood, work her into a frenzy, and then have the gall not to feel a thing. How dare he torture her all day with sexy innuendos and no intention of backing them up. How dare he turn his emotions on and off like a faucet, while she suffered like this.

Between the hurt of ten years past and the gnawing tension of the past few days, Tracy's frustrations were on the verge of erupting. She dug her fingers into the snow, glaring at John's back.

Tracy scooped up a handful of snow and packed the biggest, hardest snowball she could carry. She stalked across the park. "Oh, John!"

He turned around. "What the he—"

Her snowball hit him squarely in the face, breaking over his nose and trickling into the collar of his shirt. Yes! Two years of pitching girls' softball in high school had paid off.

Tracy stood, so caught up in her self-satisfaction that it took her a moment to notice the red haze clouding John's eyes. When he sprang forward, it was almost too late for her to run.

She turned around, running toward the jungle gym, but she couldn't get any traction. Her feet kicked out from under her. Fwoom! She landed flat on her back. Winded, she was just getting her breath back when her vision filled with white.

John dropped an armload of snow in her face. She batted at her face with the oversized gloves, sputtering to clear her nose and mouth of snow.

When she could see again . . . another load of snow came down on her. She rolled over, shaking the snow out of her face. "I'll get you, John!"

She scrambled to her feet, planning to run after him. Fwomp! Face down in the snow. She lifted her head and a gloved hand shoved a snowball into her face.

"Ahhh! Okay, okay. I surrender!"

He straddled her back, preventing her from getting up. "Do you swear to be good if I let you up?"

She spit out a mouthful of snow. "I swear."

"You won't hit me with any more snow balls?"

"I promise."

"Okay, you're free." He stood up and backed away from her.

She got to her feet, taking her time dusting herself off.

He must have decided that she was going to keep her word and turned away.

Tracy ran up behind him and jumped on his back bringing *him* face down in the snow. But he was too strong for her to hold him there for long. He made a strangled noise and flipped over, pinning her beneath him.

"You swore that you were going to be good." His face was inches from hers.

She gave him a weak smile with her cold-numbed cheeks. "I promised not to throw any more snowballs. I didn't say anything about running tackles."

"Oh, and you consider that being good?"

She giggled. "It was good for me. Was it good for you?"

He shook his head. "You have a smart mouth. Did I ever tell you what I do to little girls with smart mouths?"

Tracy closed her eyes, waiting for the snowball to crush into her face. Instead her mouth was met with heat. Incredible, searing heat.

His mouth slanted over hers and her cold, numb lips began to warm. Sensation spread from her lips outward like warm brandy, waking her cold limbs.

His body settled into hers, pressing her deeper into the snow, which she was sure was melting all around them. He opened his mouth over hers, finally giving her full access to his heat. Her tongue desperately searched for the source.

"Hey, get a room!" a teenager shouted.

John levered off of Tracy and rolled to the side, allowing her to see the two boys running past them with sleds in their hands.

"Yeah, get a room," the younger boy mimicked, then he ran to catch up to his brother. "Tommy? What's the *room* for?"

Chapter Six

Tracy burst into John's apartment, stomping her feet to release the snow. "Brrr. I don't think I'll ever be warm again. And once again, you don't have any coffee, tea, or hot chocolate and . . . I just don't think chili will do it this time."

She was rambling, and John knew it was because she was trying desperately to pretend the kiss in the snow had never happened. He also knew she fully expected him to follow her lead. Well, not this time.

He'd made that mistake after the prom. He'd wanted to kiss her the moment he saw her in that long shimmery blue dress, but he'd forced himself to wait. He'd wanted the moment to be special. Instead, he'd blown it. He couldn't wait any longer, so he'd kissed her in the parking lot. Not very romantic.

But he knew he'd make up for it at the end of the date, but he'd had to pull back a little so he didn't lose control the way he had the first time. At the door, in front of her house, he was going to tell her how he felt about her. To explain how he'd wanted their first kiss to be somewhere special, not in a crummy parking lot. But she hadn't let him get the words out. He'd gotten as far as "I'm sorry for kiss—" and she jumped right in, agreeing that it had been a mistake.

He couldn't tell her that wasn't what he'd meant. She believed the whole thing had been a mistake.

This time he wasn't going to let her pretend their kiss had never happened.

He watched her struggle to unhook the safety pins with his huge gloves. "Here, let me."

Her teeth chattered as he slipped them off. "My hands feel like ice."

"Don't worry, you won't need chili this time. I'll warm you up." He lifted the hem of his sweater and placed her icy hands flat against his stomach.

"Oh!" She shivered and his stomach muscles jumped at the contact. She moved her hands experimentally as his skin absorbed the cold. "Your skin is so hot. It must be torture to feel my cold hands on you."

She tried to pull back, but he wouldn't let her. "Ah, the suffering I do for your sake."

As her hands took in his heat, she continued to move her hands upward. Finally they covered his pectoral muscles and he felt his nipples tighten against her palms. Her fingers curved around to his side and he dropped his arms, pinning her hands under his arms.

She closed her eyes for a moment. "Mmm, that feels good." He didn't know what thoughts had crossed her mind, but her eyes suddenly popped open and she pulled out her hands. "Thanks. They feel better now."

She started to move away.

He caught her hands and held them away from her body. "Not so fast. You haven't returned the favor."

Her eyes widened, but he didn't lift the hem of her shirt. Instead, he reached around her and pulled out the elastic of her sweat pants.

"What are you—"

He reached in and cupped her buttocks over her panties. He shook his head. "No. That's not good enough." He slipped his cold hands into her underwear, letting his hands mold her firm cheeks. "Much better."

Tracy sucked in a shuddering breath. With his hands still cupping her, he pulled her closer, leaning down to nuzzle her neck.

He heard her gasp and her arms slid shyly around his neck. She took a step back and pressed her mouth to his.

They kissed with an urgency that sent heat streaking through his body. He dragged his hands over her buttocks and up her back, pressing her closer. Finally. This was the way it should be. Her breasts crushed against his chest. Her foot hooked around his ankle. She wanted him just as much as he wanted her.

John lifted Tracy until her feet no longer touched the floor and carried her over to the beanbag chair. He gently sank down and settled her onto his lap. In an instant, he'd rolled flat onto his back with her sprawled on top of him.

She squirmed around above him trying to find a comfortable position. Her body rubbing against his was driving him insane. He reached up and gripped her around the waist. She stopped wiggling.

He pushed up her sweater, reaching around for the hook on her bra. He didn't have the patience to fool with it, so he pushed it up over her breasts. His hands were filled with the soft honey-brown mounds and she straddled him, with her hands on either side of his head. They kissed wildly, sipping and sucking from each other's lips.

Tracy finally sat up, gripping the hem of her sweater. She was about to pull it over her head and . . .

The phone rang.

The shrill sound didn't even register in his head, until Tracy let go of her sweater and moved off him. "Answer the phone, John," she said, breathlessly.

He wanted to scream in protest, but it was already too late. Slowly he got to his feet and picked up the phone.

"Hello? Oh hi, Mom." He shot Tracy an apologetic look that didn't begin to cover what he felt inside. "I am? Uh, I just got off the stair climber."

While John talked to his mother, Tracy went to the bathroom to pull herself together. When she returned, she heard John say, "No, Mom, it's just Trace."

Just Trace. She could imagine what had preceded those words. *John, is there a girl in your apartment?* No, Mom, it's just Trace. *John, is that anyone important?* No, Mom, it's just Trace. That just about summed up their relationship.

She and John had been about to make love, and she still didn't rank any higher than *just Trace?*

They'd been friends for nearly twenty years. She was used to John referring to her in a casual way, but today, she suddenly required more.

Things had changed between them, and this time, she couldn't let him ignore it. But how could she define what they were to each other now? Their relationship wasn't laid out like a fast food menu.

Extra Value Deal Number One: Strong, supportive friendship, and warm mutual respect.

Extra Value Deal Number Two: Strong, supportive friendship, with a side order of kissing.

Extra Value Deal Number Three: Supportive friendship, kissing, and an extra large portion of physical intimacy.

Extra Value Deal Number Four: Supportive friendship and intimacy with a double order of love.

If Tracy could order from a menu, she'd choose number four, no question. But did she and John have the same taste? From what she'd seen in the past, he might go for number three, heavy intimacy, hold the commitment.

She glanced up. He was still talking to his mother on the phone. Did she love John? Of course she did. But now it was so much more than the steady warmth of the familiar. Now she was dealing with desire and passion. She started to feel something she never thought she'd face with John. Insecurity.

How did men do it? How could they separate sex from all these emotions? He knew everything about her. The good and the bad, and somehow he liked her anyway. He knew things other people didn't know and things she hadn't even admitted to herself. She *did* hate painting. How could he be so intimately involved in her life and not feel this connection she was feeling?

Where did they go from here? Their essay was complete. What would happen to their friendship if the romance didn't survive? Suddenly Tracy was overwhelmed by her emotions. If John didn't love her, she didn't want to know. Not today. Today she wanted to go home and savor her new memories.

Tomorrow was another day.

"Why did you not tell me you were getting married!" Lisa jerked open the door, her Jamaican accent booming into the street. "I had to hear it from a stranger. I'm always the last to know."

Tracy dashed inside before Lisa attracted any more attention from the people on the street. "What are you talking about? I'm not getting married." And how did she know?

"Don't lie to me now, girl. I went into the diner for karaoke Saturday night and they told me all about it. Said that boyfriend of yours proposed in front of one and all. Sooo romantic, she said. And before you bother denying it again, she showed me the sketch you left behind."

Tracy swallowed hard. How could she possibly explain this? "Lisa, I know this is going to sound outrageous, but I'm not lying to you. I'm *not* getting married."

Lisa shook her head sadly as if Tracy were a spokesmodel for lobotomies. "He proposed and you said yes. Patty never gets her gossip wrong."

"That's right, Lisa. John, my *friend* did propose, but it was a joke."

Lisa shook her head, making her coppery curls swirl. "A joke? I don't understand you, girl."

Tracy took a deep breath and slowly explained, from the beginning, how she and John ended up entering the contest sponsored by the Rainbow Room. Just in case their motives still weren't clear, she threw in the chocolate story to show that she and John had a consistent history with irrational behavior.

Lisa let out a hearty laugh when Tracy had finished. "This is fantastic, Tracy-girl. If you win the contest, you can put in a plug for Ribbon-in-the-Sky. There will be tons of media coverage. All you have to do is drop my name, ah?"

"I would, Lisa. Believe me, I would. But you don't understand. Even if we win the contest, we won't be getting married."

"What's this? You don't want to marry him?"

"I didn't say *that*. I just said it wasn't going to happen."

"You love him, ah?"

Tracy nodded.

"Then it will happen."

"No, Lisa. Not this time. You see, John—"

"Tracy, you listen to me. I've been in this business a long time. I don't have to know this John to know true love when I see it. Come on, girl, let's be real."

Tracy lifted her head to stare at Lisa.

"Two people don't enter a contest that gives away a wedding as the prize if they aren't in love." Tracy started to protest, but Lisa wouldn't allow it. "There are easier ways to make a point . . . get money . . . win a bet," Lisa said, ticking off each item.

Tracy's face heated. That was true. It didn't make sense for two single people to work hard to win a contest that dictated they get married if they won. Tracy shook her head. And yet that's what had happened.

It was clear why she'd done it. She'd been in love with John for years, even if she didn't readily admit it. But why would *John* go along with everything? The proposal. The ring. Could he . . .

"No. No," she said out loud.

"Tell me something, what will you do if you win? If you call it off you certainly won't be given any prizes."

"I know. I can honestly tell you we didn't think it through. That's what happens when we get excited about things. We just get carried away."

Lisa patted her hand. "Sounds like the two of you are made for each other. I don't know any other two people in the world who get themselves into messes such as these."

"Welcome to my life. I just wish this had a hope of working out."

"I'm telling you that it will."

"How? I know John has feelings for me, but I don't think they're what I want them to be."

"Have you asked him?"

"No."

"Have you told him how you feel?"

"No."

"Then how do you know he's not sitting somewhere right now feeling just as you do?"

"Because I know. John is writing a screenplay. His dream for as long as I can remember has been to move to Los Angeles where he can mingle with all the right people. He already told me that he doesn't want a relationship that will complicate his life. He's leaving."

"Then you have to make him stay."

Chapter Seven

"This tuxedo shirt itches," John said, tugging at his collar.

Tracy reached over and smacked his hand. "Stop fidgeting. We're next. Besides, I wouldn't have had to promise Lisa that we'd do this bridal show if you hadn't made such a spectacle at the diner."

"Well, didn't you tell her the proposal was fake?"

"I already explained this to you," Tracy said through her teeth. "She didn't care. It sparked this brilliant idea for us to be the grand finale in the show and dance at the end of the runway."

"Just don't blame me if I trip on your train."

So much for romance.

Tracy bit her lip. Lisa promised her this would work, that once John saw her in this incredible wedding gown, spent the day with her dressed like this, he'd develop tender feelings for her.

It seemed the only thing tender about him right now was his skin under that shirt. Though the tuxedo was too avant-garde for John's usual taste, he had grudgingly admitted that it suited him more than he would have expected.

The shirt he found so bothersome had a banded collar with a dark strip at the base that met in an elaborate marcasite and onyx button, eliminating the need for a tie. The jacket, also having a banded collar and no lapels, showcased the shirt's thin straight pleats and simple onyx buttons. The crisp lines emphasized John's broad shoulders and slim waist. When he stopped fidgeting, he was dashing.

John's heart might not have been in it, but Lisa had outdone herself nonetheless. The dress she'd picked for Tracy was perfect. The bodice, covered with beautiful lace in an elaborate floral pattern, had an off-the-shoulder, sweetheart neckline. The sleeves were thin bands sculpted from lace and tiny white satin rosebuds that encircled her upper arms. At the waist, the dress exploded into billowing layers of delicate white tulle that swirled as she walked.

The long satin gloves that cupped her elbows and a simple bouquet of buttery yellow roses completed the picture. If John didn't appreciate her now, he never would.

She heard their musical cue and looked up at him. "Are you ready?"

He dropped his hand from his collar and straightened. "As I'll ever be." He offered her his arm and they stepped forward.

The curtain parted for them and they began their walk down the long red carpet. Tracy knew flash bulbs were going off around them and a sea of people stretched out before them, but when she looked up at John, all that melted away. He looked down at her and winked with a tender gleam in his eye. Gone was the recalcitrant John who fidgeted with his tie. At that moment, Tracy knew she was looking into the eyes of her Prince Charming once again.

They reached the end of the runway and John went off to the left and she to the right, where they spun and posed for the audience. She walked to the end of the runway, turned, and threw her bouquet into the audience.

The crowd applauded and she met John in the center of the stage. First John bowed to her, going down on one knee to kiss her hand. Then Tracy bent low in the deep curtsey she'd practiced for hours.

They stood and clasped hands for the grand finale. Tracy gasped as Luther Vandross came over the speaker system. This wasn't the song they'd rehearsed to. Lisa remembered her prom night story. Though it wasn't the same song, Luther singing "Here and Now" still stirred Tracy's memories. Did it mean anything to John?

She looked up at him and he gave her a very intimate, private smile. "Not our song, but close," he whispered.

For the rest of the dance, Tracy floated on air. Halfway through the song the other models and their escorts came out on the runway to dance with them.

Tracy knew that if she never had the opportunity to do this for real, at least she'd had this moment. But she also knew from experience that memories were a poor substitute for a real relationship.

When they were alone, she had to confront John about her feelings. She couldn't go on pretending nothing had changed. Everything had changed. This time she had to have an answer.

After the show, John tugged on his collar. He wasn't off the hook yet. Each vendor hosted a reception in their room and perspective brides and grooms wandered from room to room, talking to wedding coordinators, caterers, photographers, and florists. The models were expected to circulate so their clothes could be admired up close.

He leaned over to Tracy and whispered, "How long do we have to stay at this thing?"

"I'm sorry if you're not having a good time," she snapped. "But I promised Lisa we would stay until the end. Four thirty.'' Then she picked up her skirts and flounced away.

John sighed. He hadn't meant to upset her. It wasn't that he wasn't having a good time. Quite the opposite in fact. With all the wedding noise that had been roaring in his ears for the past two weeks. It was all too easy to get caught up in it. He needed constant reminders that this was a charade.

Especially after seeing Tracy in that dress. When he'd noticed some of the other groom models admiring her, he'd felt possessive. She looked so darn feminine, a tightness formed in his chest every time he looked at her. Her face was so delicate with two wings of hair curving around her cheeks, and when they'd danced, her face literally glowed.

John's hand shot up to tug at his collar. The shirt didn't itch, but how else could he explain the constriction at his throat every time he thought about his feelings for Tracy?

Had he been half in love with her all these years? Did that explain why things had gotten out of hand lately? In addition to the normal flow of caring and respect he was accustomed to, a hot gut-twisting sexual attraction had been added to the mix. Impossible to ignore.

They'd almost made love in his apartment last week. They'd been interrupted and it was probably for the best. What could he offer her? Nothing. And Tracy deserved the best. She knew his history. That's probably why she was running in the opposite direction. He couldn't handle commitment. Not yet. Not until he'd proven himself.

He looked across the room to where Tracy was eating hors d'oeuvres. Trace deserved the whole enchilada. Her dream wedding and a perfect marriage to a man who could give her everything. John knew he had a long way to go before he could fit in that picture frame.

Tracy floated over and grabbed his arm. ''John, you've got to try these.'' She dragged him over to a buffet table. ''They're fabulous.''

She picked up a rolled crepe stuffed with a creamy filling. She held it up to his mouth. She'd taken off her gloves to eat, and he sipped from her fingertips as she nudged the last bite into his mouth.

"What do you think?"

"It's delicious."

"I knew you'd love it. They're so elegant."

He took her elbow. "They were nice, but did you see these crab things?" He prepared one and fed it to her. He couldn't help watching as her tongue darted out to catch a dot of the spicy sauce left on her lips.

"Mmm. It's delicious, but I'd have it all over my dress in no time."

"I don't think so. Besides, it's very colorful and avant-garde." He winked.

She smiled back at him. "I'm going to taste wedding cakes."

He started to follow her when another groom stopped and introduced himself.

"Hey, man, how are you doing?" John said, shaking his hand.

"I've been meaning to ask you, you two aren't models are you?"

John grinned. He hadn't realized that it was that obvious. "No, we're not."

The man's face lit up. "I knew it. I could tell watching the two of you that you were a real couple. You look great together. When's the big day?"

His eyes widened. "Oh, no, we haven't—"

"Set a date yet? Well, congratulations, man. Good luck." He shook John's hand again and walked off.

John watched the man walk away, then looked over at Tracy. She popped a piece of cake in her mouth, delicately dabbing frosting from her lips. He wanted to walk over and kiss the frosting away. If he wasn't careful, all this wedding business would get the best of him.

* * *

Tracy unlocked the door to her apartment, then stepped back for John to enter.

He went inside. "I still can't believe Lisa lost the key to the room where our clothes were stored. I felt ridiculous getting on the Metro dressed like this."

"Relax, she'll find the key and have our things messengered over first thing in the morning."

"Yeah, and in the meantime I have no wallet, no credit cards, no keys."

"Look on the bright side. If I hadn't locked my purse in the reception room with Lisa's, neither of us would have had money to get home."

"You're right." He threw himself down on the couch.

"Look, John, I know today was horrible for you—"

He looked up, startled. "Is that what you think?"

"Yes. Your tux is uncomfortable and now you're stuck in it. I'm so sorry. I didn't know it would turn out this way."

He stood up. "Actually, I've gotten used to the shirt. It doesn't itch anymore. And today wasn't so bad. I actually had a good time."

"Really?" Maybe there was hope. Now was as good a time as any to find out. "I'm so glad to hear you say that because there are a few things I think we ought to talk about."

He walked over to her. "Before you say anything, there's something I've been wanting to do all day." His hands slid around her waist and he slowly leaned forward, pressing his lips very gently against hers. It was a sweet kiss, full of tenderness, unlike the others they'd shared recently, there was no hesitancy or urgency.

He pulled his head back and smiled down at her. "You're so beautiful."

Tracy knew she was blushing and dropped her eyes shyly. John lifted her chin and dropped kisses on each of her cheeks. She couldn't stand this slow tender torture, so she reached up with a gloved hand and cupped the back of John's neck. She pulled his head down to hers and kissed him with the full force of the pent up tension she'd been feeling.

When the kiss ended, John laughed against her lips. "Now that's what I call a kiss."

She giggled. "You ain't seen nothing yet."

"Really?" He moved back to lean against the arm of her sofa, pulling her into the space between his legs. Her dress puffed like a cloud all around her. "How do you move with all this material?" He asked, fluffing it with his hands.

She laughed. "Very carefully."

He pulled her closer, then bent his head to spread kisses around the bare expanse from one shoulder to the other.

She reached around him, trying to pull off her gloves.

"No. Let me."

He picked up her right hand and bit the tip of her satin glove, then dragged backward with his teeth. She pulled back her hand, allowing the glove to slip off. John dropped the glove and took her hand, pressing a kiss into her palm. Then he kissed his way up her arm.

She giggled and he lifted his head. "Does that tickle?"

"Yes!"

He winked. "Good." He grasped the fingers of her left glove, this time kissing the skin exposed by the glove as he worked it down her arm.

When her hands were free, she pushed off his jacket. As she started to work on the tiny buttons of his tuxedo shirt, his hands began to roam around in the gathers of her dress.

"I've always wondered what brides wore under these."

She gave him a wicked look. "My ensemble is authentic from top to . . . bottom."

He widened his eyes. "Does that mean you have on a garter?"

She stepped back. "See for yourself." She raised her

hem slightly, first revealing the point of her satin pump. Then the arc of her ankle and the curve of her calf. She lifted more, exposing a knee cap and then a portion of her thigh. When she reached the lacy garter, she lifted the skirt quickly and then let it float back into place.

He groaned. "You little tease. That was too fast. Show me again."

She shook her head coyly. "If you want to see it, you'll have to look for yourself."

His brow rose. "Is that so?"

She took a step back and nodded.

He took her by the waist and settled her on the arm of the sofa. Then he knelt at her feet and gingerly removed her shoes, taking time to massage her insteps. "That feels good," she whispered, letting her eyes close.

She'd become so relaxed it took her a minute to realize that he'd stopped massaging her feet and had rested them on his shoulders. She felt her skirts ruffle and her eyes popped open just in time to see his head duck underneath.

She swiped at his head. "Get out of there."

"Oh, yeah." That told her he'd discovered her merry widow.

"Oh!" she moaned when she felt his lips on her inner thigh. He kissed his way down her leg and came up with her garter between his teeth.

Laughing with him, she snatched it and threw it over her shoulder.

He frowned. "I thought that was my prize."

She spread her arms. "I'm your prize."

"Even better." Before Tracy realized what was happening, he tossed her over his shoulder and carried her into the bedroom.

She was giggling when he set her on her feet, but that was the end of the games. She looked up into his eyes and found a desire there that was dead serious.

She reached up and curved her arms around his neck, and he lowered his mouth, kissing her like a starving man.

He spun her around so he could undo the fastenings of the wedding dress and ease her out of the gown.

When she stood before him in her lingerie, Tracy suddenly felt shy. Until she noticed the effect it was having on him. She'd never felt so feminine or so powerful.

She pushed his shirt over his shoulders, admiring the beautiful dark skin she'd revealed. He stood patiently as she unbuttoned his pants, easing the material from his legs.

Then he picked her up and placed her on the bed, covering her with his body. It felt good to feel the hard muscled length of him pressing against her.

The sensations inside her were too much to bear. "John, please," she whispered.

His fingers trembled as he finished undressing her. "You're so beautiful," he told her again.

He cupped her breasts with his palms, gently kneading them with his strong but gentle fingers. He let them pucker under his touch then bloom between his lips.

His kisses stroked downward and she ran her hands all over his body, moving against him urgently.

When it was time, she made sure they were protected, and then wrapped her legs around his waist, clinging to him. He pulled her close and began the slow, rocking motions of love.

She moaned under his touch and he shuddered in her ear. They found heaven in each other's arms.

Much later, Tracy rested her head on John's chest, while his fingers played in her hair. She stared down at the dark expansion of skin under her head, trying to comprehend the reality of being in John's arms.

His fingers combed her hair away from her neck. "Trace, I'm sensing that our friendship is moving to a new level." She heard the humor in his voice.

She propped her chin on his chest, looking up at him. "Ya think?"

He nodded. "Yes, yes. I don't want to alarm you, but I think I've fallen madly and hopelessly"—the humor faded from his eyes—"in love with you. I love you Tracy Fields." He repeated the words as if he'd just come to believe them.

She closed her eyes and hugged him tightly. "John, I love you, too." It was remarkable. He'd actually said the words.

He leaned down and kissed her forehead. "This is strange, isn't it? Us, like this?"

She looked down at their tangled limbs. "Yes. It is."

"But it feels right."

She smiled. It did feel right.

"Okay, now that we've gotten the heavy stuff taken care of, can we get to what's really important?"

"What's that?"

John rolled over in Tracy's arms and whispered in her ear, "I'm hungry."

She giggled. "How romantic. If I weren't hungry, too, I'd punch you for your insensitivity."

He chuckled.

"There's only one problem."

"What's that?"

"I don't have a lot of food in the house."

"I'll take whatever's in that white box that Lisa begged you to take from the reception room."

Tracy smiled, remembering how Lisa had sent everyone home with food. "Are you sure?"

"Yeah. At this point, I'll eat anything."

Tracy slipped on her robe and dashed out to the kitchen. John loved her. Their tender exchange of emotion clearly made him shy, but that was okay. Everything was still awkward and new, but that would change over time. Now she felt like they had all the time in the world to explore these new feelings. In the meantime, he was hungry.

She smiled wickedly as she opened the box and pulled

the lid off of a large tub of *chocolate mousse.* He'll eat anything, huh?

It was high time John got over his dislike of chocolate, and she knew just how to tempt him.

She went back to the bedroom and stood in the doorway, her left arm wrapped around the plastic tub as she dipped her index finger into the mix and slid it into her mouth.

John sat up on the bed. "What's that?"

She grinned. "Chocolate mousse."

He warded her off with his hands. "Stay away."

She took a step closer, dipping her finger again. "You said at this point you'd eat anything."

He scooted back on the bed. "Anything but that!"

She climbed onto the foot of the bed and perched there licking chocolate from her finger. "Come on. Don't be such a baby. How can a grown man be so afraid of a little chocolate?"

"I'm not afraid of it. I hate the stuff and you know why."

"I had the same experience you did, and I got over it. When was the last time you tried it?"

He crossed his arms over his chest, shaking his head stubbornly. "I don't want to try it."

She dipped her finger in the mousse and leaned forward. Spreading it over his lips, she slowly sipped it off. "Are you sure?"

She followed his gaze to the spot where her robe gaped low over the curve of her breast. He dipped his finger in the chocolate. "Well . . . maybe I will have a taste."

Chapter Eight

John hadn't even left a note. Tracy couldn't identify the range of emotions that swept through her the next morning when she realized she was in the apartment alone. The box Lisa had sent over with their clothes was sitting on the counter. John's tuxedo was in a garment bag beside it.

When Tracy called John's apartment that day, she got his machine. Just as she did for the next three days. She had to face facts, he was avoiding her. He'd told her he loved her, and now he couldn't face her.

Feeling restless, she pulled out her sketch pad. She flipped it open and almost closed it again. Most of the sketches featured John.

John sprawled across the carpet with his jaw propped on his palm, grinning up at her with his heartbreaker smile.

John standing beside a karaoke machine with a microphone in his hand.

The two of them kissing in the snow.

Were these memories all that was left of their relationship? They were supposed to be in love but, true to form, John had run away when things got serious. Why had she expected more?

When Tracy came home from Lisa's shop Thursday evening, there was a message on her answering machine. "We need to talk." Tracy's heart rate picked up at the sound of John's voice. "Meet me at Spotlight at seven thirty sharp."

A comedy club? Of all the weird places to talk. Still, Tracy was anxious to confront John. So Thursday evening, seven thirty sharp, she was sitting at a table at Spotlight. It was no great surprise that he hadn't shown up yet. John's internal clock was ten minutes behind the rest of the world.

Tracy looked around. John must have sold some jokes to one of the performers tonight. In the past, anytime John sold a routine to a comedian, they got together at the comedy club to watch the delivery. It had been a long time since they'd done that. Maybe this was John's way of putting their friendship back on its old footing.

Tracy sighed heavily. She knew what tonight was about. John was going to tell her that their relationship had become too complicated. He may have said he loved her but, he was going to California and blah, blah, blah. She knew this whole routine.

Quite frankly, she wasn't in the mood to hear it. She loved him, and that had better mean something to him. Didn't friendship, years being there for each other count for anything? Whatever happened tonight, she wasn't going to let him off easy. They had started something, and like it or not, he was going to have to finish it.

The show was scheduled to start at eight o'clock and at seven fifty, the lights dimmed. Tracy began to worry. Had John decided not to show up? Something had to be wrong. He wasn't usually this late.

Seven fifty-five, no John. At eight o'clock, theme music started piping through the club. When the show's host came out on stage, Tracy decided to give John a call. No answer at his apartment. By the time she returned, the host was welcoming the first comedian on stage.

"Okay, folks, tonight we have an amateur with us. He hasn't been doing stand-up for long, but he's clearly a natural. Hailing from right here in Washington, D.C., please give a warm welcome to John Fitzgerald."

Tracy couldn't believe her ears, this had to be some mistake. But sure enough, it was her John who walked out on stage.

"Good evening, ladies and gentlemen. You all may be wondering what I'm doing here, and I'm gonna have to be honest with you. The fact is, I've failed miserably at nearly every legitimate job I've ever tried to hold down, and stand-up comedy is my last shot at being a productive member of society."

The audience chuckled.

"If you folks can't spare a few laughs, I hope you can spare some change when you see me out on the street corner after the show."

He got a smattering of laughter out of the audience, which grew to a roar as he described his jobs as a stuttering jingle writer, a geographically challenged cab driver, and a fry cook with a certificate from the Montgomery County fire department banning him from cooking in public facilities. His voice was rich and alive as he acted out each job, and the audience responded to his natural charm.

John went on to talk about the fact that he was writing a screenplay and moving to California.

"After all, folks," John said. "You haven't failed miserably unless you've failed in L.A."

Tracy felt her body grow cold. It hurt to hear him talk about his plans to move away from her. Those plans were still foremost in his mind. Maybe more so because of what had happened between them.

She remembered Lisa's instructions to make him stay. Tracy didn't know if it was possible, but after all they'd been through, she was determined to make an effort after the show.

Her resolve was unshakable. Until she heard John's next line of jokes. He began to talk about the dynamics of friendship between a man and a woman. Tracy's little pinky nail found its way between her teeth, and she chewed fervently even though she'd given up the habit in high school. She was terrified of what was coming next.

Sure enough, John began talking about their relationship. Though most of the jokes were fictitious, Tracy recognized the undertones of their situation. The jokes may have been funny, but she felt raw and exposed. How could he betray her like this?

Finally the sting of embarrassment became too much and Tracy walked out.

John was able to catch up to Tracy in the parking lot. "Tracy, Tracy," he shouted at her back. Halfway to her car, she stopped and turned around.

He ran up to her. "Why did you leave before the show was over?"

Tracy rolled her eyes. "Maybe I got tired of being on display."

John felt heat creep up his neck. He shoved his hands into his pockets. "Come on, Trace. You know—"

"No. I don't *know* anything. What happened after I left? Did you continue your monologue on how the transition from friendship to romance is so awkward? Did you tell them how you made love to me all night long and then didn't call me for days?"

That statement piqued the interest of a couple hurrying by. Despite the cold weather, they slowed their pace to listen. John grabbed her arm and pulled her to his car. He unlocked her door but she wouldn't get in. "Tracy, we're in a parking lot for goodness sake."

She laughed bitterly. "That's interesting, you didn't

mind making our relationship a spectator sport when you were on stage. Is public humiliation only allowed when you're getting paid for it?''

John winced. And this was from a woman he had to beg to send food back in a restaurant because she hated controversy. He hadn't seen her this mad since high school when he'd promised her front row seats at the Prince concert and they'd ended up sitting in the nose-bleed section because he'd procrastinated.

"Trace, do you really think I would have invited you out tonight if I'd known you were going to take it this way?"

"How should I know what you were thinking? I left messages all week, but you didn't seem to have anything to say to me. Then you call and say we need to talk, and I find out you intended to 'talk' in front of a room full of people. Isn't this your way of letting me down easy—not to mention indirectly?"

John's eyes widened in surprise. He'd had no idea she'd see it that way. It was true he hadn't returned most of her calls. He'd been rehearsing every evening. And he'd called her as soon as he'd sorted everything out in his head. He'd hoped they could have a long talk after the show, but now he'd blown it.

She had this way of looking at him that made him feel two feet tall even though he towered over her and out-weighed her by almost a hundred pounds. Getting out of this mess was going to be very tricky, but they couldn't hash it out in this parking lot.

He sighed. "Look, Trace, I can see that I've handled this whole thing very badly. But I never meant for tonight to turn out like this. Let's go back to my apartment and I'll try to explain."

She seemed resistant at first, but she finally agreed to follow him back home. When they entered his apartment, John knew they had some heavy issues to cover, so he tried to loosen her up.

"Guess what I've got?"

She looked at him with a blank expression. "What," she asked warily.

He went into the kitchen and returned with a box of Swiss Miss hot chocolate. He shook the box in front of her. "It's the kind with mini marshmallows."

A tiny smile fought through her stubbornly closed lips. "Did you buy that for me?"

"Who else? Although, my appreciation for chocolate has improved recently." Heat filled him at the memory. Her cheeks stained a dusky rose. "Do you want a cup?"

She nodded shyly. He could tell she was beginning to warm toward him. The lines of tension around her mouth had begun to fade and she was no longer rubbing her palms against her jeans.

When he had two steaming mugs of hot chocolate ready, he carried them over and sat across from her on the floor. There was no easy way for him to say everything that needed to be said, so he decided to plunge right in.

"Tracy, I know you think that because I didn't return your phone calls this week, I've been avoiding you."

She took a sip of her drink and nodded. "The thought did cross my mind."

"I wasn't avoiding you." He held his mug without drinking from it, letting his fingers absorb the heat. "I was rehearsing my act for tonight. It was sort of my comic debut."

"So, this is the new career opportunity you'd been hinting at." She set her drink aside.

He nodded.

"Congratulations. I don't think I mentioned during my tirade earlier that you were very good. But I don't understand why you couldn't tell me about this."

"I wasn't sure how it was going to work out. It started out as kind of a dare from one of the comics at Spotlight." He grinned at her. "And you know how I respond to dares. He and a few of the other acts agreed to give me some pointers after closing this week. I wanted to talk to you about it, but things were so mixed up in my head."

He put his drink aside and leaned toward her. "I don't want you to go on thinking I was making fun of our relationship tonight. I wasn't, in fact, I wasn't going to use the material, but my other jokes just weren't working. They told me the audience responds best when you talk about stuff that's personal to you. Things they can relate to."

"Your jokes were funny. Especially the stuff about all your jobs. You were great, but why did you have to talk about us?"

He shook his head, rubbing his hands over his face. "I don't know. Because us has been the only thing on my mind lately. Darn it, Trace, you're my best friend. You're the person I usually turn to when I get confused about stuff like this. But how can I talk to my best friend about being in love with my best friend?"

Tracy nodded. "I can understand that. The change in our relationship is going to take some getting used to. Things are more complicated between us."

"That's right. So much has happened, I needed to be sure I'm doing the right thing."

She stood and faced him, light shining in her eyes. "So, did you mean it?"

"Mean what?"

"What you told me. Do you love me?"

"Yes. Of course."

She stepped up to him and wrapped her arms around his neck. "I'm so relieved to hear you say that. I love you, too. So much."

Their lips came together like two souls connecting.

John still wasn't used to the effect the news had on him. Women had said those three little words to him before but it had never set off such an explosion of joy in his heart. Tracy loved him. He'd never felt more powerful, exhilarated or . . . scared.

So many changes were going on at this point in his life.

He loved Tracy, the news that she loved him in return should have made things perfect. Instead it made things worse. He had to tell her the rest.

How could he tell her he loved her then tell her he was leaving in the next breath?

She pulled back from him. "You feel tense. What's wrong?"

"Well, there's something else we need to discuss. You know I'm leaving—"

Relief crossed her face. "Of course, California. I know this doesn't change your plans. I understand that. But in the meantime, we can still begin to explore—"

Pain knotted his stomach. "No, you don't understand. I'm leaving in three days."

She stilled. "What?"

He pointed to his plane ticket on the counter.

"Three days?" She walked over and picked it up. "But this doesn't say California. It says New Orleans. I don't understand."

"The guy who got me into this comedy gig, Trevor, he thinks I have real potential. He knows about my screenplay and California. He offered me the opportunity to travel with his comedy tour, opening his act and learning the business. This way I'll get to California and make a little money on the way."

Tracy didn't say anything for a long while. The tightness had returned to her mouth. "How long have you been planning this?"

"Trevor's original opening act was offered a movie role Monday. He saw me practicing, and I was a quick, not to mention cheap, replacement."

"So what is this? Some new form of relationship avoidance. You tell me you love me and then you leave?"

"I didn't plan for things to turn out this way."

"Maybe not, but it is awfully convenient, isn't it? The first time you get involved with a woman you can't run away from emotionally, you find a way to run physically instead.''

''Tracy, please—''

''This is your standard mode of operation. You panic the minute things get serious. What is so important about that screenplay? When is something real and alive going to matter as much to you as that stack of paper?''

''This is something I've got to do. You know that, Tracy. I've got to make this work *because* I love you.''

''What? That makes no sense.''

''Yes, it does. What can I offer you, right now? Everything I have is tied up in this dream. I have to take this shot, prove myself. Then I'll be ready—''

Tracy looked at him, and in one glance, saw all his secrets. She shook her head. ''No, this is about more than you proving yourself. You don't think any woman can be happy with you now. You think you have to do this to be worthy, and it's not true.''

John opened his mouth to respond, but he couldn't find the words. He hadn't set down any roots. He didn't hold down a conventional job. Part of him did wonder how he could make a woman happy when so much of his life was still up in the air.

''Tracy, you deserve the best. A man who can give you everything you want. Right now, I just don't think I can—''

''No, it's not that you can't, you won't. You won't stick around and find out if we can make this work.'' She picked up her purse from a chair. ''If you're not willing to try, there's nothing left to be said.''

He watched her walk to the door. ''Tracy, where are you going? Wait. Trace—''

The door clicked shut behind her.

He'd blown it again.

Tracy punched the button for the elevator. How had things gotten so mixed up? She and John had been friends for nearly twenty years and he was throwing it all away. He'd said he loved her. Didn't he realize that he may never see her again?

The elevator chimed. She almost stepped on board, when a thought struck her. He was leaving. In three days. After that who knew when she'd see him again. She couldn't let him leave with things the way they were.

This was his dream. He'd wanted it for as long as she could remember. She couldn't blame him for that and she couldn't stand in his way. But she could make sure he remembered her. . . .

Tracy spun around and knocked on John's door. It was a few minutes before he answered, and when he did, he looked at her as if he couldn't believe she was standing there. "Trace?"

Without saying a word, she went into his arms. "I'm sorry I walked out on you. I was hurting, but I realized I couldn't let you leave like this."

He squeezed her tightly. "I never meant to hurt you, Trace. You've got to believe me. I know I'm always making a mess of my relationships. That's probably why you didn't want to get involved with me back in high school after the prom—"

"What are you talking about?"

"I think I fell in love with you the moment I saw you in that blue prom dress. I wanted to kiss you and so I did, but afterward you said it was best that we remain friends."

"I didn't say that. You said that."

"No, I—"

"You were apologizing for kissing me."

He shook his head. "I was going to apologize for kissing you in the *parking lot*. I'd planned to wait for somewhere more romantic."

She pulled out of his arms. "You mean you didn't think that kiss was a mistake?"

"No, but you jumped in and told me that you agreed we should just be friends, so I went along with you."

She slammed her palm into her forehead. "Stupid, stupid, stupid. We've wasted all this time, because I have a bad habit of interrupting." She looked up at him. "Now we've run out of time."

He pulled her back into his arms. "Not just yet."

He pressed his lips to hers and Tracy felt all the love and tenderness of ten years of waiting behind it. His mouth was gentle and impatient at the same time.

When the kiss broke, she clung to him. "We've been through so much together. I can't believe that's going to end."

He stroked her back. "It doesn't have to end. Maybe when I come back—no, I can't expect you to wait that long."

"How long?"

"That's just it. I don't know."

"I understand. The timing isn't right." She reached up and began to unbutton his shirt, trailing tiny kisses over the exposed skin. "But we still have tonight."

Chapter Nine

John tossed a green and blue sweater into his suitcase. Tracy had given him that sweater for Christmas last month. He picked it up from on top of the pile of T-shirts in the suitcase and studied it. They hadn't been able to get together during the holidays, so it had arrived on his doorstep wrapped in Tracy's hand-drawn wrapping paper—this edition had little naked reindeer shivering in the snow. The wrapping paper always gave a clue to what was inside.

He put the sweater back down in the suitcase. Would he need sweaters in California? Probably not. He started to lift out the sweater but couldn't bring himself to do it. He hadn't been able to see Trace for Christmas this year, but it hadn't stung as much because he knew she was just a twenty-minute drive away. Next Christmas she would be thousands of miles away.

He pushed the thought aside. People made a stronger effort to see each other when they were farther apart. They'd see each other.

Wouldn't they?

What if she became too busy with art shows and commissions? What if the long-distance and travel costs became too much for her to handle? What if . . . she were married? To someone else.

The thought turned his body as cold as stone. He dug his fingers into the soft wool of the sweater. Next Christmas she might be making sweaters for some other guy. What else could he expect from so far away? They hadn't even had the chance to investigate this new stage of their relationship. Would it be easy for her to forget him?

He sank down on the bed, pushing the suitcase aside. What was he doing? Taking his shot in California was what he'd always wanted. Why wasn't he happier?

Tracy. He *really* wasn't going to see her anymore. The knowledge finally became clear to him. He would be in California and she would be here. He couldn't just jump into his car and go see her when things weren't going well. He couldn't fall asleep with her on the other end of the telephone snoring in his ear.

He couldn't make love to her all night and listen to her saying his name in that soft husky voice she only used when she was satisfied. He'd known her for twenty years and that was something he'd just learned about her. How many other intimate secrets, shared only between lovers, would he miss out on? Who would learn those secrets in his place?

He shoved the suitcase off the bed violently. He couldn't stand the thought of—

No! He wouldn't even picture it. John picked up his plane ticket from the night stand. The plane would leave tomorrow morning at ten fifteen. He was supposed to be on it. But maybe he and Tracy could make it if he stayed. Or maybe he'd stay and damage their relationship more than he already had.

How could he leave when he still had so many doubts?

The telephone began to ring and John decided to let the machine pick it up. He had too much on his mind to deal with Trevor's last minute instructions or his mother's incessant worries.

He left the room to get a soda as the machine clicked on. When he returned, the sound of Tracy's voice froze him in place.

". . . to bother you. I know you're probably very busy packing and everything."

He wanted to leap the length of the room and grab the receiver but his legs were paralyzed.

"If you don't have time to deal with this, don't worry about it. I think I can handle it myself, I just thought you ought to know . . . um, I got a call from New York. We won the contest."

Her words jolted him to life. He snatched up the receiver. "Trace? Trace, are you still there?"

"Oh, John, I didn't think you were home."

"Did you just say what I thought you said?"

"Yes. We won the Rainbow Room essay contest. Crazy isn't it."

Her voice sounded shy and distant. He thought he knew her various tones and expressions, but this one was new.

"But don't worry about it. I know you have a lot on your mind right now. I'll take care of everything."

"Are you kidding me? I'm not letting you deal with this by yourself. They've probably started the media coverage already. Getting out of this isn't going to be easy."

"You're right. Valentine's Day is only two weeks away. What should we do?"

"I'm not sure. Give me some time to think about it. I'll call you back."

John hung up the phone and began to unpack his suitcase.

Tracy went to Giuseppe's Pizzeria after work Monday evening. She was surprised when John called the day before and asked her to meet him. Especially since he should have been on a plane to New Orleans yesterday.

She almost tripped over her own feet when she saw John

sitting at a table waiting for her. "What's going on? How could you possibly have gotten here before me?"

He shrugged. "I live closer than you do."

She shook her head, sliding in across from him. "That never made a difference before."

He didn't answer. He just took a sip from the mug in his hand.

"What are you drinking?"

"Hot chocolate," he said, winking at her.

Tracy didn't smile back at him. She dropped her eyes and turned her head toward the window. Of course he was going to sit there, looking so handsome in the sweater she'd knit him for Christmas. Everything about him from the curve of his lips to the way he let the mug dangle from two fingers had a memory attached to it.

And they were all tearing her up inside.

"I already ordered the pizza. It should be here soon."

"Sounds good." She fiddled with the table's salt and pepper shakers so she wouldn't have to look John in the eye. Things were so awkward between them. "I thought you'd be in New Orleans by now."

"I called Trevor and told him I wasn't going to be able to make it."

Tracy's heart leaped with joy. John wasn't leaving? It was too good to be true. She was afraid to hope. "So, does this mean you're not going at all?"

He tapped his fingers on the table. "It means that Trevor gave me a couple weeks to sort this out—he thinks it's a family emergency. He said I can meet the tour in Texas. I won't make as much money, but . . ." He shrugged.

Tracy stared out the window, trying to hide the acute disappointment forming in her eyes. "Well, don't worry. It won't take a couple of weeks to sort this out. All we have to do is cancel the wedding."

"I don't know if it will be that easy. What did they tell you when they called?"

"The woman caught me off guard. She congratulated

me on a beautiful essay then started spouting wedding
details right away. I told her she was talking too fast for me
to absorb anything. She said we'll also be getting detailed
letters in the mail, and she offered to fax me the information."

"Did you bring it?"

"John, I don't have a fax machine. Besides what would
be the point? I can't believe they're going to put together
a whole wedding in two weeks. We should let them know
we're canceling right away."

"Well, it's not going to be that simple, Trace."

"What do you mean?"

"Right before I left to meet you, I got a call from Darrell
Sanders at the *Gazette*. He wants to interview us, the happy
couple."

"What? How did he know about the contest?"

"The Rainbow Room sent press releases to our local
newspapers. Sanders does human interest stories."

"Okay, so we just tell this Sanders person that we're not
interested in being interviewed."

John shook his head. "It's not going to be that easy.
Sanders is the type who will dig even harder if we refuse.
You'd have to work with him to understand. He's always
wanted to be an investigative reporter. He'll write about
us anyway."

"How can he write about us without our permission?"

"Very easily. It's news, at least to him. He'll probably
cut out our old yearbook pictures and get quotes from our
friends and family. In no time he'll figure out that we'd
had no intention of getting married. Then it will be all
over the media that we were trying to run some scam on
the Rainbow Room. I don't know, they might even sue us
for fraud or something."

Tracy felt her blood run cold and dropped her face into
her hands. "Oh, no. How did we get into this mess? What
are we going to do?"

"The only thing we can do. We have to do the interview."

She dropped her hands, letting them slap the table. "Are you kidding me. My parents will see that. They'll go nuts wondering why I didn't tell them we were getting married."

"Hey it will be the same with my folks, but what else can we do?"

"We cancel the wedding. Then we tell this Sanders guy that we no longer intend to get married."

"I keep trying to tell you, there will still be a story and then the word fraud may come up."

"Oh, man, what were you thinking when you talked me into this."

"Me? Excuse me, Ms. Fields, but this was all *your* idea."

"Oh, yeah, this is my fault just the way you said it was my fault when you climbed Mrs. Fenton's crabapple tree then fell out and broke her ceramic lawn animals."

"Okay, *that* was my fault, but this was definitely your fault. If you hadn't started working with Lisa we never would have seen that flier. Then you challenged me to—"

She grinned, feeling a normalcy between them return with their bickering. The pizza arrived and Tracy began making a neat stack of pepperoni on the side of her plate. "Instead of pointing fingers, why don't you put your energy to good use and figure out how to fix this mess?"

His face became serious. "Look, when Sanders called, I told him we'd go ahead and do the interview."

"How could you without discussing it with me first."

"Because, as I just explained to you, we have no choice."

"Okay, so we do this interview, then what? The Rainbow Room is going to expect us to start communicating with them about our wedding plans."

He pressed his fingers into his temple. "Let's just get through tomorrow's interview first. I need some time to think this through."

"Tomorrow? The interview is tomorrow?"

He nodded.

"Great," she said, dropping her pizza. "What on earth am I going to wear?"

Tuesday morning, John paced Lisa's shop. Tracy had insisted that if they had to do this interview, then they had to do it here. John glanced at his watch. For the second time in two days, he was actually early. This crazy mess was definitely getting to him.

Lisa opened the door for Tracy a few minutes later. Tracy took off her coat and John's eyes widened as he took in the clingy rose sweater she wore with a long matching skirt and high heeled leather boots.

Lisa hung up her coat. "Good, Tracy-girl, you took my advice about the scarf."

Tracy touched purple and blue silk tied elegantly around her neck. "Thanks for loaning it to me. You were right, it was just the touch this outfit needed."

John walked over and took her hands. "Wow, look at you."

She smiled shyly. "You said they'd take our pictures. I wanted to look my best." She reached up to adjust the lapel on his sport coat. "You look pretty good yourself."

Lisa placed a hand on both of their shoulders. "I have a couple upstairs looking through the wedding books, but they should be gone by the time your Mr. Sanders gets here." She gave their shoulders another squeeze. "I do appreciate all you've done for me." Then she hurried upstairs to attend to her customers.

For a few minutes, John and Tracy were left alone. They both looked around for an escape from the awkwardness.

"Um, Lisa has a nice little buffet set up for us. Can I get you anything?"

She shrugged. "I'm not hungry, but some punch would be nice."

John turned the corner into the kitchen and filled two glasses with punch. When he returned, he saw Tracy flipping through some sort of book. She realized he was approaching and shoved it back into her bag.

He handed her the punch. "What was that?"

The color in her cheeks deepened. "Nothing."

He put his drink down and faced her. "Come on, Trace, what was it?"

She shrugged, looking away. "Just some memories. No big deal."

"If it's no big deal, why won't you let me see?"

She rolled her eyes, plunging her hand into her bag. "All right, fine. Here."

She handed him a tiny book that she'd bound with ribbon. He opened it. The first page was a sketch of him. He turned to the next, a drawing of them kissing in the snow. He continued to flip. All the sketches were of the two of them. The next one was very familiar. He looked up at Lisa's walls. This sketch resembled the photograph of the man's hand placing a diamond ring on a female hand, but it wasn't a diamond being placed on the finger in Tracy's sketch.

"What is this?"

Tracy didn't answer, she fixed her eyes on the ceiling, clearly embarrassed.

He looked back down at the drawing. "It's a ring isn't it. A twist-tie ring." John felt his throat constrict. What had begun as a joke, suddenly touched the core of his heart. That ring, had meant something to her.

He looked at the other sketches. It was a chronicle of their relationship. From the proposal to the two of them standing on top of a wedding cake.

He laid the book down on the table and reached for Tracy. She had folded her arms over her chest and was facing the wall. He turned her to face him with a hand on her shoulder.

She came easily into his arms, burying her face in the arch of his neck. He bent his head to her ear. "Tracy, sweetheart, I'm so sorry things got so messed up. But I'll make it up to you, honey. Do you hear me? I *do* love you.''

He felt her nod against him, but before she could respond further, they heard footsteps on the stairs. They immediately broke apart.

Lisa came down first with a couple in tow. ''Tonya, Jacob, I'd like you to meet Tracy and John.'' The four of them shook hands and exchanged polite conversation.

Tonya picked up Tracy's book from the table and began to flip through it. ''Jacob, look it's a memory book of their relationship.''

John heard Tracy gasp and she instinctively reached out. He grabbed her hand and squeezed her fingers. ''It's okay,'' he whispered in her ear.

''This is incredible,'' Jacob said, turning to Lisa. ''Do you have these made for all your clients?''

Lisa didn't skip a beat. ''That's a special option. You can only purchase a memory book with the deluxe planning package.''

Tonya handed Tracy back the book. ''I just love it. It's so intimate. We've been to several wedding consultants and none of them offered anything with such a personal touch. Please tell me more about this deluxe planning package.''

Lisa went into her pitch, and when Jacob and Tonya left, Tracy and Lisa went into her office upstairs to hash out the details.

John was still reeling with the affects the memory book had on him. He and Tracy had a long history together. She was probably the only person in the world who knew him inside and out.

''John. John, you'll never believe this.'' Tracy came skipping down the stairs and threw her arms around his neck.

''What is it?''

''Lisa and I have finally come up with something that will set Ribbon-in-the-Sky apart from all the other wedding coordinators. We're going to do a line of specialty packages to offer along with the various wedding plans, like a portrait of the bride and groom, or memory books, or portrait invitations."

"Wow, you two were really busy up there."

"And as a payment for my creative services, Lisa is making me a partner in her business."

"Whoa, isn't that kind of sudden?" He lowered his voice. "You haven't known Lisa for very long."

"John, I can't explain it, but there are some people that from the moment you meet them, you click. I just *know* it's right."

He stared into her caramel-colored eyes. "I think I know exactly what you mean."

Lisa answered the door, calling over her shoulder, "Your Mr. Sanders is here for your interview."

Chapter Ten

For the interview, John sat down on the sofa next to Tracy, who immediately picked up one of the colorful throw pillows and clutched it in her lap. She was chomping away on the nail of her pinky.

Lisa hovered in the background and Darrell Sanders sat opposite them, tapping the eraser on his pen against his teeth. He turned on his tape recorder, signaling the beginning of the interview.

"Okay, John, Tracy, what made the two of you decide to enter the Rainbow Room contest?"

Tracy leaned forward to answer and the pillow on her lap popped through her arms and landed on the floor. John leaned down to pick it up and stuffed it behind him. He put his arm around Tracy to steady her. He'd never seen her this nervous.

She clasped her hands on her lap. "Well," she looked over her shoulder and smiled at Lisa. "We learned about the contest through Lisa. She runs Ribbon-in-the-Sky. Uh, that's one word, separated by hyphens. R-I-B—"

John squeezed her shoulder, then answered the question

Sanders was really asking. "Actually, Tracy and I fell in love at our high school senior prom. We spent years avoiding it until we finally admitted our feelings to each other recently. We really hadn't made any formal plans to get married. Tracy had been working with Lisa, and we entered the contest on an impulse. Now that we've won, Lisa is helping us get the details straightened out."

Sanders nodded and moved into some easy questions about their backgrounds, how they met, and so on. Tracy began to relax, and finally stopped trying to give Lisa's shop the hard sell. John thought the interview was going very well, much better than he'd expected until Sanders asked what their dream wedding would be.

They'd talked a lot about weddings lately, but he didn't think Tracy really had anything special in mind. He was surprised to see Tracy's face take on a dreamy look. "I've always dreamed of a candlelight wedding."

Tracy continued to speak and Sanders scribbled notes furiously. Then he turned to John, "Do you have anything to add?"

John picked up Tracy's hand. "Tracy is already my dream girl. Just being able to marry her will fulfill all my dreams."

While Sanders' head was dipped over his notebook, Tracy shot John a look that told him she thought he was overdoing it.

He frowned. She didn't believe him. Of course, why should she believe it. He wasn't going to marry her. Instead, he told her he loved her and was moving across the country in the same breath. Why should she believe anything he said, especially now.

He'd said the words for Sanders' benefit, but he was surprised at how true they were. Tracy *was* his dream girl. When he told everyone he was going to write a screenplay and move to California, everyone had laughed except for Trace. When he ran through job after job like water, Tracy was the only person who understood where his heart was.

Where was his heart now? He looked at her. His heart was with Tracy.

"Okay, last question," Sanders said. "Your wedding will take place on February fourteenth. What does that mean to you."

"I owe Tracy so much," John said. "I have to make up for so many Valentine's Days and romantic nights. Tracy deserves the best. Which includes getting married on the most romantic day of the year."

Sanders nodded, apparently satisfied with the material they'd given him, then his photographer posed them for a few pictures. While Tracy was chatting with the photographer, John pulled Lisa aside.

"Lisa, I'm going to need your help with something." He let his gaze rest on Tracy. "There's something very important that I've got to do tonight."

That night, Tracy rode up on the elevator with a heavy heart. Their interview had gone very well, but she still didn't know how they were going to resolve their problem. They had to cancel the wedding, but the article was going to complicate things considerably.

She'd tried to talk to John after the interview, but he claimed he had a plan and would tell her in due time.

Due time. What did that mean? They'd already wasted so much time, and the longer this charade continued the more painful it was becoming for her. She was going to be a partner in Ribbon-in-the-Sky and right now the sight of wedding favors made her want to cry.

It would have been so much easier if she could have avoided falling in love with John. But that would have been like avoiding breathing.

She stepped out of the elevator and trudged down the hallway to her apartment. What was that attached to her door knob? A white balloon filled with helium bobbed on a string.

She untied the balloon from the door knob. The words "Pop Me" were written in black marker on the outside. A long stick pin was taped to her door.

Puzzled, Tracy brought the balloon inside and sat down on her sofa. She could see some kind of note through the transparent walls of the balloon.

Feeling a rush of anticipation, she gently pricked the skin of the balloon with the pin. With a loud burst of air, a tiny white invitation fell into her lap. Only two things were printed inside. John's address. And a time.

Midnight tonight.

John wanted her to meet him at his place at midnight? What was going on? She picked up the phone and tried to call him, but she only got his machine. She left a brief message detailing her confusion and confirming that she'd be there.

At eleven fifty-nine, Tracy knocked on John's apartment door. She wasn't quite sure what apparel was appropriate for this particular midnight rendezvous, so she wore a simple sweater and slacks.

John pulled open the door, stepping aside for her to see the room beyond him. Every flat surface in the room held a candle, filling his barren room with intimate dancing light.

"John?" She walked in slowly, not believing her eyes. "All the candles? What's going on? Are you joining some new religion, or did you forget to pay your electric bill?"

He shut the door behind her, then walked over to her. "I don't know if the Rainbow Room will give us a candlelight wedding, but I can at least give you a candlelight proposal."

"Proposal? I don't under—"

He nodded, placing a finger to her lips to halt her words. "I know. Let me do this right."

With her standing before him, John got down on one knee. "I know the first time I did this it was in front of a large group of people, and it was a sort of joke. This time it's just you and me, and I mean everything I'm about to say."

Tracy's head was spinning. She felt tears welling in her eyes. Could this really be happening?

"Tracy, I know I've been surrounded by confusion lately and I haven't been very clear on what I want, but today it all became very clear to me. I want you. I want you to marry me. For real. Please, Tracy, will you be my wife?"

Tracy couldn't stand towering above him, plus her knees were giving out, so she sank down in front of him. "But what about California? You'll be leaving and I just worked out an agreement with Lisa here . . ."

"These past few days, I've really had to take a look at what I want for my life. I've spent many years telling everyone that I was going to California when I finished my screenplay, but do you know what? I have yet to finish it and I finally realized why those last hundred pages have been so difficult. It's not because I don't have time or because my other jobs have interfered. It's because I don't want to go."

Tracy shook her head in confusion. "You don't want to go? What do you mean? You were just about to jump on a plane to New Orleans."

He squeezed her fingers. "That's because the opportunity to travel with Trevor's act came up suddenly. Right at the time our relationship became serious. I thought it was a sign—if I didn't go after my dream, I'd never get the chance again. This was my last chance to make something of myself. Make myself into the kind of man you deserve."

"That's crazy." Tracy reached out to cup his chin in her palm. "You're perfect right now, just as you are. You're funny, talented, intelligent, and an incredible lover."

"Thanks for the vote of confidence. I finally believe in myself as much as you've believed in me all these years. I don't need to go to California to fulfill my dreams. All my dreams are right here.''

"What are you going to do if you're not going to California?'' she asked.

"The manager at Spotlight is going to put me on the rotation of local comedians. Also, talking to Sanders this morning gave me an idea. I called my old editor at the paper and proposed an idea for a new column. It's called 'Comic Watch.' I'd interview local comedians, spotlight the hottest clubs, etc. He loved it. He gave me the job.''

"Are you sure this is what you want?''

"You are what I want. Please say you'll marry me.''

She threw her arms around him, knocking them both off balance. They rolled to one side and sprawled on the carpet. "Of course, I'll marry you!''

John stretched out above her and kissed her with slow loving passion. They cuddled and kissed in the candlelight, basking in the glow of their happiness. Then he lifted his head suddenly.

"What's wrong?'' she asked, lazily.

He sat up. "I almost forgot the most important part.'' He started digging in his pocket.

She sat up, too. "Did you upgrade to pipe cleaners this time? I hope it's blue because that would match my sweater.''

He pulled out a box and flipped it open. "Sorry to disappoint you, but all I have to offer you is this.''

The diamond caught the light of the flickering candles reflecting the brilliant light of their love. "Oh my,'' she gasped.

He removed it from the box, and Tracy's hand shook as she held it out. "It's beautiful.''

She admired the ring on her finger and the man at her side. Dreams really did come true. "Can I ask you something?''

He smiled at her. "Sure. What is it?"

"Why did you want me to meet you here at midnight?"

He looked down at his hands and a stain of color deepened his cheeks. "It was midnight when I first kissed you after the prom. You remembered so many of the details of our relationship. I wanted you to know that those memories are important to me, too."

She wrapped her arms around him. "John, I love you."

*Mr. and Mrs. Gregory Michael Fields request the honor of your presence at the marriage of their daughter Tracy
to Mr. John Lloyd Fitzgerald
Saturday, the fourteenth of February at six o'clock
Rainbow Room
New York*

Tracy gripped her delicate bouquet of white rosebuds tighter between her gloved hands as she heard the first strains of the "Wedding March." The Rainbow Room staff had helped them weave tiny reminders of the night they first fell in love into their wedding. The white rosebuds resembled the flowers from her corsage, and all her bridesmaids wore blue taffeta, similar to the gown she wore to the prom.

Her father leaned down and kissed her on the temple. "You look beautiful, sweetheart. I'm so proud of you."

Tracy took her father's arm, hoping she wouldn't burst into tears. Her heart was filled with so many emotions, she couldn't believe she was about to get married to her childhood friend, her teenage crush, and now her lifelong partner.

The music reached a crescendo and she took the first tentative step down the red-carpeted aisle. She looked to the center of the room where John waited for her, under a magnificent crystal chandelier surrounded by a shimmering rainbow of lights.

The guests circled the altar from all sides. She couldn't believe all her friends and family were there. She could see her mother in front, smiling with joy and pride.

Her eyes returned to John. She met him at the end of the aisle and he took her hand. As the minister spoke, they forged a lifelong bond of love and family. She looked up into his warm rum-colored eyes, and when the minister asked for her pledge, she spoke loud and confident. "I do."

John promised to love and cherish her and sealed the promise with a shiny gold band which he placed on her finger.

At the words, "You may now kiss the bride," Tracy's heart felt as though it would burst. His lips descended on hers and she felt all their love pouring through their kiss.

The reception was held in a section of the Rainbow Room that looked over the New York skyline. The lighted city below against the night sky made Tracy feel like she was sitting on top of the world. The room was lit with candles and each table had a centerpiece of heart-shaped wreaths for Valentine's Day.

Her mother reached for Tracy's elbow. "It's time to cut the cake."

Everyone gathered around as Tracy and John stood before their wedding cake, which was made from three-tiered heart-shaped cakes with white satin icing and striking red sugar roses. The wedding couple standing under a heart shaped white lace arch, bore an uncanny resemblance to John and Tracy.

"If you shove this cake in my face, I'll kill you. Do you understand?" she asked from the corner of her mouth.

He leaned down to whisper in her ear. "Don't worry about your face, but I hope it's not chocolate cake, because you know where I like to li—"

She gripped his arm, stifling a giggle. "Shh, our parents are here." She picked up the ceremonial knife.

They held the knife together, cutting the first slice from the frosted heart. John broke off a small portion and raised it to her lips. "Here, Trace, have a piece of my heart."

The wedding guests cooed over John's quip as the photographer clicked the shot of him feeding her.

Tracy picked up a piece of cake for John, unable to think of a cute remark. Instead her naughty streak kicked in. John took a bite of the cake she offered him, but a large white dollop of icing was left on her thumb. She saw the photographer raise his camera, and at the last moment, she swiped her thumb over John's nose.

He laughed, reaching for a napkin. "You're going to pay for that tonight, sweetheart."

She winked at him. "I'm looking forward to it."

They both turned, becoming distracted by a conversation between their parents.

"I always knew you two would end up married. I wasn't a bit surprised when you sprang the news on us," John's father said.

John's mother slapped his arm. "Now you know that's not true Reginald. You almost fell over flat when Tracy and John announced their wedding plans."

Tracy's mother smiled an I've-got-a-secret smile. "I knew Tracy and John were made for each other the day I sent them off to the prom together. John had that same look in his eye that Greg had on our first date. It took him a while to realize it, but it was there."

Tracy and John exchanged looks of amusement as their parents argued over who was the first to realize their children were in love.

John leaned down to whisper in Tracy's ear. "Well, whichever of them figured it out first, I wish they'd clued us in. Clearly, we were the last to know."

Tracy laughed and one of her bridesmaids rushed over. "Come on, Trace, it's time for you to toss the bouquet."

Tracy went to the head of the room and they helped her stand on a chair.

"Okay, here it comes." Gripping the bouquet between two hands, she bent her knees and tossed the flowers over her shoulder.

She heard a flurry of movement behind her, and when she turned around she saw Lisa dive past two smaller girls to catch the bouquet. "I've got it! I've got it, Tracy-girl! All these years of planning other people's weddings, it's about time I got to plan one of my own."

Tracy laughed. She and Lisa had become good friends in the short time they'd known each other. That's why Tracy was thrilled that Lisa had agreed to be her maid of honor. It was a perfect way to begin a new business partnership.

Lisa had been a big help preparing for the reception. It had been her idea to put a karaoke machine by the bar. She'd gotten them all started by singing Roberta Flack's "The First Time Ever I Saw Your Face" for Tracy and John.

It had been fun watching their parents sing a quartet of "We Are Family" by Sister Sledge. Tracy and John had even joined in on the chorus. Lisa finished them up with her rendition of Stevie Wonder's "Ribbon in the Sky," her moment of shameless self-promotion.

Tracy had pretended not to notice Lisa leaving her business cards next to each place setting at every table.

The celebration continued on through the night and it was everything Tracy had hoped it would be. The band began to play the instrumental of Luther Vandross's "Any Love," their song, and John led Tracy out onto the dance floor.

She looked up at him and smiled. "Are you happy?"

"Happier than I ever thought I could be." John spun her around and brought her into a low dip, just as a large clock struck midnight. "Okay, Cinderella, you aren't going to turn into a pumpkin on me, are you?"

"Not a chance."

He brought her out of the dip and tugged her tightly into his arms. "Then, do you want to get started on our honeymoon."

"Right away, my Prince Charming," she said, raising her face for his kiss.

This time, after midnight, the magic was just beginning for Tracy and John.

A PERFECT MATCH

Gwynne Forster

Susan Andrews curled up in a burnt orange barrel chair that dominated her ultramodern living room and sipped tomato juice as she watched the New Year's Eve revelers in Times Square. How could human beings be so frivolous and so foolish as to crowd into that small space in freezing temperatures, sleet, and wind just to watch a ball drop a few feet when they could see the same thing in the comfort of their warm living rooms? She thanked God that she had better sense. That she wasn't scatterbrained. She sipped more juice. At least those people weren't alone, a niggling thought intruded; they had each other, if only for those few moments. She wouldn't cry. She never cried, no matter how much a thing hurt. Crying denoted weakness. But why couldn't she meet a loveable, eligible man who could appreciate an educated, independent woman. Not that she planned to lose sleep over it. She had a good life. How many women anywhere could boast a two hundred thousand dollar condo, a six-figure income, and the respect of their peers? True some of the men with whom she worked had nervous hands and couldn't keep them off of her, but she could handle that. Still, she'd like to go to work once in a while wearing makeup, a skirt above her knees, and her hair hanging down the way those secretaries did—the girls that men chased and married. Marriage. She longed to find someone to love, marry, and to have children with, but she was thirty-five.

She sucked air through her teeth, disgusted with herself. She didn't care. She'd made her choice. She had the best of all possible worlds; she didn't have to be home by six, and she didn't cook dinner if she didn't want to. She carried the half empty glass of juice to her modern, fashionable, and rarely used kitchen, emptied it and put it in the dishwasher. No, she wouldn't exchange places with any woman, not for anything. She stepped into the shower, wiping the moisture from her eyes. Darn that steam. Half an hour later, wrapped in her silk dressing gown, she couldn't blame the shower for the moisture dripping from her eyes.

Susan awoke early New Year's morning to the insistent chimes of her doorbell.

"Aunt Grace, what are you doing here so early this morning? You're not working today, are you?"

"Honey, I never went to bed last night. I made over two hundred and fifty dollars since midnight. You must have been the only person in town who wasn't in Times Square, and I sure drove a lot of 'em home in my limousine. Never saw such a happy bunch of people. Honey, you got to do something about yourself. You can't make me believe you're content to split your life between work and this chrome mausoleum." Susan yawned exuberantly, hoping to warn her aunt that another topic would be more welcome.

"Aunt Grace, this is New Year's morning. Please don't make me start the year with that lecture."

"Alright. Alright. But you're wasting your life. You're

already thirty-five, and in a few more years, you'll be past your prime—at least according to my book. You can't make me believe you don't want a man in your life.'' She looked around and waved her hand disparagingly. "This is just a lot of pretense; you can't fool me. I'm fifty-six, but your manless life would drive me crazy. 'Course, I didn't do your cause a bit of good coming in here like this. A man should have been the first person across your doorsill this year to bring you good luck.''

She loved her aunt Grace, but she had no tolerance for superstitions and, since Grace knew that, she didn't respond.

"Would you like some coffee, Aunt Grace? I'm just getting out of bed.''

"Coffee? No thanks. I'm going home and go to bed.'' Susan watched an expression roll over her aunt's face and knew she could expect one of the woman's brilliant ideas.

"You know what?'' Grace asked, her eyes alight with anticipation. "I'm going to do your chart. Let's see now, I know your birth date; weren't you born at noon on a Sunday?''

"You're the one who keeps tract of these things. How would I know?''

"I'll look it up in my book, and I'll call you tomorrow. I should have done this years ago, but you're so scientific, never believing anything. Happy New Year.''

Susan looked out of her bedroom window early the next morning, saw torrents of rain, and decided that she'd better telephone her aunt Grace.

"Are you on call this morning? I'll never be able to hail a taxi in this weather.''

"I can take you downtown, dear, if you're in your lobby at quarter to eight.''

Susan dressed hurriedly in a yellow-green woolen suit that set off her silky, ebony complexion and complemented it with lizard accessories and a brown, mink-lined raincoat. She stepped into the rear seat of Grace's private taxi and paused, surprised to see a passenger. A man. *And what a man!*

"Honey, this is August Jackson, one of my regulars. Mr. Jackson, this is my niece, Miss"—she emphasized the word—"Susan Andrews. Susan works about six blocks from you." Susan turned to greet the man and had to swallow the lump that lodged in her throat. Someone should have prepared her. She wouldn't classify him as handsome; that was too commonplace a description. He was riveting, that's what he was. Flawless dark brown skin, thick silky brows and lashes, lean face, square chin, perfect lips, and mesmerizing light brown eyes. She shook herself out of her trance and extended her hand. *Pull yourself together, girl,* she silently admonished herself.

"I'm glad to meet you, Mister Jackson." His hand clasped hers gently, and she noticed that he looked directly at her eyes and didn't flirt. But he continued to hold her hand and a smile slowly traveled from his lips to his remarkable eyes.

"Hello, Susan. This is a pleasure." She was sure that her blink and swiftly arched eyebrow betrayed her surprise. The man looked the epitome of sophistication, but his drawl and slow speech were not that of an urban sophisticate. He glanced toward the driver's seat. "Why are you stopping, Grace? Anything wrong?"

"Have you looked out of the window recently," Grace asked him and stopped the car just beyond an exit on the FDR Drive. "I can't see two feet in front of me, it's raining so hard."

"I hadn't noticed," August said, his eyes back on Susan "Did Grace say 'Miss Andrews'?"

"I sure did," Grace put in quickly.

"How is that? I can't believe such a lovely lady isn' married."

"I suppose if I'm single, there's something wrong with

me," she said in cool even tones, pulling her hand from his. He's only a man, she told herself, though her pounding heart and racing blood belied it.

"Ah, Susan, how could you imagine such a thing? You're very beautiful, and I just think it's strange that some man hasn't convinced you to marry him. That's all." She didn't respond, but she noticed that peculiar smile of his start toward his eyes again.

Then he said, "I hope you're not against marriage." She wished he'd get off the subject of her and marriage, and she turned to him with the intention of putting the matter to rest. She just hoped he didn't notice how her heart jumped in her chest when she looked straight at him.

"Mr. Jackson," she said coolly, refusing to use his first name, "I am not against marriage, but the time, energy, and imagination spent on courting and pretending not to want what one knows one wants is a waste of time. It's a phoney process, but that's the way it's done, and I don't have time or the inclination for it."

"Hmm. I see," he replied drolly and glanced out the window as though inspecting his chances of getting more agreeable company soon.

"What do you see? In developing countries, marriages are contracted by a very simple procedure. Either the parents or the individuals engage a marriage broker or a matchmaker to find a mate. In some places, an astrologer makes the selection. The marriages work just as well, and divorce is rare by our standards." Satisfied that she'd made her point, Susan crossed her legs and looked out of the window as the water cascaded from above.

"Susan, I'm disappointed that you aren't romantic," August drawled in what was clearly a mild reproof. "I thought most women bloomed with lovely music, candlelight, and romance." Hurt and hiding it, Susan lifted her chin as though that gesture would silence him.

"Most women don't have my responsibilities."

"Or your beauty and poise," he added.

"Why is it, Mr. Jackson, that men can't talk without getting personal?" She caught his grin from the corner of her left eye.

"Oh, they can, and they do. And when you get to be fifty-five or sixty, you'll know just what I'm talking about." Surprised at his dig and concluding that he was smoother than she had surmised, she changed the subject.

"You don't speak as if you're a New Yorker. I think I hear a drawl."

"Right on both counts," he agreed, "I'm from North Carolina. Down there, we men aren't getting familiar when we pay a woman a compliment. And our women know that." Evidently Grace had been quiet as long as she could, because her words seemed to rush out of her.

"Don't worry about the time, you all, nobody's going to be on time for work today. I can just about start now, though it's still pretty dense. Mr. Jackson, did you say you were looking for your son?" Susan sat forward, aware that with her occult abilities, Grace knew whether August Jackson was looking for anyone and for whom.

"No," he replied. "I don't have any children, unfortunately. I'm looking for my brother. We were separated when he was eight and I was ten. I've been looking for him ever since. How did you happen to ask?"

"Oh, I dabble in astrology and clairvoyance, though I'm at my best when I do charts," she said proudly, "but since I saw a young boy in the stars, I thought it was your son."

"I've never married. Wasn't in a position to until just recently and, now that I could consider it, I find that these New York women are too much. I'm not going to start running around in a tuxedo every night, hanging out in bars, and competing for the attention of maître d's. This place is a mad house. Aramis cologne is out; some kind of 'noir' is in. Would you believe one of our secretaries looked down at my feet and said 'oh gee, are those . . . ?' Her voice seemed to die, literally, before she said, 'no, I see they're not Guccis.' Those shoes cost me one hundred and thirty-nine dollars plus tax, and she scoffed at them because they don't have a Gucci label.''

''Not all of our New York girls are like that,'' Grace hastened to say, having discovered his single status. He continued as though it were his favorite grouse.

''These women have such superficial values, Grace. Do you think one of them would get on a public bus, however clean, with you? When she's by herself, yes. But if you're paying, these New York girls are subject to demand a stretched out limousine just to go to a neighborhood movie. I'm used to a different type, one who wants to be with me for myself rather than for the admiration and envious looks she gets from other people.''

''Now, don't you worry none,'' Grace insisted, ''we've got nice girls here that's different. You just quit hanging around those corporate secretaries and take a good long look at some of the other ones.''

Susan refused to look either at her aunt, whom she wanted to throttle, or at August Jackson, who excited and infuriated her at the same time. She got out at her office building after biding the man a cool goodbye.

August leaned back in the corner of the cab, doing his best to keep the grin that he knew Grace could see in her rear view mirror off of his face. He hadn't lied, but he'd phrased his conversation in such a way as to tell Susan Andrews that she could get off of her high horse or not, he couldn't care less. She was cut from cloth that he liked, and when he liked something, he explored it. Fully. Talk about a double whammy. She'd poleaxed him. No indeed; she hadn't seen the last of August Jackson.

''Is she really like that,'' he asked Grace, ''or was she putting me on?''

''Well, Mr. Jackson, she thinks she's like that.''

"Thinks? You mean she isn't?" This was getting more interesting by the minute.

"She hasn't given herself a chance to find out *what* she's like. She thinks life is work and chasing goals."

"Nothing wrong with going after a goal, depending, of course, on what it is. Maybe what she needs is a new one. Maybe more than one." He found himself warming up to the subject. Susan Andrews had some traits that he liked, and one of them was a distaste for superficiality. He tuned in to Grace's next words.

"That's what I keep telling her. She wants to get married, but she doesn't want to. No, Mr. Jackson, the truth is she refuses to be bothered with the nice little rituals that you have to go through before you get married." He smiled inwardly, appreciating Grace's niece more with the seconds.

"Very interesting."

"Is it?" an obviously disapproving Grace wanted to know. "She's really a wonderful person, socially conscious and all that . . . you know . . . a good girl. But she's just so cut and dried."

"Hmm." Socially conscious, was she? His adrenalin stepped up. He intended to get to know Susan Andrews.

"What does she do for recreation?" he asked, trying to get a rounded picture of her.

"I'm not sure she knows what that is, Mr. Jackson."

"Hmm," was all he said as Grace pulled up to the curb in front of the forty-story office building in which he worked. After giving her a receipt for the ride, he turned to go with just seven minutes in which to get to the twenty-second floor conference room. He pivoted around when Grace called out to him and beckoned him to her side of the cab.

"Could you give me your date, day, and time of birth? I'd like to do your chart." August smiled. He had become fond of Grace. She wasn't old enough—maybe fifty—to be motherly, but she'd pass for a wonderful older sister. "I won't misuse whatever I find," she quickly assured him.

"I'm not afraid of that," he said and gave her the information.

Susan bumped into one of her peers as she stepped off of the elevator. "Keep your hands to yourself," she warned Oscar Hicks, one of the other senior lawyers. She had stopped trying to figure out whether he touched her because he found her irresistible—something she doubted —wanted to control her as a woman because he couldn't best her as a lawyer or whether he was an insensitive clout who'd been lucky enough to get a law degree. She went into her office, closed the door, and got to work. August Jackson wouldn't try to demean a woman. Now where had that thought come from? She picked up the phone and buzzed her secretary.

"Lila, cancel my nine-thirty staff meeting and reschedule it for two this afternoon. I'm sure this morning's storm delayed a few people."

"Yes, Ms. Andrews." Susan maintained strict protocol; none of her staff addressed her by her first name. She sat back in her chair. And she was going to put Oscar Hicks in his place once and for all, next time he gave her the opportunity.

Three afternoons later after dropping off three of August's colleagues, Grace said to him, "Well, I did your chart, and I'll say you're one fine human being."

"Thank you, Grace. I take it that's not all." He leaned forward, waiting to hear what she had to say.

"Well, if you don't mind my saying so, you and Susan are a perfect match. I'm never wrong, Mr. Jackson, and believe me, you're perfect. I've been doing charts since I was a teenager, and I've never found such a perfect pair. I just did hers earlier this week.''

"What else did you see?"

"You don't shoot pool, do you?"

"I wouldn't know how to hold a cue stick. Why?"

"Well, this showed you getting out from behind a ball that had an eight on it. I'll work it out further, if you want me to."

"Well, I don't know, Grace, I've never paid much attention to this sort of thing." He didn't want to hurt her feelings, but he doubted you could look at the stars and determine a man's future.

"If you don't believe me," she argued, "next time Susan rides with us, ask her if I've ever been wrong in anything she knows about. Just ask her."

Anxiety knotted his insides, and he couldn't help smiling at himself. "When will that be?"

"I can pick her up when I take you down tomorrow morning. Okay?" She'd played into his hand. He'd already decided that he wanted to see Susan Andrews again; he'd state his own case.

Her aunt's offer of a lift surprised Susan; Grace usually waited to be asked. She had reliable corporate clients whom she drove to and from work weekday mornings and, occasionally at other times, if she was free, when they beeped her. But she didn't solicit anybody's business, including that of her niece. She had her customers, and they gave her as much work as she could handle.

"You're picking me up this morning?" she asked Grace.

"Well, I'm not doing you a favor," Grace said bluntly. "August doubts my word, and I want you to verify what I told him. I'll be there at quarter to eight." Grace hung up. Susan stared at the phone for a minute, then shocked herself by tossing her pin-striped suit aside and grabbing the royal blue one. She draped a red scarf around her neck and left her fur coat hanging open as she walked from the building to the taxi in twenty-one degree weather. Let him think what he liked.

"Good morning, Susan," August greeted her. "Are you always so lovely?" She jerked around to give him a good silent censure only to find him grinning broadly.

"Oh, you . . ." she sputtered, unable to hide her pleasure at his compliment.

"Grace says her charts are never wrong."

So that was it, Grace had done his chart. "She never has been, at least not to my knowledge." Why did he fold his hands and lean back in the seat looking as though he'd just won a big lottery?

"Aunt Grace, what's going on here? What have you been doing?"

"Nothing. I just did his chart, and he acted like he wasn't going to take it seriously. I did yours, and I did his, and I never saw the likes of it in my life. If I was superstitious, I'd quit charting."

"You are superstitious." She turned to August. "My aunt doesn't tell things she sees that are really bad, so what did she say?"

"Well, if you're sure you want to know."

"I want to know."

"She said you're the woman for me. My perfect match."

Her handbag slipped to the floor as she half stood, forgetting where she was. "She said *what?*"

Grace took charge. "I did your chart, and then I did his two days later. There ain't no mistake. None. And if y'all don't do something about it, you're cheating yourselves."

"Aunt Grace, you've gone too far."

"But you said she's always right."

"Nobody's perfect."

Grace aligned the taxi with the curb, and Susan got out. She'd tell her aunt Grace a few things she wouldn't soon forget. That man didn't need any help getting a woman.

* * *

August let his head loll against the back of the cab. It had been an interesting trip. Remarkable. Susan Andrews spiked his blood. "I think she's upset, Grace."

"Sure she is. Trouble is, she knows I tell the truth, and she doesn't want to accept it. She never learned how to play games with boys when she was a teenager, and she doesn't understand courtship; that's why she hates it."

August laughed out loud.

"What's funny? Are you laughing at my Susan?"

"No indeed. I'm fascinated. The more you talk about her, the more certain I am that I want her telephone number. Don't worry. I won't court her." Grace gave him her niece's numbers at home and the office.

"Good luck."

"Thanks. I don't doubt that I'll need it."

Susan knew she might be playing into her aunt's hand, but she decided to risk it, nonetheless. She dialed her home phone number. "Aunt Grace, you're pushing August Jackson on me. What do you know about him? He could be a criminal."

"Just what I see on the chart, honey."

Susan hooked the telephone between her chin and her shoulder and applied more nail builder to her big toenail. Not for anything would she admit being excited and anxious to know more about him.

"That's all?"

"Well, the men he works with treat him like he's a big shot, but he acts like a regular fellow. And he sure has got nice manners. I'm driving him down tomorrow morning, so I'll pick you up at the usual time."

Susan knew from that click of the receiver that if she called a dozen times, Grace wouldn't answer the phone. Monday morning, when she stepped into the taxi at seven forty-five, she had to admit that she wasn't there because she didn't want to disappoint Grace, but because she hadn't been able to get August out of her thoughts.

Grace got right to the point. "The moon is in Venus and Saturn is rising, so it's your season, Susan. Truth is, the stars say you two should get married during the next full moon."

Susan couldn't believe the eagerness in August Jackson's voice. "When is that?" He wanted to know.

"Second week of February," Grace hastened to say.

Susan turned sharply toward August and quickly switched back to her position. That slow-moving smile seemed to take possession of his face, which was already too beguiling.

"Do you really believe in this stuff?" he asked Susan.

"Well, I told you that I don't as a rule, but Aunt Grace has a flawless record. Still, even perfect people eventually make mistakes. Don't forget Napoleon."

"I see." As she got out of the taxi, she thought she heard him say, "I'll be in touch." Tremors continued to roll through her long after she got in her office and closed the door. What kind of a man was he? He didn't behave as if she were a challenge as men usually did. Maybe he didn't understand executive women. She rubbed her arms, trembling as a chill slammed up her spine. Maybe he did understand them, and maybe status didn't bother him.

She sat at home that evening seeing her green and blue bedroom with new eyes. The room didn't portray an arresting quiet, a cool elegance as she had thought; it was harsh and unfeminine. She jerked herself up from the side of the bed and started toward her dressing room. Was she losing her mind?

"Hello. Yes, this is Susan," she said and groped for her boudoir chair. Surprised.

"Susan, this is August. Would you see a movie with me

this evening?" She had to lock her left hand over her right one to steady the phone. She hadn't been invited to a movie in seven years.

"I . . . uh . . . Well, I don't know. This evening?"

"Yeah. Throw on a pair of jeans or something, and I'll pick you up at about eight. Okay?"

"Jeans? August, I don't have any jeans. I . . . Well, I never have an occasion to dress that casual." She thought for a moment. "I could put on a pants suit, but it's wool crepe." She wondered what he'd think of her. It had never occurred to her to buy a pair of blue jeans.

"Never mind, wear whatever you like; that pretty blue suit, maybe. I'll put on a business suit. Will you come with me?" He spoke so softly, so gently in his deep and lilting southern drawl that she could have listened to him forever.

"Okay, I will. Do you want me to meet you somewhere?" She knew the minute the words left her mouth that she shouldn't have said them.

"Susan, I'll call for you. What is your apartment number?" She told him.

"I guess I'll never overcome my small town, southern upbringing, Susan, but I can't think of an occasion when I'd ask you to meet me somewhere. I'll be there around eight, and we can make the nine o'clock."

A movie date. What did people do on movie dates? She knew how to act at the opera and at such four-star restaurants as Twenty-one, *but the movies.* Well, he'd said wear the blue suit. She put it on and answered the door minutes later.

"You must have been around the corner when you called me."

"Hi. You look pretty. I was a few blocks away. Ready to go?"

She got her coat and would have put it on, but he took it and helped her into it. Somehow, he didn't make her feel helpless the way most men did when they took over; he made it seem natural.

"When did you buy the tickets?" she asked as he presented them to the usher.

"Soon as I called you. I didn't want you to stand in that long line; it's cold."

"Thanks," she felt compelled to say. "You're very considerate."

He stopped in the lobby. "Two bags of popcorn, please, and make that lots of butter."

"That's fattening," she protested, her voice suggesting the horror of it.

"You're nice and slim, so what's the problem?" he said, regarding her appreciatively.

"And I hope to stay that way, too." That's the trouble with men, she thought; they like you one way and are always trying to make you into something else.

"Forever?" August asked, his expression suggesting that the idea was ludicrous. "You're supposed to develop a little contentment around the middle as you grow older." He sampled some popcorn. "Hmm, this is good."

Susan couldn't believe what she heard. The men she knew wouldn't look twice at anything larger than a size twelve and then only if most of that was in the bra.

"You couldn't be serious," she said, a tone of incredulity shrouding her voice.

"Of course, I am. All this New York City fixation on skinny is ridiculous."

Appalled, she asked him, "You don't like the way I look?"

"Sweetheart, you are definitely not skinny. It's all exactly where it's supposed to be." He handed her a bag of popcorn and enveloped her other hand in his big one. "Come on. Let's get our seats." She felt a little strange when August released her hand while helping her to her seat, and she got a shock when she realized that she wanted him to hold it. He could have been reading her wishes, because he obliged her immediately, locking the fingers of his right hand through those of her left one. Don't give in to him, she pleaded with herself.

"How am I supposed to eat this bag of calories if you're holding my hand?"

He squeezed gently. "Maybe I could hold both our bags between my knees. If you don't mind, I'd like to keep this hand."

Exasperated, she fumbled for words. "You ... oh, you're ..." She couldn't even convince herself.

"What? I'm what?" Susan released a deep breath and knew she was about to give in.

"Different, I guess."

The beginning of his slow smile unnerved her, and she locked her gaze on the movie screen. Halfway through the movie, she dipped her hand into an empty bag.

"That wasn't so bad, was it? Here. Have some of mine."

He'd never know how grateful she was that he couldn't see her face. She couldn't remember when she'd last enjoyed anything as much as she had that high-calorie popcorn. I'm too comfortable with him, she thought, as delicious shivers snaked through her when he locked their fingers again. This wasn't like her; she was sensible. She tried without success to withdraw her hand.

"I need my hand," she told him, half hoping that he would ignore her. And he did.

"No, you don't. You're supposed to hold hands in the movies. It's one of the reasons why you go." Now she wished for light so that he could see the look of incredulity that she knew blazed across her face.

"You're putting me on," she said, but she wasn't certain of her ground, because very little of her life had been spent in a movie theater and almost none of that with a member of the opposite sex.

"I should have taken you to a horror movie," he went on, confusing her further. "And before you ask why, that's because if you got scared enough you'd be glad to hold onto me. Girls have been known to crawl all over guys when Godzilla pops up on the screen. You see, you're already scared."

"Why do you think I'd do that? I can look after—"

He interrupted her, obviously enjoying himself. "Because you're squeezing my fingers. Here, have some more popcorn."

August slid an arm around her shoulder as they stepped out of the movie, claiming that he had to keep her warm. "Want to stop for some ice cream and coffee? I know a nice little place about a block from here."

Ice cream and coffee. Was he from Mars? In her world, the words "would you like" were the beginning of an invitation to a drink or a visit to a guy's apartment, and her answers always began with the word, no. The man was intriguing.

"Okay, but make mine espresso."

"The ice cream or the coffee?" She stared at him; surely he wasn't that unsophisticated. He smiled down at her and tightened his arm around her. "Just pulling your leg. You don't know what to expect of me, and I've decided to reveal my secrets slowly and in small doses." Susan laughed. She broke one of her rules of decorum and let the sound of laughter escape her. He hugged her.

"I enjoyed the evening, August."

He shook his head as though reprimanding a small child. "Susan, you loved it. Come on, be honest."

"Alright, I loved it."

He smiled in his usual mesmerizing way and asked for her door key. She wondered what he would do next, but the possibilities didn't worry her, because she knew without a doubt that August Jackson was a gentleman.

"This has been wonderful, Susan."

Warm anticipation increased the fluid in her mouth as

the back of his index finger drifted tenderly down her cheek. She wished he'd give her a signal as to what he intended to do. A goodnight kiss was normal after a guy took a girl out, though she couldn't swear what they did after having been to a movie. She'd let him take the lead. So she waited while his gaze roamed over her face and his smile brightened as though his pleasure increased the longer he looked at her. She couldn't restrain a gasp when he suddenly leaned forward and kissed her cheek. Didn't he know where her mouth was?

"I want to see you again, Susan. Truth is, I want to see you a lot. What do you say?"

She fidgeted, something she'd taught herself to stop doing when she joined the law firm.

"August, I told you, I don't like . . ."

"Shh. I'm not going to court you, because I know you don't like it."

"Then what do you call seeing me, as you put it?" His deep sigh suggested that she had, completely misunderstood him.

"Just spending a little time together. What do you say?"

She wanted to be with him. She couldn't remember when she had been so relaxed, so completely unwound. She hadn't thought once of the office . . . horrified, she realized that she couldn't remember which case she was to present in the senior staff meeting the next morning. She'd gotten so carried away with him that she'd practically forgotten who she was. She'd better break it off right now, before she cultivated a taste for this man—if indeed, she hadn't already done that. But he let her know that he had other thoughts about their relationship.

"I'd like to show you something, Susan."

"What?" She hoped she hadn't sounded as eager to him as she did to herself.

"Heaven from the back of a horse."

She could relax; horseback riding in winter held no fascination.

"I've already seen things from the back of a horse, August."

"But not heaven. I'd bet anything that only I can show that to you."

She couldn't decide whether he was egotistic or naive, but she suspected that it wasn't the latter. Trouble was, he didn't appear to be too involved with himself, either. So what was he?

"Would you kindly define heaven for me," she asked, deciding to play along.

"It's hills lightly covered with snow and evergreen pines that sparkle with white, cloudlike crests and sun rays that take on hundreds of hues dancing against the pines; icicles trying to find their way to earth, stymied by the frosty breeze, and lighting your way at sundown; squirrels and chipmunks frolicking around the tree trunks; an occasional, lonely leaf that whispers a love song as you pass; and not a track in the pristine snow until your horse puts one there. It's all that and just the two of us. You can't prove to me that it wouldn't be heaven."

She stared, tongue-tied. Bewitched.

"You're nodding your head. Does that mean you'll go with me?"

She nodded again. How unpredictable he was and how wonderful. Where could a person find a pair of jodhpurs on such short notice? Barney's, maybe.

A light snow fell as they took the horses over a trail in Harriman State Park. The scene was all that he had promised and more. So much more. Scattered snow flurries floated down around them, adding allure to the fairyland setting. The stillness, the enchanting quiet gave them a world of their own. A restful, spiritually renewing world— the antithesis of stressful board rooms, cut-throat competition, crowded streets and blaring traffic. A doe with her young fawn stared as they passed, and stepped forward as though to greet them. She glimpsed a squirrel as it hustled up the trunk of a great oak carrying its treasure of acorns in its mouth and thought, how free and happy it seems. August had been mostly silent while they rode, but she hadn't felt the need for conversation. And she didn't remember ever having experienced the sense of oneness with another person that she enjoyed with August that morning. He had an almost magical way of lulling her into contentment, of giving her a sense of completeness. She looked over at him astride the big bay and smiled when she found him looking at her. His lips smiled first, then his cheeks seemed to bloom and, finally, his eyes sparkled. He might as well have kissed her. She wrung her gaze from his when she realized that she could stay with him forever. They took the horses back to the stables, got into the car that August had rented, and drove back to the city.

They stood at her apartment door, and she knew he didn't want to leave her. She knew, too, that she didn't want him to go.

"I found a theater that's showing Godzilla tonight. How about it?"

She had to laugh. This was courting; even she knew that, and she'd never done any of it.

"I have some work to do tonight." It was true but, as she looked at him, anxiously awaiting her answer, she thought, oh what the heck.

"Okay, I'll go, but I am not going to make a habit of going places with you."

He grinned. "Alright. I won't expect you to. This isn't a steady thing. We'll negotiate it each time." She shook her head in amazement. He behaved as if nothing was complicated, but she didn't plan to be taken in by his easy, laid-back manner. "You going?" he urged.

"Okay. I'm crazy, but I'll go."

She hadn't ever seen a horror movie and, at the monster's first appearance, a scream escaped her throat that would have rivaled the best efforts of a great coloratura soprano. August immediately slipped an arm around her, but that was soon insufficient protection, for the monster threatened to leave the screen and leap into the audience. Not even the richly buttered popcorn held an interest as she dealt with her fears. The beast roared and she couldn't help clutching August with both hands. Thank God, he didn't seem to mind, but gave himself over to the task of banishing her consternation.

"Do you want to leave, honey?" Godzilla overturned a dozen cars, and she couldn't speak. She tugged him closer.

"Do you?" he asked again. She came to her senses; it wouldn't be ladylike to spoil the evening for him, especially since he obviously loved the monster. But scared as she was, she couldn't walk away from the thrill of it.

"Oh, no," she whispered. "I wouldn't want you to miss the end of it."

"But you haven't even eaten your popcorn. I don't want you to be miserable, and you must be if you barely opened the bag."

She reached into the bag and brought a few kernels toward her mouth just as the monster's claws whirled something or someone into the air. She screamed and buried her face in August's strong, protective shoulder. The movie ended, and they walked out into the chilly air.

"Oh, August, it was wonderful," she exclaimed. "I don't know when I've enjoyed anything so much. It was just smashing." She offered him some popcorn, but he shook his head.

"Are you serious? You enjoyed that movie?"

"Why, yes. I could go back in there right now. It was fabulous."

"But you were scared to death the whole time. I thought you might cry."

"Sure I was scared, but it was such fun."

He stared at her. "Well, I'll be doggone."

* * *

"Susan, honey, I think Grace is right," he said, standing in her foyer after taking her home from the movie. "We ought to get married."

"What? Us get married? You can't be serious, August." She stared at him, but saw that he was no less serene than usual.

"Why shouldn't I be serious? We've got a lot in common, and you said yourself that Grace is never wrong. So why do you want us to waste time shilly-shallying about it. Let's give it a shot." Susan closed her mouth slowly just before he added, "For keeps, though. I mean we get married 'til death does us part."

"August, do you know what you're saying?"

"Sure I do. You don't want to waste time courting; I'm uncomfortable negotiating this New York City scene with these New York women; I know what I want; and Grace says we were made for each other."

The abrupt disappearance of his warm, teasing smile unnerved her as he stepped closer, his expression unmistakably serious.

"I'll always be there for you, Susan, for better or for worse. No matter what." Suddenly, he grinned. "Nothing will ever change that, and I'll be faithful to you for as long as I breathe." She gasped aloud. He was serious. She hoped he'd ignore her trembling, but he didn't. "I'll never do anything to cause you to regret marrying me, so don't worry."

August wondered whether he'd moved too quickly, but he didn't think so. He'd learned to go with his instincts, and if he followed them this time, his search for a mate had ended. An inner something told him that Susan was the woman for him and that he'd still feel that way aeons into the future.

"Uh . . . I'll call you," he heard her whisper.

"Alright. I'll be in Washington for a few days. I'm leaving tomorrow evening."

"Work?" Her voice was tentative, he noted, as though she had no right to ask.

"My work rarely involves travel. I did tell you that I'm a criminologist, didn't I? Honey, I wish it was something as simple as work." He had to camouflage his sudden feeling of distress. "For the last twenty years, I've been trying to find my younger brother, and I'm going to Washington to check a lead with my private investigator. It could be another wild goose chase, but I never assume that; any bit of information is checked. We'll talk about it when I get back."

"I hope it works out this time. I can imagine what this means to you, August. Will you call?" It surprised him that she would ask him that, but he took pleasure in it.

"As soon as I get in my hotel room." He looked at her upturned, worried face. He wanted to kiss her. Badly. But it was too early for that. She trusted him a little, but he was after more. Much more. He tweaked her nose, opened her door and playfully pushed her in.

"Lock it." He walked off. She wanted to throw something at him when it dawned on her that he'd been protective, but she could start right then to get used to him; he was in her life forever.

Susan hung up her mink coat, got out of her blue designer suit, kicked off her Susan Bennis/Warren Edwards shoes, and paced the floor in her stocking feet. What in the world was August Jackson thinking about? And he was serious, too. In her mind's eye, she recalled how his face sobered before he told her he'd always be there for her. She stopped, nearly panicking. She didn't know anything about men who talked as he did and acted the way he acted. He had meant every word. Good Lord, he had actually pledged himself to her. She wrapped her arms around herself, seeking assurance that she was still a separate entity, that she wasn't a part of him. What had he done to her? Without his having touched her, she'd felt enclosed securely in his arms, warm and protected. She rushed to the kitchen and got a glass of water. If she'd ever thought about the kind of man she wanted, she wouldn't have dreamed his type existed, but there he was, and . . . She picked up the phone and dialed her aunt, praying that she wouldn't get the answering service.

"Aunt Grace. I'm so glad you're home. I went to the movies with August tonight, and he . . . well, he . . ."

"He asked you to marry him, did he? I knew he was going to; it was right there on the chart, plain as your face."

"Aunt Grace, marriage is a serious business. How can he take it so lightly?"

"Don't be fooled by that easy, charming front of his, honey. That man means business. You take my advice and quit pussyfooting around. Besides, you know you want to do it. You're intrigued with him, plain loco. He heated you up the first time you saw him. That was in *your* chart. Don't you get stupid and try to string him along, now, 'cause that won't work with him."

Susan had to sit down. "Aunt Grace, be reasonable. We don't know anything about him." Her heart hammered in her chest, and she tried to calm herself.

"He's nice, Aunt Grace."

"Sure he is; his chart doesn't show a single thing against him that I could see. And, honey, he's so handsome, it's sinful; and he acts like he don't even know it. He ain't faking, either. He wants to marry you, and he'll do what he says, 'cause that chart of his shows he's solid as a rock."

"Don't you ever doubt your charts?"

"Never. And something else. How many men like him will you find that's equal to a woman like you? Most of his kind go for those cute little clinging vines, which, Lord knows, you are not."

"But we're not in love."

"Shucks, honey, your cousin Ella fell head over heels for Richie, went home with him the same night she met him, stayed with him for fours years before they got married, and left him three weeks after they said 'I do.' You're the one with the college degrees; you figure it out."

"But Aunt Grace, that's . . ."

"Please spare me that logic of yours. You want to marry him. Do it. You two are going to fall so hard for each other, you'll think lightening struck." Susan didn't want to believe it.

August prepared himself for another disappointment. He'd had so many where Grady was concerned that he'd almost become inured to the pain. He unlocked the door of his posh room in Washington's Willard Hotel—too much for his taste, but that was what his private investigator had reserved for him—dropped his bag beside the bed, took out his NYNEX card, and called Susan. Mere thoughts of her elevated his spirits. For once, he didn't feel alone in it.

"This is August. Did you miss me?" Susan laughed, giving him the reaction he wanted. He'd only heard her actually laugh just once before.

"Hi. You're impossible." He caught the warmth in her voice.

"Well did you?" That lovely laughter again. He could listen to it forever, because it meant he'd get what he was after.

"Not yet," she teased, "but if you stay away long enough, I might."

Joy suffused him, and he let it flow out to her in his speech. "When are we getting married?"

"Soon as you get back."

His back went up; that was a subject about which he refused to let her joke.

"I'm serious."

"Me, too."

The sudden acceleration of his heartbeat made him grab his chest.

"What size ring do you wear?"

"That's unimportant; I don't want a ring."

"I don't remember asking whether you wanted one. I want to wear your ring, and I'd like my wife to wear mine."

"But I won't . . ."

"Don't draw the line, honey. You haven't seen it yet." He'd ask Grace what size ring Susan wore. He teased her for a bit and hung up.

He'd had over a hundred so-called leads over the past twenty-six years, but this one really sounded promising. He felt as if he could run the five miles to the Sheraton Hotel where he was to meet his P.I. and the man thought to be his brother. The man was about his height, and vaguely resembled him, but August didn't feel a connection between them. He'd planned to ask him some key questions but first, he'd have a look at the birthmark— the black quarter size spot on one shoulder that had a thick patch of hair growing in it. The man obligingly removed his shirt, but he didn't have that birthmark, and neither was there evidence that it had been removed. August thanked the man and offered to pay his expenses to and from Charlotte, North Carolina. He couldn't help feeling relieved, though, because the man wasn't the kind of brother that he'd want. The search would continue, as it had for the past two and a half decades.

Later in his hotel room, he called Susan again, her expressions of sorrow that he hadn't found his brother touched him deeply. He hadn't known how much he needed her caring and understanding. She was there for him, solidifying her niche inside of him

"What will you do now, August?"

He'd keep looking, he told her.

"Do you believe he's alive?" she asked, and he admired the strength that her ability to ask him that difficult question communicated to him.

"I know he is, Susan. I feel it. Besides," he said, changing to a lighter mood, "Grace's charts say I'm going to find him and, remember . . ."

"I know," Susan finished for him, "she's never wrong."

He rolled over, heat beginning to pool in his belly just from the sound of her sultry voice.

"I'll see you tomorrow night, honey, and every night."

"But we're not . . ."

"Right. We're not courting. We'll just see each other." He hung up and laughed.

He got back to New York the following afternoon and went directly to Tiffany's and chose a size seven diamond engagement ring of one and a half carats flanked by half carat diamond baguettes set in eighteen-karat gold. He tucked the red velvet, satin-cushioned box into his shirt pocket, and hailed a taxi for A Hundred Thirty-Fifth and Malcolm X Boulevard, where he had a fourth-floor co-op. His coworkers had asked him why he lived there when he could afford the upper east side. It wasn't their business that he used his wealth to find his brother. Besides, he also lived there, as he told them, because he loved Harlem. It was the closest thing to rural southern living that he'd come across in New York. Turnips and mustard greens in every market, not to mention spareribs and plenty of fresh fish. He liked filet mignon, salmon, and lobster as well as anybody, but when he got good and hungry, he wanted some collard greens, baked sweet potatoes, and fried Norfolk spots, and he didn't want his greens cooked with olive oil. He put his bag down and called Susan.

"What time can I see you tonight?"

"Auuuugusssst." She drew it out. "We're not supposed to . . . I mean, I thought we weren't going to . . ."

"Honey, we're not courting. I promised you, didn't I? We're making plans. What time?"

She told him seven thirty and asked where he planned to take them. He had to suppress a laugh. She was priceless. He'd never seen a woman so reluctant to come down to earth.

"Well, I thought we'd just eat dinner at a real nice restaurant. Anything else would be, well, courting." He hung up and called the Plaza Athené. He didn't intend to have but one engagement dinner, and he wanted his fiancée to remember it forever. Thinking about that, he called back and ordered pink orchids for their table.

Susan kicked herself for putting on her full glamorous armor, but she wasn't going out with him to a swanky restaurant looking like a poor relation. She knew what those other women would look like, and she intended for him to keep his fantastic eyes on her. She scurried into a red silk shift that was cut low in the back and front and would give him just enough cleavage to let him know there was a lot more. She put on a light makeup, gold loops at her ears, and dabs of French perfume. It was a come-on, but she wasn't sure where he stood, and she hadn't gotten where she was by taking foolish chances. She looked down at her feet. That's it, she decided, experiencing a mild rebellion at herself. I will not put on heels; he has a big enough ego. She put on black silk ballet slippers, and wouldn't admit that the effect was more striking than heels would have been.

Her neighbors could have heard his whistle of approval, she decided, lowering her head in acute embarrassment. But she was glad he liked what he saw, even if it did remind her of the wolves in her office.

"August, I'm glad you like my dress, but that whistle is

the same thing I get from other guys.'' She glanced up at him and excitement raced through her at the adoration his eyes revealed.

''When those men whistle at you, honey, they're tom catting. I was expressing appreciation for my woman.''

''I'm not your woman,'' she huffed, giving him an arrogant twist of her head.

''Sure you are, and it doesn't make sense to argue about it.''

She had to admit that if she was going to marry him, he did have a point.

''Well, not yet, I'm not.''

''Ah, Susan, you're so beautiful and so sweet.'' His warm hand on her bare arm tugged her gently to him, and she couldn't help trembling with heady anticipation. Frightened at what she felt, she attempted to move away, but his strong fingers caressed her arms and back, stroking her until she relaxed against him. Her deep sigh must have encouraged him, because he tipped up her chin and let her see the desire in his eyes, stunning her. She knew he felt her shivers when his arms tightened around her, and she grasped the right lapel of his coat with her left hand and clung to him. She couldn't help it; she was sinking as sure as her name was Susan Andrews.

''Darling, I want to taste your mouth. Kiss me.''

She couldn't make herself raise her head, but she didn't object when he did it for her. His lips touched her tentatively, burning her, sending hot darts all through her.

''Honey. Ah, sweetheart,'' he murmured, ''take my tongue.'' She parted her lips slightly at first, but when he claimed her, she opened wider loving the taste of him, the feel of him. He groaned, and she stifled the urge to move against him. His hands stroked her back, and she wanted to beg him to sooth her aching breasts. She wanted . . . Her hips moved to him, and he turned and held her to his side. She stepped back, shocked at herself. What had she been thinking? She shook her head as though to clear it; August was behaving as though what they'd just done was perfectly natural. She had known him two weeks and, in her whole life, she'd never kissed a man with such—there was no other word for it—fire.

Later, she sat across from him in the swank room looking around at the lovely mirrors and the gold leaf that adorned the pale blue walls and ceiling, the French Provincial chairs and crystal chandeliers. A nice restaurant, he'd said.

"The orchids are beautiful, August. Thank you." She wondered about the low regard in which he held New York night life, including its fancy restaurants, and she said as much.

"I said I didn't want to do it on a regular basis. Besides, if I'd suggested hot dogs and a fast food place, you would have been perfectly agreeable."

She stared at him. "How do you know?"

He shrugged carelessly. "Am I right?"

Susan nodded in agreement, wondering what he'd do when he took her home. She wasn't sure she wanted to be left raw after another one of his kisses.

They lingered inside her foyer until he said, "How about some coffee?" She made it quickly.

"I wasn't sure you knew how to make it," he teased.

"Well, if you had asked for anything more complicated, I probably wouldn't have."

August looked at his future wife, hoping that his heart wouldn't burst.

"Did you tell your office associates that you're engaged?"

"Did I . . . Is it their business?"

He didn't like the sound of that, and he was going to set her straight.

"That's a courtesy, and it'll let those bulls know you're not available." Now was the time, he decided, taking her left hand and beginning to slip the ring on her third finger.

"I told you I didn't want a ring."

"But, honey, that was before you kissed me."

"Before I . . ." she sputtered. "I didn't kiss you; you kissed me. How can you . . ." Her glance swept the ring on her finger, and she gasped aloud.

"Oh, August. It's beautiful. Ooo. It's . . . it's . . ." Evidently at a loss for words, she threw her arms around him exuberantly, and he pulled her closer.

"Will you wear it? I want everybody to know that you're engaged to me. I'm so proud of you. Will you?" His heart turned over. Had he fallen so deeply in love with her already? She nodded assent and snuggled up to him, and August knew he'd made the right move.

"You feel good in my arms," he told her, but she wiggled nervously, and he figured she hadn't accepted her reaction to him, hadn't come to terms with her feelings.

"Don't move away," he soothed. "We're not courting; we're just getting to know each other." He smiled down at her, hoping to raise her temperature by several more degrees.

"Honey, I saw the loveliest little white ranch house while I was in D.C. It had a white picket fence, trees, and shrubs. Perfect. I could see the two of us living there years from now with our hair as white as the white bricks of that house. I wished you were there so I could show it to you." Was she tensing up? There certainly wasn't any reason for that; his arm was around her and he was describing the most . . .

"Susan, don't tell me you dislike ranch style houses."

"Okay. I won't. I'll tell you I hate them, because I do. There's nothing imaginative about them. An entire block of sameness. It's a wonder people living in them don't let themselves into the wrong house. Oh, August. They're so . . . so, well, you know." She waved her hand as if the subject were of little moment. So much for the little white house of his dreams.

* * *

She'd had the ring for almost twenty-four hours. Anybody who knew her would think she'd lost her mind, looking at her left hand every two or three minutes. She could have bought a ring for herself, but she hadn't, and he had. She stared at it. It made her long fingers look daintier. Shocked at the change in her, she bawled up her fist and contemplated putting on a glove. How had he ever persuaded her to do such a thing. Promise to marry him? She could figure that out, because he was perfect from head to foot, and sweet. But wear a ring? Why she was a feminist, for heaven's sake. She took another look at her ring, twirled around, and dashed to the phone. But just before reaching the table on which it sat, she slowed to a dignified walk. Don't forget yourself, she counseled. He answered on the first ring.

"Hi."

"Hi. I was just about to call you, but it's nice to answer my phone and hear your voice. How are you?"

"Fine. Want to come over?" she asked him as casually as she could. "You don't have to get dressed up."

"Give me twenty-five minutes."

She hung up, dashed to her closet and found a green corduroy jumpsuit. It wasn't dressy, she reasoned, and she looked good in it.

If she expected a frenzied kiss, she didn't get it. "Hi. You're a treat for my eyes," he stated, as his slow smile claimed his face.

"Want to hear some music?" she asked, for want of something to say.

"I'd love it. Got any country? Charley Pride, Vince Gill, or George Strait?"

Susan opened her mouth and couldn't close it, certain that her jaw had locked.

"You don't mean you like that . . . er, that kind of music, do you?"

"Sure I do. What's wrong with it? What do *you* like?"

"Well, if you don't want classical, how about just plain old pop? Or Dixieland, if you insist on southern stuff?"

He laughed. "No thanks. When are we getting married?"

If they did, she thought, they'd better not have any music in the house.

She said, "If we get a license tomorrow, we can get married Monday at lunch time."

August sprang from his seat. "Calm down, Susan."

"What?"

He shook his head. "Sorry. I was talking about myself." He sat down beside her and took her hand. "Susan, we need a decent engagement period so we can get to know each other. I won't court you. Honest. But we need time to get our affairs in order. Give me a reasonable date that fits in with Grace's charts. She said something about the full moon, didn't she?"

If she laughed, he might be offended. Grace's charts, for goodness sake.

"Alright. According to her that's the second week of February. About a month from now." She marveled at the way in which his face beamed and that special gleam lit his eyes.

"How's Valentine's Day. Alright?" he pressed eagerly. "That should give us time to arrange things."

She nodded. "Okay."

He leaned back, seemingly content now that plans appeared to proceed to his liking, holding her hand. "Do you want me to wear a tux or tails?"

"For what?"

"For the wedding, honey."

"*Our* wedding?" She figured her eyes were the size of saucers. He had to be kidding.

"Yeah. Whose did you think I meant?"

She sprang up.

"August, I agreed to wear this ring—"

He interrupted her. "Wasn't such a bad idea, was it?"

"Oh, you ... I haven't finished. And I agreed to an engagement, but a formal marriage is too much. We're getting married by a clerk of the Court or a Justice of the Peace. And that's that."

He stood up, walked over to her and put his arms around her.

"Honey, I grew up in church. I want to get married in one, and I charge you right now with the responsibility of having my funeral in a church."

"But, August . . ."

"I've got the most beautiful bride-to-be in New York, and I want to see her walking up a church aisle toward me in a veil of white lace with rose petals beneath her feet. It's a picture I'll take to my grave. You won't deny me that pleasure, will you?"

Why did she feel as if she'd done something terrible to him? He trained those bedroom eyes of his on her, softened his honeyed voice and stripped her of her will. She wanted to curl into him when he began to stroke her back gently, almost seductively.

"August, you're making too much of this." She knew her protest was a weak one and tried to summon her usual stern manner. "In a joint venture, the parties have to come to an agreement. You know that."

"I do. But, sweetheart, this isn't a business venture; this is us getting married to each other, and I'm holding out for seeing my bride in white satin and lace. You don't want to deprive me of that sweet vision that other brides give their grooms, do you, honey?"

Susan took a deep breath and summoned her wits. He wasn't going to steamroller her. "Slow down, August. That's your dream; what about mine? I told myself ages ago that if I ever got married, I wanted the ceremony to take place in the Rainbow Room."

From his expression, you'd think she'd shot him. "*What?* You couldn't be serious. Why?"

She didn't succeed in staving off her nostalgia. "I spent a New Year's Eve there. I was twenty, and it was my first adult date. I had on a long white silk gown, and the room was pure paradise. Low hanging, silvery clouds hid the ceiling, and millions of twinkling stars danced around a crescent moon. Icicles glittered on great snow-covered trees, candles glowed in the windows, and soft, romantic music came alive all around us. Heaven. I'd even wear white satin, lace and a long train if we could be married there. Oh, August, it was magic."

He laid his head to one side and scrutinized her. "Where's the guy now?"

She grinned. "I have no idea. It wasn't him, but the Rainbow Room that was memorable." A sigh floated from her. "I walked on air and danced in the clouds."

"I don't want to say my vows to a woman decked out in pants," he grumbled.

Laughing, she stroked his cheek. "Suppose they have wide bottoms."

He wasn't placated. "Nothing doing. We'll have to work that out."

Susan folded her arms to signal *his* defeat. "You won't snow me on this one." His wink sent hot arrows to her middle, but she was not giving in.

He frowned. "And since the Rainbow Room is a pipe dream, it's pants and the court clerk. Right?"

"What's wrong with that? We'll still be married?"

"How'd it go at work today? Did you tell them?" he asked, settling them into her big barrel chair. She snuggled as close to him as she could get.

"I don't know why they were so surprised. Oscar—he's one of the more senior lawyers—was mean. He said he'd like to meet the guy who pulled it off. Getting me to say yes, that is. They figured I'd stop working, but I reminded them that this is the end of the twentieth century, and I'm not giving up my chance at that full partnership. I worked too hard for it." The stroking stopped.

"Have you been promised a partnership?"

"Over six months ago." Where had his sweet, coaxing tone gone?

"Then, if they welch, we'll go to court. If you're entitled to a partnership, I'll see that you get it."

Her brows arched sharply, and her mouth dropped; he wasn't as laid-back and homespun as his manner often suggested. She asked if he was serious.

"Didn't I say I'd be there for you through thick and thin, whatever comes?"

She nodded.

"Well, in my book that's pretty thin."

"It's eight o'clock, Susan. Don't you think we ought to eat? I'm beginning to feel a pinch. Let's get some dinner and talk things over." She twisted around in his arms and looked into his face. He wished she'd be still; he had enough problems with his self-control as it was.

"We've been talking for nearly an hour," she complained. "What else do you want to talk about? You want us to sign a marriage contract?" She sat up straight, but he pulled her back into his arms.

"No. I don't. When we get married, whatever's mine is yours. There're a lot of things to talk about."

In that case, she'd better fortify herself. "Then let's get some Chinese food delivered and eat right here."

"Nothing doing. Monosodium glutamate is bad for your health. I'll run out and get some stuff and I'll cook. It'll be simple."

"How simple?"

He laughed. "Hamburgers. For a woman who can't cook, you're awfully fussy."

August thought his chest would spring open when she wiped her mouth and smiled at him. Happy. "That was delicious," she declared, when they'd finished and were cleaning up.

"My pleasure. I'd better go."

"What's the hurry?"

He raised an eyebrow. Did that question have a provocative undercurrent? "It's getting late."

"Oh."

"What's the problem, honey?" He believed in dealing with trouble head-on, so he took her into the living room and sat with her in the barrel chair.

"Well?" he pressed.

"Nothing. I mean, aren't we supposed to make love?"

He wasn't going to laugh. He wasn't. He did his best to put on a stern face.

"Where does it say we're supposed to? I'm planning for us to wait."

She jumped out of his lap, spun around, and stared at him, clearly aghast. She'd kill him if he laughed, so he put his hands on his knees, leaned forward and waited.

"You . . . you're willing to buy a pig in the poke?" she sputtered.

He had to laugh. "You're not concerned about what I'm risking, and you know it. You're the one who's skeptical about me. *Come here.*" She'd asked for it, and she was going to get it. She started toward him, and he stood to meet her.

"Come here to me, baby," he coaxed, "and put your arms around me. Come here and let me love you." She stood there staring at him, obviously perplexed. If she wanted sophisticated seduction, he'd give it to her. Her tongue rimmed her soft brown lips and in lightening fashion, heat shot to his groin. He watched transfixed as her eyelids half lowered, the muscles of her face relaxed and her left hand clasped her bosom while she swallowed what he knew was evidence of desire. Caught in a prison of his own making, he reached for her, no longer interested in teaching her a lesson, but in sating his need for her.

"Woman. My Lord, I'm on fire for you. *Come here!*" He clasped her hips as she sprang into his arms. Her parted lips took in his tongue and he searched her mouth with its velvet smoothness until he knew every crevice of it, and she slumped limply against him. He pulled her up until his full arousal rested against her nest of passion so that she could know him, feel him. Every bit of him. He was paying for it, and he didn't care. Tremors raced through him when she sucked on his tongue, and he tightened his hold on her hips longing for the heavenly sweet release she'd give him. She had to feel the shudders that racked him as she twisted in his arms, letting him feel the softness of her full breasts. He wanted to taste them, wanted to pull her sweet flesh into his mouth, to nourish himself and drive her wild.

"August . . . please . . . If you're going to make love to me. Do it. Please stop torturing me."

Stunned, he recovered his senses, and held her away from him. He shook his head in wonder. He might have planned to teach her something, but he'd gotten a lesson of his own.

"I guess there's a first time for everything," he said, as much to himself as to her. "I don't ever remember losing control like that. I . . . I'm sorry, honey, but I do intend for us to wait." She stared at him as though seeing a mirage.

"August, what you just did would be grounds for divorce, and we're not even married yet." He'd deal with her disappointment in a few minutes, but right then, he had to get himself in order; she had really sent him into a tailspin. He risked putting an arm around her and hugged her lightly.

"That surprised me as much as it did you, honey, but I hope I set you straight. I was born in the country, but I do know how to love a woman. You trust me; we're going to wait."

She nodded. "I still haven't agreed to that big church

wedding you want. That's for people who court each other.''

He resisted the impulse to pace the floor and settled her more securely in his lap. "Honey, the Rainbow Room is for eating and dancing. You can't expect the management to turn it into a church—''

"I don't want it to be a church, but it's the only place where I'm prepared to wear a formal wedding or any other kind of dress.'' He tried to get her to look at him, but she ducked her head. So much for his winning strategy.

"We'll have to discuss this some more, Susan. I won't feel married if you show up at our wedding in a pants suit.''

"It'll be silk and a lovely gay color,'' she said airily.

He'd love to shake her. "Susan, please be reasonable.'' He made up his mind to talk with Grace about it.

The next afternoon, Susan raised her head from her work just enough to identify the intruder. "What is it, Lila?''

"I'm sorry to disturb you, Miss Andrews, but a Mr. Jackson is on the phone, and he insists that you'll take his call.''

"Thanks.'' She lifted the receiver, furious with herself for having shown her embarrassment. "Hi.''

"Hi, honey. Want to drop by my office after work?'' Her immediate response was to say that she would. Then she remembered.

"Oh my! This isn't a good evening for us to get together. It's my night to serve dinner at the homeless shelter.''

"You do that? That's wonderful. We've finally got something in common. I mean . . . we agree on something.''

"Like what? We should take care of the homeless? Everybody should do that.''

"Yeah. What I mean is we're both caring people. I cook at the Wesley soup kitchen Sunday mornings from six to nine, and I've gotten to the place where I can make a decent batch of biscuits."

"How'd that happen?"

"Quite by accident, believe me. I was there to serve breakfast one Sunday morning, and the cook didn't show, so I had to cook. The people ate what I gave them and, as far as I know, nobody got sick. From that time, I've been the Sunday morning breakfast cook."

"You're full of surprises. Tell you what. We can eat early, and you can pick me up about nine after I finish at the shelter."

"You want to see me?"

She heard the eagerness in his voice. Something akin to longing. Did he really like her so much? She swung around in her desk chair.

"Yes. I . . . I want to see you, August." The softening of his rich, velvet voice told her that his face had given itself over to that slow, beguiling smile. At his next words, she was sure of it.

"I'll meet you, and we can get desert."

"What kind?" she asked, serving herself a helping of fun at his expense.

"Have you ever got a one-track mind. I told you we were going to wait."

"What did I say?" she protested. "You're the one whose mind is in a rut." August had a wicked streak, and she was going to have to learn how to get the better of him. She would, too.

Susan waited near the shelter exit, hoping that poor Mrs. Butcher wouldn't find her before August arrived. Mrs. Butcher arrived at the shelter every evening precisely at six o'clock, and whoever was on waitress detail had her for company during the entire evening. She ate quickly and followed the help around until closing time. Tonight, she was reading her latest poems. They weren't bad, Susan decided, but by the tenth reading, she longed for ear plugs. August walked in at exactly nine o'clock, his face glowing with the smile she had begun to cherish.

Mrs. Butcher saw him at about the same time as Susan did. "Mr. Jackson. Mr. Jackson. You're going to work here, too? I didn't like my grits, Sunday. I found a lump in them. 'Course, I'd rather have grits than oatmeal. If you start 'em in cold water and stand right there and stir until they're done, they don't get lumpy. I could come in early Sunday and show you if you want." Susan knew that her valued decorum had finally failed her, when she couldn't close her mouth nor erase the look of astonishment that she knew was ablaze on her face. She tried to shake herself out of it and would have succeeded if August hadn't grabbed the untidy old woman and given her a big hug.

"I don't work here, Carrie. I'm meeting my fiancée. You come in early Sunday morning, and we'll work on those grits together. I'll see you Sunday." To Susan's astonishment, the old woman made no attempt to detain him as she usually did when she got someone's attention. She smiled at him and said, "Have a nice day."

"Close your mouth, honey. Carrie has that effect on everybody."

"Carrie? What about you?" The happiness that radiated from him warmed her heart. She wasn't making a mistake; every move he made increased her assurance that, for once, her instincts about the opposite sex had been perfect. And don't forget Grace's charts, an inner voice whispered.

"How'd it go today?" But before she could answer, he kissed her hard and quickly on her mouth.

"August!"

"Yeah?" He was a consummate actor, too, she decided, taking in his contrived look of innocence. She braced her hands on her hips and glared at him.

"You mustn't do that here in front of these people." She looked at his irreverent grin, capitulated and let his joyous mood envelop her.

"Sorry," he said, feigning repentance, "but it wasn't so bad, was it?"

"Are there any other women under your spell?" Susan asked August as they walked down Adam Clayton Powell Boulevard.

"Other than who?"

She was learning that August's mind worked with trigger speed; well she wasn't bad herself.

"Other than Carrie," she rejoined, laughter rising up in her throat. "Thought you'd caught me, did you." He stopped at the bus stop.

"This one coming will take us to Eightieth and Lexington. Okay?" She knew he was testing her.

"August, if you said 'let's walk,' I wouldn't object, because I'd know you had a good reason. The bus is fine." They reached her building on Eightieth between Lexington and Park, and he said he'd tell her goodnight in the lobby.

"Just like when I was in college, right?"

His eyes darkened with what she'd come to recognize as desire, and a thrill of anticipation teased her senses. She rimmed her lips with the tip of her tongue and wanted to vanish when she saw the answering flame in his eyes. He grabbed her elbow and held it until they reached her door. Inside, he wasted no time. Within a second, she was in his arms where she'd wanted to be since he arrived at the shelter. With her hands, she lowered his head, unwilling to wait longer for the sweet pressure of his lips, and took what she needed.

"Is this what you wanted?" he asked in a voice that betrayed his passion, that trembled for want of control. "Is it?" With his tongue, he simulated the loving they would soon share, and she clung to him, asking for more. Needing more.

"August, why can't . . . ? Oh. Oh, Lord." She'd never

let a man fondle her breasts, and fire shot through her when his hand went under her coat and his fingers rolled her nipple.

"Is this what you wanted, Susan? It will happen every time we're alone, and you know it." His deadly serious mein nearly unnerved her.

"This isn't a game, honey. I don't want us to make a habit of going this far without consummating what we feel. I don't approve of it. But no matter what, we're going to wait. Eventually, you'll understand and appreciate my point of view. I don't want you to wake up in bed with me and think, 'My God, I'm in bed with this stranger.' Another thing. Your bark is loud, but I've learned that you won't bite. If you had any idea how much I want you, how badly, you'd probably run."

She pursed her lips. "How can you be so sure of that?"

August leaned against the wall and folded his arms across his chest. "I read you well. In this and other things. You've decided that I'm easy to handle, that I'll be putty in your pretty brown hands if you put me to a test. So you aren't afraid to challenge me. Grace said she did my chart, and you say she's always right. Ask her to let you see it."

She didn't like the tenor of the conversation; she didn't want to discover that she'd been foolish to let herself like him so much.

"Have you misrepresented yourself to me?" she asked, attempting to summon her pre-August personality, her executive demeanor. Her shoulders slumped in defeat, when she realized that she couldn't shield herself from his look of penetrating evaluation. She didn't want him to judge her harshly.

"No, I have not. But there hasn't been an occasion for me to let you see how quickly I'll put the record straight if someone misjudges me for a person of little consequence, or for an unsophisticated country boy."

She bristled at that and stalled for time, while she pulled off her coat and hung it in a nearby closet. "Do you think

I'd agree to marry that kind of man, even if he agreed that courting is for adolescents, a waste of time? Do you?''

"A country boy's no threat to a Wall Street lawyer. I didn't attempt to mislead you; you let me be myself, and I enjoy it, because it's what I've always wanted, always needed in a woman. And you've given me that. I'm trying to tell you that there's more to me."

"Alright, I'll look for it. Are we still engaged?"

The slow smile began at his lips, revealing his beautiful even white teeth, and moved upward, stealthily it seemed, to envelop his wonderful eyes. Then he laughed aloud.

"Ah, sweetheart. How could you ask that? Didn't I give you the responsibility of looking after my funeral? Baby, you'll never get rid of me."

Tremors coursed through her as his strong hands brought her gently to him, and her body shook as the fire of his hungry mouth drew her into the orbit of desire. Her parted lips begged for his tongue, but he denied her and let his mouth brush her eyelids while he stroked her arms and back.

"Our time will come, sweetheart. If we're going to make a go of this, we'll have to wait. Lovemaking is a part of love, anything else is sex. Everybody needs that, but if we're planning a life together, we have to have something deeper. I get good and high when I feel how you want me, but I'm going to try and nurture that into something deeper, something stronger and permanent."

She expected the smile to start again, and there it was. She had to fight to resist it as she gazed up at him. "August, why do you think you can turn on your charm and get me to do, think, and accept whatever you want?"

"Now, honey, I haven't ever tried to seduce you. Not once."

He had to know from the expression on her face that she didn't believe him. "Be serious."

"I'm serious. I've never done that."

She shook her head. "Well please do. I can't wait to see what you're like when you *really* get going."

August looked down at the woman nestled so sweetly against him and smiled. He didn't think he'd ever get used to the feeling of total contentment he got whenever he felt her in his arms.

"We're going to have a good life together. Trust me?" He loved her shy smile, the way she seemed to submit to her feelings and enjoy being with him. He mused over that for a second and amended the thought. Submissive until they got into an argument. He asked her again.

"Sure you trust me?"

"Yes, I do. I have from the first."

He'd always made it a point to remember his origins and try to stay humble, but when she got like this, so cuddly and agreeable, it was all he could do to keep his chest from swelling. He buzzed her on the forehead.

"What if I tell Grace to go by for you and bring you to my office tomorrow around five?"

"There you go again. Treating me as if I'm an infant. August, I can walk; it's only a few blocks." A deep sigh escaped him. So much for cuddly and agreeable.

"I know you can negotiate a couple of blocks, but it's pitch dark at five o'clock. Let Grace bring you over. Okay?" Her laughter curled around him. By Jim, she was beginning to get his number.

Susan stared at the shiny brass plate on the office door. T. AUGUST JACKSON, VICE PRESIDENT. She hadn't had any idea. Vice president of a highly regarded criminal law firm. She'd thought he worked there as a salaried criminologist. That explained a lot—those flashes of sophisticated taste and behavior, his flawless enunciation and grammar, even with that drawl. What was she supposed to think now? Her light tap on the door was rewarded with a deep-voiced, "come on in." A male secretary? She looked around for a chair, figuring that her knees might not withstand her next shock.

"Mr. Jackson is waiting for you," the young man told her, as his glance swept her from head to foot with obvious approval.

She opened the inner door just as August reached it, sidestepped his open arms, glared at him and demanded, "Explain yourself, mister. You told me you were a criminologist. What other tales have you got me to believe?"

"You asked what I did, and I told you. When a lawyer friend and I started this firm, he was president, and I was vice president. Since then, we've added fourteen lawyers and a dozen criminologists. I'm responsible for the research and investigation, and my partner handles the legal aspects. Come on, I'll introduce you to my secretary." She noticed that the gleams faded from Harold's eyes when August introduced her as his fiancée. As he took her through the office, she didn't doubt that August had his staff's affection and respect.

Susan wasn't sure she wanted Grace's company right then; she was dealing with August's surprises, and she didn't want to hear a word about Grace's charts and lines. He settled in the cab, comfortable as always and slid his right arm around her shoulder.

"How y'all getting along?" Grace asked.

"Fine," Susan answered with a halfheartedness that she knew wouldn't escape her aunt.

"Terrific," August said simultaneously.

"Looks to me like there's some disagreement on how well you're getting along."

"She doesn't want to admit that you were right," August boasted, "but she knows you were. Take us up to my place."

"A Hundred Thirty-Fifth and Malcolm X Boulevard is a long way from Wall Street—and in more ways than one," Susan observed as Grace headed up the FDR drive well above the speed limit.

"That's true, but I love Harlem. Its sounds and pungent smells are unique, and if you speak to people, they speak back. Reminds me a little bit of home."

He waved to an old woman as they entered the lobby of his apartment building.

"How are you, Miss Effie?" he greeted the woman. "Haven't seen you lately." The woman's pleasure was reflected in her broad smile.

"August. I do declare. You're going to live a long time, son. I was thinking about you when I turned around and saw you standing there. Heard anything about Grady, yet?"

"No. Not yet, Miss Effie, but I have a feeling we're getting closer."

"Me, too," the woman said. "I just feel it deep down in here." She pointed to her heart. Susan felt August's arm gather her to him.

"Miss Effie, this is Susan, my fiancée." Susan greeted the woman with a proffered hand and received a powerful grip in return.

"You look after him good, honey. You hear? This man is a prince." Susan wanted to tell her that she knew it, but she settled for a warm smile and said goodbye.

Susan looked around the attractively furnished, spacious apartment. It didn't look as she'd thought it would. "We don't have similar taste in furnishings."

August seemed unconcerned, but that was as she would have expected. "I know, but we'll get around that."

She braced herself for another tug of war. "How? Just tell me how your French Provincial"—she paused and glanced around when an odd object caught her eye—"a couple of Queen Annes and"—she threw her hands up in despair—"and I don't know what else are going to mix with my clean modern lines?" Why was he laughing? Couldn't he see that their furniture didn't belong in the same house?

"Honey, when it comes to what I've got mixing with your sleek lines, you needn't worry. I've got the key to *that*."

"August, I'm talking about house furniture and things like that."

His laughter filled the room. "And what do you think I'm talking about? Come on, baby, loosen up. Chrome and glass are out of place in suburban and country living."

Her voice dropped to a low contralto, barely above a whisper, her words nearly trapped behind her clenched teeth. "What did you say? Suburbs? *Country?* I don't ever plan to live more than walking distance from the Metropolitan Museum of Art and a fifteen-minute taxi ride from the Schomburg Center. Anybody who thinks differently would do well to see a shrink." Let him pace and throw his hands up. See if she cared.

"You want to live in *Manhattan?*" he asked her at last, pronouncing the word as if it foretold a doom of indescribable horror. "*Manhattan?*" He stuffed his hands in his back pants pockets and thoroughly scrutinized his bride-to-be. "What's the big deal? The Met doesn't open on Mondays and, except for Fridays, it's closed on weekdays when you leave work. You've got until quarter to nine in the evening on Saturdays. You have to shackle yourself to Manhattan for that? Same with the Schomburg. You won't miss a thing."

"You want to take me to the *country?*" she asked with both hands planted on her hips. She turned her back quickly as the beginnings of that smile appeared. She wasn't going to be lured into agreeing with him just because he was the most handsome . . . the sweetest . . . He walked around to face her, lights already beaming in his eyes as though he was impatient to give her a lovely present. He tipped up her chin and trailed his thumb down her cheek.

"Honey, come with me to Tarrytown Saturday. Please. I found a nice house for us that I know you'll like." He couldn't have sounded sweeter or sexier, she thought, if he had been whispering words of love. "Then you can put your foot down," he added.

She stamped her left one, though mainly for effect. "It's already down."

"Aw . . . now, honey. I'm never going to ask you to do anything you just don't want to do. Like courting. Have I made you do any courting?" He caressed her back and gently squeezed her arm. "Have I? No, and I'll respect your wishes about everything else, too."

"August, I'm not going to live in the country, and that's that." His grin broadened.

"Fine with me. They've got street lights all over Tarrytown, not like where I grew up, where it was so dark at night the moon had trouble lighting up the place."

"Oh, stop it. You promise not to try and persuade me if I tell you I don't like it?"

He nodded, and she had a chilling feeling that the house would be perfect.

"It isn't so bad, now is it?" he asked her, standing in the dining room of the Tarrytown house that he hoped would be theirs, unable to hide his eagerness. "You like it, don't you?"

"But I'm not having any gold leaf on my chairs and no curlicued candelabrum anywhere in my house."

"Well, alright. I'll give my Queen Anne chairs to Grace, maybe." When she didn't reply, he said, "She can have them auctioned off at Christie's, if she doesn't want them. They're authentic."

She turned to face him and jerked on his lapels.

"Melt them down if they're so precious, August, and have them deposited in Fort Knox. They are not going in my dining room, not even if they're solid gold. Got it?"

"Alright. Alright. Can't win 'em all. But is there such a thing as modern without chrome and glass?"

"You don't like my cocktail table?" His right shoulder bunched upward in a quick shrug.

"Well, first time I saw it, I thought you'd sawed the legs off of your dining table. 'Course it might be alright out by the swimming pool."

"August!"

"On sunny days, I mean." She opened her mouth as though to speak, and he wondered why she didn't say anything. He waited. After a few minutes, she walked over and leaned against his chest.

"August, we have to stop this. Every time we have to decide something, we fight. You think maybe Aunt Grace doesn't know what she's talking about? We don't seem like such a perfect match to me." He put both arms around her.

"This is healthy, sweetheart. We're just sublimating our libidos. Now don't move away. Trust me; every criminologist has to be a good psychologist." He had to laugh when she groaned, not believing what he'd said.

She hadn't said any more about where they'd get married and what she'd wear, and he didn't like it. Getting a wedding dress made might take weeks. That night, he phoned Grace, and reached her at home. He summarized the problem briefly and added, "I want her to be happy. If I could, I'd buy that room for her. Grace, have you ever heard of a more ridiculous idea?"

"Can't say that I have," Grace replied. "Say, wait a minute. Seems to me I remember reading about a contest they're having. The couple that wins will get married in the Rainbow Room. Yes, indeed. I read it in the *Times* one day last week. I'll find it and—"

"Grace, that's too iffy."

"Don't trash it. I can look in—"

"Never mind. Don't do that." He'd had enough crystal ball logic to last him the rest of his life.

Undaunted, Grace told him, "I'll find that newspaper and bring you that notice. What's meant to be will be, so don't close any doors. All you have to do, if I remember right, is tell them in a hundred words or less why you or Susan always wanted to get married in the Rainbow Room. You can do that, Mr. Jackson. And there's a fat prize, not that you need it. What can you lose? Just the time it takes to write a hundred words. I'll bring it to you Monday morning."

He expelled a long breath. "Alright, Grace. I'll think about it."

August got through his chores at the soup kitchen on Sunday morning without too much interference from Carrie. She had walked in clean and reasonably tidy and had been content to stand by the stove for half an hour stirring grits. For once, it was free of lumps. He had a mind to pay her to do it. He walked into his apartment with the intention of dressing hurriedly and getting to church, but a call from his private investigator altered his plans. Could he fly down to Washington that morning? The P.I. was almost certain that their long search was nearing an end, that he had news of Grady Jackson. August telephoned Susan. He had always fought his own battles and taken pride in doing that but, for the first time in his memory, he needed someone with him—a buffer against disappointment. He needed Susan.

"I've got a new lead about my brother, and I'm going to Washington. I'd love to have you with me, if you can be ready in a little more than an hour."

"I'd be happy to go, but I'm just waking up. Will you call me as soon as you know anything?" He promised that he would.

He looked at the two women who greeted him with warm smiles when the P.I. introduced them. Somewhere around thirty, he guessed, roughly in Grady's age group.

"Our family makes a line of cosmetics," Jessie, the older of the two, told him, "and this man supplies our chemicals." August tried to calm his breathing. The two women were apparently intelligent and, had it not been for the differences in eye color, he might have thought that they were twins. As they talked, he searched for reasons why two young, white women would travel from Knoxville, Tennessee, to Washington to mislead him about his brother when they had nothing to gain. He found none.

"When we saw your picture in the paper, we thought it was him and, looking at you, I'm convinced there's a close connection," Jessie continued. "He's just a tad younger, though. Same height, face, and build."

"Would you say we're identical twins," he probed, seeking firmer assurance.

"I don't think so," the younger one answered. "I think his eyes are darker than yours."

"I agree," Jessie said. Tremors danced down his spine; his brother's eyes were nearly black. He tried to stem his feverish anticipation. He had carried the burden for twenty years, used every resource available to him trying to find Grady. Please God, he didn't want his hope built up this way without cause.

"What does he call himself?"

"Grady Jackson," they replied in unison.

He sat down. Could there be two men with that name who looked almost enough like him to be his twin? He thanked the women, opened his check book and began to write.

"No don't give us any money," Jessie said. "Our expenses were paid, and that's enough; I know how I'd feel if I couldn't find my sister. Here's his address." He read, Grady Jackson, Chemist, 37 Rond Point, Ashville, North Carolina. Could it be that he'd looked all over the country, and Grady had never left North Carolina?

Nearly crippled with anxiety and his shirt wet with perspiration in spite of the frigid January weather, August decided to check into the hotel room that his P.I. had reserved for him. He wasn't sure he could find the strength to do anything else. He fell across the bed, couldn't stay there, got up and went to the window. He needed Susan. He honestly believed it was the first time he'd ever needed her right down to the recesses of his soul. He called her.

"Any luck?" she asked him. He heard the fear in her voice.

"It's the best lead I've ever had. I don't know what I'll do if it fizzles out."

"Are you okay?" That hesitant speech, the attempt to hide the tremors in her voice. She was there for him. He hadn't known how much solace it would give him to have that assurance. And he needed it.

"Yeah. I'm handling it," he lied.

"I'll come down there, if you want me to."

The temptation to say yes, to scream it, was powerful, and he almost said it. But impulsiveness was foreign to him, and the consequences of her being in his hotel room flashed through his mind. He couldn't put her in a separate room, not even an adjoining one, and if she stayed with him, he'd make love to her all night long.

"I'll never forget your offer, Susan. I appreciate it more than you could know, but I'll be back tomorrow morning. We can be together in the evening."

"I thought you might need me." Her voice betrayed a feeling of rejection, but he knew himself and knew the awesome strength of his desire for her. And he knew, too, that if they made love for the first time under those conditions, he'd be out of control. He'd destroy the feelings that he had nurtured in her with such care. And he'd ruin her trust in him.

"I need you, Susan. God knows I do. And that's the problem. Our relationship is still fragile, and I don't think it can withstand what I'd put you through tonight if you came down here."

"I . . . I thought I should be with you if you're having a hard time. I'm a big girl, August."

He couldn't help laughing. "I know that, honey. But I think we'd better do it my way. Okay?"

They finished the conversation, and he hung up. *If I wouldn't take her to bed when she practically asked me to,* he told himself, *I'd be less than a man if I used her to ease my personal torment.*

"Stop beating a dead horse," Susan snapped at Oscar Hicks just after the Monday morning senior staff meeting got under way. She sat one place down from the head of the conference table as the firm's protocol demanded, and Hicks sat one place farther down across from her. His antipathy toward her was common knowledge among their peers, and he scowled furiously at her stern reprimand.

"Our client is wrong," she continued, "and if you hold out longer, he'll lose it all. Settle out of court."

"My, aren't we testy this morning," he sneered. Two senior partners agreed with her, ending what could have been an unpleasant session. He cornered her in the hallway as she walked toward her office.

"You think everything's going your way, don't you? A smart person wouldn't make an enemy of me, Ms. Andrews."

She didn't break her stride. "I told you when the two of us discussed it that you would lose that case if you persisted in going for a killing, but you didn't take my advice," she explained patiently. "And you won't take it now. But if that case goes to court, you won't win. There isn't a judge anywhere who can't see that your client is lying, that his documents are not authentic, and that it's a trumped-up charge. For your own reputation, you should settle now. You and the firm will get something, as well as our client. But if you go to court, we'll end up paying the cost of court and probably getting sued." She wasn't surprised that her gentle tone failed to placate him, because he seemed to thrive on conflict.

"You know it all, don't you? This is my biggest case, and you're telling me to turn tail and run. You couldn't be jealous?"

She slowed her steps. "Oscar, suit yourself. As for me being jealous of you, let's just admit that your imagination has gone berserk." She didn't look at him, because she knew he'd appear crushed; Oscar thought himself wise, imaginative, and dashing. Poor misguided man. She didn't have the time nor the inclination to polish his ego; she had problems of her own.

She went into her office quickly and closed the door. It hadn't been necessary for her to go after Oscar as she'd done in the staff meeting. His performance lacked competence, but she could have put it in a memo. She resisted dropping her head in her hands and giving in to her feelings. She knew that August had been tormented last night, but he'd nevertheless refused her offer to be with him and, while she didn't claim to understand men, his refusal hadn't made sense. She couldn't force herself to work, a new experience, so she called her aunt.

"I knew it was you when the phone rang," Grace said. *I'm not going to cry,* Susan lectured herself. Instead, she went on the attack.

"Aunt Grace, this whole thing with August is ridiculous. What do I know about him? How do I know he isn't seeing someone down there in Washington?"

"Well, at least he's put a fire under you. If you're worried about that, you care about him."

"Of course I c . . . I don't give a snap what he does. Oh, Aunt Grace, I do. I do. I really care for . . . Oh, what am I saying?"

"That's your heart speaking, girl. You better listen to it."

"I'm hanging up."

"Now. Now. I can pick you up at about five, if that isn't

too late, and we can get a little something to eat. Might make you feel better. Did August tell you why he went to D.C.?"

"His brother."

"That's been a long hard trial for both of them. They're looking for each other."

"I'm ashamed of myself." And she was, she told herself.

"No need for that. You're human, you care for him, and you're not sure of him though I don't know why not. This should have happened to you when you were a teenager. But no, when other youngsters were learning the opposite sex, you decided the most important thing in life was cybernetics. I think that's what you called it. Where'd it get you?"

"Aunt Grace, I don't need this lecture. See you at five." *I'm going to get some work done if it kills me,* she told herself after hanging up, but within seconds, her secretary buzzed her.

"Mr. Jackson on line two."

"August, where are you?" Her breath seemed trapped in her throat. Had he found Grady?

"I'm at La Guardia airport. I'm still looking, but I have hope now. I want to see you tonight. How about seven-thirty at your place?"

She breathed at last.

"I'll be there," was as much as she could manage. She hung up, phoned Grace and canceled their date. Might as well clear her desk; nothing related to that office was likely to push August from her thoughts. She couldn't help wondering how she had become so strongly attached to him this quickly. Admittedly, with his mesmerizing brown eyes, high cheek bones, smooth dark cleanly shaven skin, pouting bottom lip, and tantalizing smile, he was better looking than a man had any right to be. But her world had a plethora of handsome men. August was more, she mused. Far more. Strong. Oh, yes. She was learning that he had enormous strength, and it had taken her a while to realize that his gentleness and tenderness with her was just that: strength, not weakness. When August had her in his arms, everything else could go skate; he made her feel as though her world and everything in it was perfect. She locked her desk, shaking her head at her new self-knowledge, snapped her briefcase closed and gazed across Upper New York Bay at the Statue of Liberty, wishing she could see that far into her future.

Susan tried to calm herself and to appear casual, her normally decorous self, when she opened the door for August that evening. She looked her best and knew it, and she wanted to behave as if his staying in Washington overnight and refusing her company hadn't bothered her. She steeled herself against his charisma and looked into his eyes but, even as she did so, she knew he could see her joy at being with him. Without a word, he stepped into the foyer and took her to him. Tiny sensations of prickling heat raced all through her body when his lips claimed her, and she let him cherish her. Her heart hammered in her chest like a runaway train as his knowing fingers roamed over her arms, shoulders, and back and his talented tongue found its home inside her mouth. If she could only get on him, under him, inside of him . . . if she could just drown in him. She felt his arousal and lost all reason. In wild abandonment, her body took control, and she sucked on his tongue, telegraphing to him the power of the need he'd provoked in her.

"Whoa, honey," he said at last, gasping for breath. She must have looked bewildered, because he didn't release her but shifted her to his side and held her there. "Honey, when you get started, you really move, don't you? Anything to eat?" She gulped. Maybe he could shift gears with the speed of sound, but she was still in that other world he was so good at creating.

"Uh . . . yeah. I ordered us a catered dinner for eight o'clock. Okay?"

"Sweetheart, can't you cook a bit?"

"If I have to; after all, chemistry was one of my best subjects in high school and college."

August closed one eye, raised the eyebrow of the other one and shook his head. "I thought we were talking about cooking."

"We are. Cooking is just a matter of blending flavors and substances, and chemistry is pretty much the same; you mix stuff and hope it doesn't blow up in your face."

August's stare would have been worthy of someone witnessing a supernatural phenomenon. "If you're serious, honey, I guess I'd better do our cooking."

Susan couldn't suppress a broad grin. She hadn't lied to any great extent: ordinarily, the average human could turn out a better meal than she, but the five menus that she'd mastered would please the most discriminating person.

"In that case, fair is fair," she deadpanned, "I'll make coffee every morning." His rippling laughter warmed her from her head to her toes. She led him toward the kitchen where she'd stored a pitcher of Oklahoma High in the refrigerator. She reached toward the refrigerator door, her lips still tingling from his kiss, withdrew her hand and looked at him. She hadn't meant to issue an invitation, but her eyes must have communicated to him her churning need and the sweet communion for which she longed. In a second, she was in his arms, caught up in wild passion. Frissons of heat darted through her, and every molecule of her body screamed to have him within her. The flesh of her arms and shoulders burned from the loving touch of his hands, and her body was his to manipulate. Flaccid. Submissive. She parted her lips for his kiss and took what he gave. Hard, possessive loving. She couldn't help shivering in frustration when, as suddenly as he'd set her afire, he released her.

"You've got to stop doing that to me, August," she said, when she could get her breath.

"What?" It pleased her that he, too, seemed to struggle with his emotions.

"You know what I mean. Isn't there anything intermediate between your mind blowing kisses and no kiss at all?" *Oh, oh, here we go,* she thought, as he started to smile.

"Honey, I don't believe in doing a thing halfway. Nothing. And that includes . . . Well, you'll see. Hmm. This is good; what is it?" he asked, savoring the cold drink.

"Peach juice and carbonated Mateuse Rosé. Aunt Grace concocted it. She calls it Oklahoma High. Don't ask me why." Her eyebrow arched sharply, but after thinking for a moment, she decided not to comment on his sudden shift in demeanor; he did it often, and she'd have to get accustomed to it.

She answered the door, paid the caterer, and served the food.

"Did you miss me?" he asked in a voice that she thought rather subdued.

"You were only gone overnight."

"I know, but that was long enough to miss me."

"I had things on my mind," she hedged.

August unfolded his napkin, dabbed at his mouth and grinned.

"Liar. Those kisses were worth a thousand words." His tone softened, and the dark sonority of his voice caressed her. "I missed you, and I'm counting the hours until I don't have to leave you."

"You don't—"

"Of course, I do," he interrupted. "Once we agree to something, we don't reopen it."

"Not even when the agreement involved duress? You did pressure me, you know that."

"No comment," August said, refusing to be drawn into it. "Did you put in for leave so we can go on our honeymoon? How much time did you ask for?"

"How much . . ." She didn't try to hide her shock. *"Honeymoon?* I thought . . . Well, it didn't occur to me that . . ." Her voice drifted into silence.

"Shame on you, honey. Do I look like a man who wouldn't give my bride a honeymoon? They could spare you for two weeks, couldn't they?"

Her napkin dropped into her soup. "But *two whole weeks!* I'm on an anti-trust suit, and I may have to argue it before the Supreme Court. I can't take—"

He interrupted in an exasperatingly mild voice. "But, honey, slow down. If it isn't on the Court's docket for this session, you have until October, almost ten months. So, as soon as you get the Court's agenda, we can make plans. No excuses. I want you all to myself where nobody knows us, and I need a lot longer than two weeks, but I'll settle for that. We need time, sweetheart." His lips curled into a grin. "Just wait. You'll wish you'd taken at least a month." He walked around to her, lifted her out of the chair and sat down.

"I care for you, sweetheart, and I'm going to make you happy."

She leaned against him. "Aunt Grace is nuts. The only thing we've had in common so far is the homeless. With everything that counts, you're odd and I'm even."

His eyebrows jerked up sharply.

"What does that mean? The fact that we're both compassionate and care about less fortunate people says more about us than our taste in furniture."

"What about the place where we'll live?"

"Country or city, ranch house or whatever, that business about where we'll live wasn't important."

"Of course not," she grumbled, "you got your way."

He got up and put the dishes in the dishwasher, claiming that she looked too beautiful to touch anything soiled. Then he smiled at her, and his tone was very casual.

"I'm glad you like the house. It's got plenty of rooms, and four or five children won't make it seem crowded."

The water glass that she'd been holding crashed to the floor.

"Did you say three or four?"

"I said four or five." She had to sit down. Ignoring her consternation, he plowed on. "I've longed for a family most of my life. I guess most people who are orphaned at an early age feel like that. And I suppose being without my brother accentuated the need."

She looked first to heaven and then at him. "And less than five kids isn't a family?"

He stopped pretending and faced her. "What are you saying?"

"I'm saying I figured two would do it."

He dried his hands and started toward her, but she was onto his methods of persuasion. She backed away. "Two? Honey, this is more serious than honeymoon, house, engagement ring, and church wedding combined. I *love* kids."

She stared at him, hoping to convey how far off base he was and to bring him around to reason before they got into another fight, because this was one that August Jackson was not going to win.

"You don't have to overindulge yourself to such an extent just because you love them. No way." She wouldn't allow herself to be swayed by his look of . . . of injury and dismay. You'd think she was attempting to deprive him of a divine right. She braced herself for his next sally, but he chose to plead.

"Honey, you don't understand. Most of my life, I've been dreaming about my little kids playing around my feet before a nice big winter fire while I read stories to them. Don't you love kids?" He took a step forward, and she took one backward.

"Sure I love children, but I'm already thirty-five and, if we're going to ensure the children and me the best chances for good health, our babies should be spaced at least two and preferably three years apart. If I have five, I'll still be having babies when I'm fifty." She threw up her hands as though in despair. "And even if I were younger, I'd have to have quintuplets if you want a crowd of them playing around your feet; babies grow up."

He frowned and ran his slim fingers over the back of his tight curls. "Honey, can't we discuss this?" She looked toward the sky as though seeking help.

"We *are* discussing it. Can't we just have two?" When he suddenly relaxed and began to smile, she prepared for battle.

"How about three? I'll help you."

Both hands went to her hips. *"You'll help me?* You're darn tootin' you will. How else do you think I'll get pregnant?"

This time, his smile began in his eyes, which gleamed lustfully, and his beautiful white teeth showed themselves in an appreciative grin that developed into a howl. When he could stop laughing, he offered an explanation.

"What I mean, honey, is that I'll do everything and anything to keep you comfortable and to ease your burden."

Thinking that her heart would burst, she ran to him and threw her arms around him. "Oh, August. You're so precious."

He hugged her to him fiercely, and she could feel a new emotion, something akin to a healing energy radiating from him. He buried his face in her neck and murmured, "Baby, this is the first time you've ever come to me like this. You always respond to me, but you haven't opened yourself to me and asked me to reciprocate your feelings. A man needs that, too." She held him as close as her strength would allow.

"Ah, sweetheart," he murmured, "can't you see that we're going to make it? We have these little misunderstandings and disagreements, but we always ride over them, don't we?" She snuggled against him.

"We're not having five children, August."

"I know, honey. I know. You agreed to three, and I'm willing to compromise."

She stepped back and glared at him.

"I didn't hear myself agree. We'll take this up again when our second is two years old."

"Okay. Okay. At least, I'll get to be a father." She had never realized that a loving relationship with a man could be so sweet and that laughing with him could be so wonderfully satisfying. August made her laugh. And he made her heart skip beats.

August figured he had to learn how to be happy. He had achieved success as a corporate executive, had the respect of his associates and employees, and the people back in Wallace, North Carolina, thought he had spun gold wings. Whenever he walked into Wallace's library, Mrs. McCullen, the librarian, ushered him into the computer room that he'd funded and introduced the children who worked and studied there to their benefactor. All of that made him feel great, but it wasn't a part of him. The woman in his arms was a part of him; he could feel it. But he wasn't sure of it, an ephemeral quality about their relationship wouldn't let him enjoy it to the fullest. He'd believe his good fortune when he saw their marriage certificate. He shifted his attention to Susan when he heard his name.

"August, I want to go to the opera. If I get two tickets, will you go with me to see *La Boheme?*" Her surprisingly seductive voice told him that she wasn't sure of their relationship, either. If she had been, she'd know that he'd do whatever he could to make her happy.

"I'll get the tickets. When do you want to go?" He made a note of that. Since she thought she had to seduce him into taking her to an opera, he'd better put her straight.

"I love opera. I learned to appreciate it from the Saturday afternoon broadcasts that I've followed since my childhood, but I've never been to one. I'll look forward to this." Joy suffused him as he savored her smile and obvious delight.

"A little thing like this can make you so happy?" he asked.

."Well . . . we've got something else in common, something we can enjoy together without getting into a fight or either of us having to compromise."

He grinned. "Don't mistake me for a highbrow, now. I love country music, too. Some of the best guitarists in the world play country." Here we go, he thought, as her smile dissolved into a frown.

"You can't sell it to me." She inclined her head toward her left shoulder and lowered her eyelids slightly in that way he loved. "If you want to hear spell-binding popular guitar music," she admonished him, "listen to some good classical jazz—Charlie Christian or Freddie Green, Wes Montgomery or Laurindo Almeida. Now, that's guitar playing. Those guys knew what to do with six strings."

He put a serious expression on his face. "I wouldn't know, being unfamiliar with the guitar." At least she had the grace to appear less sure of herself.

"But you said . . . Oh," she murmured, remembering that he'd studied guitar for many years, "I guess I can't tell you who knows how to play a guitar."

"Sure you can," he said with a shrug of his left shoulder, "but you don't have to be right, you . . . ." The roll of paper towels sailed straight at him, but he caught it, tossed it on the sink and went after her.

"Throw things at your future husband, will you? Well, we'll see about that," he said, reaching toward her. Warned by the fire she must have seen in his eyes, she raced down the hallway, but he charged after her, grabbed her as she whirled into the living room and tumbled with her onto her big velvet sofa. Gales of laughter pealed from her throat while he mercilessly tickled her side. He watched, transfixed, as her giggles dissolved into sudden and sober silence when she opened her eyes to the passion he knew his face betrayed.

She squirmed beneath him, and his response was swift, hard and hot. *I'm going to get him this time,* she told herself, when heat pooled in the pit of her belly and shot to the center of her passion. He turned to his side bringing her with him but, as she struggled in the grip of desire, his effort to slow them down only vaguely penetrated her consciousness. When he didn't respond to her parted lips, she wet his mouth with her tongue and luxuriated in his hoarse groan as he opened up to her. Wanting more and demanding it, she threw her right leg across his hip but, with what sounded like a wrenching sob, he moved her away from him.

"Susan," he said, sitting up straight and seeming to drag the words out of himself, "we're going to wait."

She sat up and moved close to him. "Can I expect you to stop doing this to me after February fourteenth?" She tried not to be vexed at his raised eyebrow that suggested he couldn't imagine what her question was about.

"Leaving me hanging like this. You know what I mean." His tender hug made up for it a little, but not much.

"Aren't you beginning to see why I'm holding back. Think how much closer we are now than when you first brought it up. The closer we are and the deeper our feelings for each other the first time we make love, the better it will be and the more binding, too. I'm flattered. I'd lie if I said I wasn't, and especially because it's me and not just the physical relief that you want." She poked his shoulder playfully.

"I'm cooperating aren't I?"

"Just barely," he muttered.

"Well, it's taking some effort on my part."

He gazed at her, as though surprised. "What does that mean?"

"It means that I am not so naive that I don't know how

to seduce you. That's what." He wasn't going to fool her with his look of solemnity, his pious sincerity.

"I'm glad to hear it," was all he said. Then he looked down at her left hand and his eyes seemed to gleam with happiness. "That's not so bad, is it, honey?"

"What?"

"Wearing my ring. It's not like I'd asked you to wear a big, bright sign on your forehead or anything." She had to laugh, he could think of the most ridiculous things.

"It gets a lot of attention. The first day I wore it, would you believe a line formed at my desk? The consensus at the office is that you have elegant taste." She paused, weighing a decision. "August, will you stop by my office tomorrow afternoon? I'd like to introduce you to my colleagues." She should have suggested that earlier, she realized, when the change in his demeanor reflected frank pride.

August called Grace and asked her to be in front of his office building at noon the next day.

"I found that clipping," Grace said, as soon as she heard his voice, "and it's got all the information you need. You don't even have to tell Susan a thing about it; you can do it on your own, it says here. But you be sure and make that deadline, now. You hear? My second sense tells me—"

He didn't want to hear about her second sense. "Alright. I'll do it, but it's just between us. I don't want Susan to be disappointed." So far, he hadn't found Grady, he told her in reply to her question, but he had an excellent lead, and his P.I. was currently checking on it.

"Shucks," she said. "Give me his christened name, birthday, date, time, and place, and I'll bring you something tomorrow. No need to wait on an investigator when he can't tell you anything that I can't." He did, adding that his mother had said Grady was born at high noon.

* * *

He had a sensation of being suspended in midair, when he saw the look of excitement on Grace's face as she greeted him at noon the next day. Her whole body seemed to vibrate and glow in contrast with her normally closed face and phlegmatic demeanor. She opened the front door of the taxi for him, something she hadn't previously done.

"It's him, alright," she said, dispensing with preliminaries. "His chart says he's looking for you, and my second sense backs that up. He's going to find you before the full moon."

"When is that?"

"Next one is February the eleventh. From the looks of this, you ought to be heading toward western North Carolina, somewhere around Pinehurst, or maybe eastern Tennessee. If that's where your P.I. went, you're on the right tract. Go for it!"

August pulled at the scarf around his neck and loosened his tie. With trembling fingers, he took a few tissues from the box on Grace's dashboard and wiped his forehead. "Slow down over there, please, Grace. I need a couple of minutes before I go for Susan. I'm trying not to hope too much, but my investigator went to Ashville, and that's in western North Carolina. I've had so many disappointments that I can't let myself expect too much. I haven't married, bought a house, or even a car. My earnings have gone for necessities and for my search for Grady. I've put everything that I could into finding him; the only kin I know about. Twenty-six long years. I wonder what he'll be like, how he turned out."

Grace patted his hand. "You needn't worry; he's a respectable citizen."

"I was prepared to love him, no matter what, but I'm glad to know he made it. Thank God, and thank you, Grace." He shook his head slowly, unable to believe that the agony was nearing an end. He recalled something that Grace had said minutes earlier.

"You said something about a second sense. Are you clairvoyant?" He noticed that she appeared ill at ease.

"I don't tell people about that, because it makes them uncomfortable with me, but since you asked, very much so. I was that way growing up, and I didn't have sense enough to keep my mouth shut about it. The upshot was people treated me like I was a circus freak. I studied astrology because a woman told me that was more scientific. I don't know. I use both together, and I've been able to help a lot of people. I didn't manage to go any farther than high school, and I didn't want to wait tables or tend a bar, so I figured driving my own taxi was my best chance of meeting a lot of people and helping as many as I could. Of course, I make a good living at it, and I ain't sneezing at that. No sirree."

That night, August decided to enter the Rainbow Room contest. What could he lose? Maybe, if he showed some originality, he'd stand a chance of winning. He wanted Susan to have her dream, and he wanted to see her in a long white wedding gown.

He wrote: I dreamed of a wedding in the Rainbow Room, because

I wanted a little church wedding
Before flying with my bride to the moon
But on a New Year's Eve long, long ago
She fell in love with the Rainbow Room.

She says she'll marry in a gay pants suit
And hurry back to her office by noon
She wouldn't think of wearing satin and lace
Unless she wears it in the Rainbow Room.

She longs to relive that star-spangled night
When the world was hers, and her youth full bloom
She'll even take her vows in a white bridal gown
If she can take them in the Rainbow Room.

He put the letter in an envelope, considered crossing
his fingers and decided a prayer made more sense. On his
way to Susan's apartment, he dropped the letter into the
mailbox.

August hadn't objected when she told him that since
he'd gotten fourth row orchestra seats for the performance
of *La Boheme* at the Metropolitan Opera House, she'd like
to wear a long dress. "Fine with me," he'd said, offhand.
So she dressed in a figure-hugging red velvet sheath supported by thin shoulder straps and her ample bosom, piled
her hair on her head, and surveyed the results. Not bad.
She barely heard August's piercing whistle when she
opened the door, nor did she notice his appreciative comment on her looks. In a black tuxedo with a pleated silk
shirt and gray and black accessories, August Jackson was
spellbinding. Not certain whether her eyes deceived her,
she blinked them several times, as she tried to reconcile
this urban sophisticate with the gentle, homespun man
she thought she knew. She took a deep breath, invited
him in and went for her coat, all the while musing over
the picture he made. This guy was poster material. Well,
she consoled herself, at least he didn't behave as if he
knew it.

"Where's your coat," she asked as he helped her into
hers.

"I don't have a black chesterfield," he told her, "but I
won't get cold; a car's waiting for us right outside."

Her eyebrows arched in spite of her effort to hide her
surprise, but he laughed, taking it in stride.

"I do know a few things, honey, including how to dress.

The first thing I did when Amos and I started to turn a profit was to concentrate on how to present myself in all kinds of situations. I hate putting on these things, but let me tell you it's worth it to see you looking like this. You're so pretty.''

Only he had applied that word to her since she was a small girl. She wanted to put her arms around him and hug him to her; he'd blindsided her, poleaxed her. He looked down at her, and his lips began to smile. She had to close her eyes, because she would be besotted for sure if she gazed at him until that smile reached his eyes.

"Come on, let's go," she urged. He assisted her into the back seat of a waiting chauffeured, Lincoln Town Car, joined her, opened the bar, and poured her a glass of champagne.

"I'm going to faint," she said, her voice low and breathy.

"Don't you like champagne?"

His grin told her that he was well aware of her problem, so she gathered her wits as best she could and sipped the icy wine. Throughout the performance, during the intermission, and on the ride back home, she saw an August who displayed every nuance of good manners and elegant taste. And at the end of the evening, she couldn't say who had sung the role of Mimi or how she'd sounded.

"You're amazing," she told him, as he left her.

He turned and favored her with his high powered grin. "There's a first and only time for everything. Wouldn't you say?"

She had to laugh, because he'd just told her not to expect that treatment often. Maybe not again.

Two days later, August kept his promise to meet Susan's colleagues. She took him first to meet the firm's president, a genial man of Norwegian decent, who gave them his blessings. August Jackson was as comfortable in that setting as she, and more than one of her male colleagues frankly deferred to him. It didn't surprise her that Oscar Hicks proved the exception.

"Man, I'm glad you're taking Susan out of the running for partner. She's a mean piece of competition, and I won't stand a chance as long as she wants a shot at it." He talked on and on, Susan observed, apparently oblivious to August's failure to respond.

"What exactly do you mean by that comment?" August finally said in a voice iced with sarcasm.

"Well," Oscar said, apparently less sure of himself now. "She'll soon start a family and, well, you know."

He cautioned himself not to show his temper. "And that's your business?"

"Well, no . . . of course not," Oscar replied, as he edged toward the door. "Good to meet you." Susan watched his departing back and couldn't restrain a laugh.

"Milquetoast, if I ever saw any," she said, as much to herself as to August. "Oscar knows a man when he sees one. No wonder he got out of here when you challenged him." She didn't let August see her misgivings. For the first time since she had agreed to marry him, doubts as to the wisdom of it and fear of probable consequences buried themselves into her consciousness. She didn't know what she'd do if she missed out on the chance to become a partner, to see Andrews added to Pettersen, Geier and Howard.

Three evenings later, Susan sat up in bed putting rollers in her hair and musing over August's inconsistent behavior. Whenever he had an option, August usually chose the traditional, the old fashioned. So simple a thing as how visitors would announce themselves had been an issue between them. She had wanted a doorbell and an intercom, but he claimed that was too unfriendly, and they'd settled for chimes. He wanted a house full of children, but when their furniture was delivered to their Tarrytown home the day before, he hadn't asked her to take the day off to receive it. He had done that himself. Maybe he wouldn't expect her to stay at home for months after each of their children was born. She hoped he'd be understanding about that. She didn't want to give up that partnership; she'd worked too hard and too long for it.

August returned the phone to its cradle and propped himself against the wall with the help of his right elbow. His left hand went to his chest as though to still the furious pounding of his heart. After all these years, was he finally going to see Grady? He didn't know if he could stand a disappointment such as he'd experienced when he'd gone to Washington to see a man who might have been his brother. His private investigator claimed to be 90 percent certain this time, and Grace's charts were never wrong, but there was still a chance that his hopes would be futile. His entire life had been one triumph after another over adversity, and he didn't fear his ability to withstand it. But this was his heart. He'd loved his little brother and had protected him as best he could against the cruelty and unfairness that they endured in foster homes. But one day their foster father had promised Grady the beating of his life, and the boy had disappeared. Soon after that, August had been sent to another home, and Grady couldn't have found him without going to the authorities. He'd been looking for his brother ever since, and he knew he'd never be a whole person until he found him. He dialed Susan's number,

"Susan, my investigator says he's found my brother in Ashville, North Carolina. I'm going there tomorrow morning, and I want you to go with me. Will you?" He didn't know what he'd do if she said she couldn't make it; he needed her, and he needed to know that she'd be there for him whenever he needed her just as he would be for her. He needed some evidence that meeting his needs was important to her. Annoyed and uneasy at her long silence, he didn't try to hide his testiness.

"Look, if you think you can't be away from your office for a day and a half, say so. I'll be back Thursday."

"Oh, August, I'm so happy for you. And of course, I'll go with you," she said, in the shadowy tone of one coming out of a trance. "I was trying to figure out how to shuffle the deck here, so to speak." They agreed on time and other particulars, but he wasn't fooled by her explanation. She had hesitated to go. He told himself to pay closer attention. He didn't intend to give her up, but he believed in correcting errors and solving problems at the root the first time he noticed them. That policy had made him a successful executive, and he'd use it to keep his marriage on track.

They had barely greeted each other before he realized the absence of the warm camaraderie and togetherness that they had shared ever since their movie date, the closeness that he'd felt with her, the indescribable feeling of oneness. He ascribed his own feeling of separateness, of there being a distance between them, to his anxiety that the man he would meet might not be his long sought brother. But to what could he attribute her quiet, somber manner? As the plane touched down on the runway, he felt her hand cover his and squeeze in a gesture of support and forced a smile in her direction.

"If it isn't Grady, we'll keep right on looking until we find him," she said. "And we *will* find him." He gave silent thanks, leaned toward her and captured her mouth. She was there for him; that was all he'd needed.

Almost as soon as they walked into the waiting area and looked around, he felt Susan tug sharply at his hand and point to two men in the distance who had begun to approach them. The taller of the two men smiled, and his heart beat accelerated. Susan grabbed his hand and started running toward the men.

"It's him!" she yelled. "August, it's him. It has to be. His smile is just like yours."

He ran with her, speechless, barely aware of his moves. They reached the men and stopped short, as the two men searched each other's faces, hope gleaming in their eyes. August thought he heard Susan say, "Oh, Lord, let it be," but he didn't move his gaze from that of the man in front of him. He found his voice.

"Grady, do you remember our father?" The man smiled and, in a nearly identical voice said, "Of course I remember him. He only had one leg. He lost the other one at the saw mill where he worked."

"I can't believe it; after all these years. My God, Grady, this has to be the happiest moment of my life." He didn't care that tears streamed down his face as he embraced the man whom he didn't doubt was his blood brother. Jessica and her sister had been right; they could have passed for twins. He tried to control the excitement that clutched at him, but couldn't manage it and finally rested his head on Grady's shoulder and let the tears flow. After a few minutes, they stepped back from each other, unashamed of their wrenching emotions and teary eyes, and smiled. Grady had a question of his own.

"I've got a birthmark, August. What is it and where is it?"

August grinned; he'd forgotten about that, hadn't felt the need for any further proof after he saw their father's smile on Grady's face. "There should be a round black, hairy spot the size of a quarter or fifty cent piece on your left shoulder."

"Want to see it?" Grady asked, laughing as though they shared a private joke, as indeed they did.

"Not really, and I'm sorry for all those times I taunted you about it." He followed Grady's glance to a tear stained Susan, reached out and gathered her to him.

"Grady, this is my fiancée, attorney Susan Andrews. We plan to be married on Valentine's Day."

"Say, that's only about three weeks," Grady exclaimed, ignoring Susan's outstretched hand and bringing her to him in a warm hug. "I'll try to make it."

August quirked an eyebrow. "Try hard; I'm having a big wedding and inviting every single person I know, so you'll have to be my best man." He could see that his request pleased Grady, who agreed and invited them all to his home, a small ranch house on a hill with a spectacular view. He didn't doubt that Susan would remind him that she and Grady had similar preferences for houses. As they walked into the living room, he saw more that his brother and fiancée shared; the room was sparsely, but elegantly furnished with modern pieces. Pleased, he smiled at her. But when he caught Susan's withering glance, he knew that her mind was centered on his announcement of a big church wedding, something to which she obviously hadn't accommodated herself. Well, if he was lucky, their crowd would gather in the famous Rainbow Room.

They sipped coffee while Grady related to them experiences he'd had growing up without August. Susan offered to leave so that they might have privacy when Grady told of personal, almost intimate and sometimes nearly tragic happenings in his young life, but August held onto her hand, though at times with unsteady fingers. He marveled that the man before him could have survived months at a time in freight cars, stealing food from restaurants by posing as a delivery boy, picking strawberries in the spring and sorting potatoes in the autumn.

"When did you go to school?" Susan asked, clearly appalled that a child should have had so painful and precarious a life.

"A pullman porter on the Atlantic Coastline became interested in me when he caught me stealing books from someone's compartment and discovered that I wanted to read them and not sell them. I was about eleven. He took me home with him, and we worked out a deal. He'd send me to school and take care of my expenses if I'd look after his mother. Mama Ada was about eighty or eighty-five, she wasn't sure, and couldn't walk too well. She refused to move out of her house, although it was little more than a shack. I made her fires, got water from her well, swept her yard, went to the store and got her groceries, and did just about everything else that she needed done. After six or seven months, I decided to move in with her, and it was a smart decision. She'd once taught grade school, and she still had a trigger sharp mind. She made me her project, and within a year and a half, I was right where I should have been in school. She tried to teach me everything she knew, and I tried to take it in. I got a scholarship to the University of North Carolina, and I was on my way. My goal was to find old Chester Faison and show him that I'd made a man of myself. I did go back to Wallace, but he'd long since died, and his daughter, Ruthie, didn't even remember that we'd once been foster children in that home."

"Where's that man who helped you?" Susan asked.

"About ten miles from here. He's retired now, and I usually run by to see him and his wife every Sunday after church. Of course, Mama Ada's been gone a long time. We'll catch up with the rest later, August. Tell me what you've been doing."

August leaned back in the comfortable business-class seats as the big plane headed for New York and draped his arm around Susan's shoulder. So much to digest, to think about. His life had been rocky at a time when he was a youth trying to get through school, but he'd had a much easier life than Grady. He gazed down at the woman whose head rested trustingly on his shoulder while she slept, and counted his blessings. He had his brother once more, and he had at his side this woman who had come to mean everything to him. More than she could know. When she'd grasped his hand and promised him that *they* would look for Grady until they found him, he'd known that, after twenty-six years, he was no longer alone.

How could so much go wrong in less than two days? Susan paced between her desk and her window overlooking the Statue of Liberty. Her contract stated that the next partnership was hers and that she should apply for it after six months—five weeks hence. But she'd just been told that partners were not expected to take extended leave and that she would have to promise not to do that. The partners knew her age and were forcing her to choose between partnership and motherhood. They hadn't put it in writing but, if she didn't cooperate, they'd easily find a reason to withhold the coveted promotion. There was no mistaking Oscar's hand in that attempt at blackmail; on more than one occasion, he had alluded to there being a conflict between her job and marriage. Upset and more depressed than she could ever remember having been, she called August.

"What's the matter, honey? You sound low, almost as if you've lost your best friend. Tell me."

"I don't want to talk about it over the phone. Why don't you bring over a great big pizza about seven and I'll make a simple salad. I don't feel like cooking, and I don't want to go anywhere."

"I'll be there. Chin up. I promised that, as long as I'm breathing, I'll be with you no matter what, and I mean that. See you at seven."

They'd eaten half of the pizza, discarded the remainder, and straightened up the kitchen, but neither had mentioned what had depressed Susan earlier that day. She knew what his reaction would be, despite his promise of support, and she dreaded the confrontation. He took her hand, walked them into her living room, sat in her big barrel chair, and pulled her gently onto his lap.

"Since it's so painful you dread talking about it, I gather I'm not going to like what you say. Am I right?"

She shifted slightly on his lap, remembered where she was and the probable consequences of not remaining still, and nodded. "You're right, and it's about the office."

"You can't get time off for our honeymoon?" he queried, and she could see that he braced himself for an unpleasant discussion.

She shook her head, sighed, and faced him. It couldn't be avoided. "They've added a condition to my partnership contract. It's unwritten, but it might as well be in black and white. I have to promise not to take any extended leave for the first three years after I'm a senior partner."

"That's ridiculous." He placed her on the floor and stood up, his face mottled with fury. "Nobody can stipulate such a requirement. Besides, I suspect it's against the law in New York. And even if it isn't," he roared, "you can't leave a few weeks old baby and go back to work. What if you got sick? They're full of baloney. You've got rights."

"I'm not being given the choice. If I want the partnership, I have to agree and in writing, and they will enforce it." She hadn't thought that August could get so angry, and it frightened her as she watched his lips tremble in cold fury. He slammed his fist into the palm of his right hand.

"If you sign that and they can hold you to it, that will be the end of our dreams of a family. You can't do it," he repeated emphatically before laying back his shoulders and cocking his head in a gesture of finality. "We'll go to court."

She couldn't help feeling as if her world had begun to dissolve into nothing, but she wouldn't allow him see how badly she hurt.

"And if I win, they'll make it so miserable for me that

I'll be glad to leave there. So what you're suggesting is that I walk away from my other dream, my dream of that partnership for which I've struggled so hard. I've worked nights and weekends, foregone vacations, lived without friends or lovers, devoted my youth to the pursuit of that dream, and you're giving me the same choice that my boss gave me. The world is full of healthy, well-adjusted, bottle-fed babies. I'm sorry, August.'' She raised her chin a little higher and shook her head.

Pain flickered in his eyes as he stood mute, waiting for her last word. Her mouth tasted of gall, and her stomach churned as she anticipated his verdict, words that would chill her soul. She felt an inexplicable loneliness, as though he had already left her. He had never seemed so handsome, so desirable, or so remote. So little inclined to shelter and protect her as she'd come to expect of him. She looked down at her hands, to shield from him the anguish that she knew he would see in her eyes.

"Think this over, Susan. Be certain of what you want, because if you tell me it's over, I'll believe you.'' He spoke in soft tones that were devoid of emotion. "You may choose that partnership and break our engagement, but you won't get over me, Susan. Not now, and maybe never. I'll be everywhere you turn, because I am the man who awakened you and made you feel, really *feel* deep down. All the way to your gut. I know you. I've set you on fire, and you'll never be content until I finish what I started. I'm willing to go part of the way with you in this, but I need some evidence that you're agreeable to making some sacrifices. Think it over.''

She watched him, too stunned to move, as he let himself out. She had assumed that they would compromise on this as they had with all of their other disagreements, but they'd each reached their limit, each confronted the future and refused to relinquish their dream. She thought of calling Grace and discarded the idea, unable to endure one of her aunt's lectures.

*   *   *

August caught a taxi and headed home. Yesterday, he'd had everything. Grady was back in his life and, in less than three weeks, Susan would have been his wife. Now, he had to cancel their wedding plans, the caterer, the white limousine that he'd ordered for his bride's trip to the church and their ride to the reception, her bouquet of white roses, the honeymoon that he'd planned as a surprise for her. He got home and paced the floors, trying to decide what he could give up. After an hour, he was determined to find a way; he wanted Susan, and he wanted, had to have children. He took their wedding bands out of a drawer, sat on the edge of his bed and looked at them, looked at his dream, the life he'd yearned for ever since he'd lost his parents. Those years when he didn't have Grady. Ever since he was ten years old. He would not accept defeat. He had to talk to her.

"Susan," he began when she answered the phone, "are you willing to give up all of our plans? Can you just forget what we feel for each other? We've built a wonderful relationship, and I know that we would be happy together, because I'll make sure of it."

"August, we won't settle anything this way. Why does it all depend on me?"

He had to resist laughing, because he knew she'd think he was trying to snow her.

"Honey, can you give me the boot as easily as that?" he asked her, trying to lighten their conversation. "What about the soloist I hired. I didn't tell you, because I wanted her to sing a love song from me to you." He was sure that his pride in the little surprise reached her through the wires.

"What singer? What song?"

"A lady from church; she has a lovely voice, and she told me that she's sung it many times."

"What song, August?" He couldn't figure out why her

voice sounded darker and stronger, unless she had gotten annoyed, and there wasn't anything for her to be upset about.

" 'Through The Years'," he said.

"But I wanted 'Ich Liebe Dich'."

" 'Ich Liebe Dich'?"

"That's German for I Love Thee," she announced, a bit haughtily, he thought.

"Thanks, but I know that."

"Did you study German, or did you spend some time in Germany?"

He had to laugh. She could arrive at some of the most far fetched conclusions. "A German girl taught me that." He waited for a ripping comment, but she fooled him.

"A Ger . . . When?"

"Before I met you. We're getting off of the subject, Susan. Now, as I was saying—"

"Did you tell her you loved her?"

He groaned. She had to be a first-class lawyer. Give her the scent of something, and she put on her blinds and went after it.

"What happened?" she persisted. "Do you still know her?"

"Sure. She sends me cards at Christmas and for my birthday. So I—"

"Your birthday? I don't even know when that is, and she sends you cards all the way from Germany. At least I hope that's where she is."

"My birthday is October nineteenth, and you are deliberately trying to sidetrack me with these frivolous questions."

"I'm never frivolous."

"More's the pity."

"August!"

"I want Miss Lewis to sing 'Through The Years' at our wedding."

"If you see things my way, and if we ever do get married, I want a man to sing 'Ich Liebe Dich'."

He thought about that for a few seconds. If she was being agreeable, he could give a little.

"Well, since it's going to be a big wedding, there's no reason why we can't have both songs, and I'll have that much more time to look at you in that lovely white satin gown."

"August we haven't settled one thing. I haven't agreed to a big church wedding and not to a satin gown, either."

"Alright. Alright. We'll take that up later. But you don't want to give up our home, do you? What about our home, honey?"

"What about it? It's in the middle of a bunch of trees, and that's country from where I stand."

"But we could have nice walks in the woods, especially in the spring." He nearly laughed again when her exaggerated deep sigh reached him over the phone.

"That's still the country. And I'd rather sip espresso in a sidewalk cafe on Columbus Avenue on a nice spring evening. No thanks."

"Aw, honey, don't be so difficult." He paused, thinking of another carrot to dangle before her. "Well, what about my music? You've never heard me play the guitar. Not once."

"I told you I hate country music."

He was beginning to suspect that, while she was serious about some of it, she had begun to enjoy pulling his leg.

"I also play jazz," he corrected, "and Dittersdorf wrote a considerable portfolio of wonderful classical guitar music, most of which I know from memory."

"Then let him play it." He wasn't sure, but he thought he heard a giggle.

"Too late. He's been dead for centuries. What about our honeymoon? Don't tell me you're not interested in *that*."

"I told you that was overdoing it," she reminded him. "A weekend at the Waldorf would have been plenty."

He didn't feel playful about that and took his time before his next point.

"We've never made love, Susan, and I planned one long trip to paradise for us. Are you willing to give that up?"

"Whose fault is that? You're hitting below the belt, August, and you know it. I was ready the first time we were alone, but you were the one with the ... with the ..." She stammered for a word. Then she said, "You were the Victorian."

August laughed. "Honey, don't you believe people didn't fool around in Queen Victoria's time; they've been doing that since Adam and Eve got in trouble with that apple. Victorians hopped in and out of bed whenever it pleased them; they just disapproved of themselves after they did it. You can't give up on us, Susan; I can't think of myself without thinking of you, too."

"August, I am not going to make you a promise that I won't keep. When I'm forty, I'll be too old to start a family. You want me to stay home for at least six months after our babies are born, and I agree that would be best for our children, but I'll lose out on the job. If that happens, I'll be so miserable you won't want to be around me. Can't you see that you're asking me to give up what I've worked my whole life to get? I won't do it."

Maybe he'd have to figure a way around that but, right now, he couldn't think of a thing. "Are you saying we're not going to have any? That's cruel, honey. I can just see our little boys and girls blossoming in our Tarrytown home. I can—"

"Why are you so pigheaded? If I have girls *and* boys, that's at least four." He tried to think of another tactic in a hurry, but couldn't.

"I'll have to get used to the change, sweetheart, I've been thinking about my five or six kids for so many years, that I'm having trouble switching to two, maybe three. But I'm trying."

"But you're not going to agree to a nanny six weeks or two months after the babies are born?"

Cold shivers shot through him. If he could nurse babies, he would, but nature had decreed otherwise. He didn't answer; if it ended, she'd have to do it.

"I'm sorry about the house. I loved that big fireplace you put in it just for me. Bye, hon." She hung up, but he heard the unsteadiness, the unshed tears in her voice. And she'd called him, "hon," the first time she had addressed him with an endearment. If she thinks this is over, he told himself, she's due for a surprise. He opened a bag of unshelled peanuts in order to have something with which to occupy his hands while he did some serious thinking. He ought to call Grace, but he didn't expect women to do his work for him. And besides, he wasn't sold on that chart business. Never had been. Where Susan was concerned, he'd fallen for her on sight and gone with his instincts. He shelled a couple of nuts and chewed slowly. Heck, Grace was the architect of this fiasco, and she'd better come up with some answers. He answered his cordless phone.

"Yeah. Grace? I was just about to call you?"

"I expect these coincidences," she said. "Why were you calling me, Mr. Jackson? I can't help you. Anybody who expects a thirty-five-year-old corporate lawyer to produce five children and work, too, is beyond help. Don't you know it takes at least nine months to make 'em? And that's if you're lucky."

"I gave in on that. We're having two, maybe three. Heck, I'll be happy if she gives me one. The trouble is that she insists on going back to work as soon as they're born." He knew she took a deep breath; he wasn't accustomed to having people sigh deeply when speaking with him, as though he might be a few bricks short of a full load, and it annoyed him. He ran his hand over his tight curls. Frustrated.

"Find a tantalizing alternative to dangle in front of her. She doesn't want to give you up, either."

"But what about us being a perfect match? If we are, why do we disagree on everything?" He hadn't heard Grace laugh many times, but he'd observed that when she did, she made a cackling sound. She cackled.

"What's amusing?"

"When it comes to my charts, I don't make mistakes. I've helped you all I'm going to. Figure out what you're doing wrong. Oh ... and send me an invitation to the wedding."

He hung up. No help there.

He paced the floor, cracking nuts as he walked. There was Inger in Germany. He could invite her for a visit and arrange for Susan to know about it. He mused over that for a while. No. It wouldn't work. Not enough time. Besides, Susan would give him back his ring, she'd be so mad. He telephoned Grady, thinking that he'd better tell him not to expect a wedding.

Grady listened to his brother's tale of woe without comment, until August stopped talking.

"Look, man," Grady began, "if you love her, don't let a little argument like that break you up."

August didn't consider it a little thing and told him that. "The first six months is supposed to be a bonding time for mother and baby, but that can't happen if the mother is one place and the baby somewhere else."

Grady did his own thinking, August learned, when he said, "Think, August. Could you stay away from your office half a year or more and not create problems for yourself?"

"Sure I could; I'm part owner of that firm."

"Then, there's your answer. Let Susan leave a supply of milk for the baby, and you stay home with it. Kids have to bond with their father, too, don't they?"

"Sure they ... Are you serious?"

"You betcha. Offer her that alternative, and the loving you get will blow your head off."

August figured he'd missed something somewhere. He had a lot to look forward to with Susan, but he hoped to be able to keep his head intact. *Le petit mort,* or the little death, as the French called climax, was one thing, but to have your head blown off. He could do without that. He laughed aloud, enjoying the warmth and intimacy of their exchange. "You seem well informed about these matters," he told Grady, though he was actually asking him what he'd been doing for the last twenty years.

"The school of hard knocks, brother. If you pay careful attention to your surroundings, you won't have to experience it to know it."

"When are you coming up?"

"Week after next. I figure you'll have things settled with Susan by then, and we'll be able to spend some time together." They agreed on the date and time of Grady's arrival, and hung up.

Grace unlocked the back door of her taxi, but August opened the front door and sat beside her. He'd never cared for Grace's highway driving, so he sat where the chances were best that she'd keep her eyes on the road while talking and not on the rearview mirror.

"For a man who's watching his lifelong dreams come true, you certainly do look sour today, Mr. Jackson. 'Course it's not my business, but you and Susan are acting foolish, if you'll pardon me. Ain't nothing going to go wrong, believe me, so just enjoy your brother and don't worry." For as long as he could remember, he'd had unshakable faith in God, Martin Luther King, Jr., and the Democrats in that order. Now, Grace Andrews Lamont wanted her name added to that list of icons, was hinting that he ought to consider her and her charts infallible. On the basis of what he'd seen of her work so far, he couldn't do it.

"You were on the button about Grady, but so far you're fifty percent wrong about Susan and me."

"Impatience and failure are bosom buddies, Mr. Jackson; February fourteenth is still ten days away." He flinched. A nineteen seventy-something Buick lumbered across their path, and Grace didn't appear to have seen it.

"Grace, I am where I am today, because I've made it a policy never to spend money before I get it in my hand. Susan has drawn a line, and won't budge past it. She has her principles, and I have mine; I'll believe you're right when I see my signature beside hers on a marriage certificate." He slapped his right hand against his forehead. "Grace, will you please keep your eyes on the highway?" he pleaded, as she turned fully toward him.

"Well, don't say I didn't tell you. My record is perfect." She pulled up to the curb and turned to him. "You're never going to give her up. *Never.*"

Never was a very long time. He saw from the incoming flight board that Grady's plane had landed. He didn't know if he'd ever become accustomed to the happiness that nearly overwhelmed him, to the sensation of walking on air that he got whenever it hit him that his search was over, that Grady was once more in his life. He found him at the baggage carousel retrieving his luggage. Grady had been reaching for a bag, but when he saw August, he let the bag go, raced over to August and embraced him.

"I can't get used to this," Grady said. "Believe me, I'm praying this isn't one of those recurring dreams that I've had for the last twenty-six years." They collected Grady's luggage and found Grace standing beside the cab. August introduced them.

"No need for that. Anybody can see the resemblance." She spoke to Grady. "You here to be best man?"

"Well ... sure," Grady answered, his tone indicating uncertainty as to how much she knew and that he was picking his way.

"I'm the one that got them together," she boasted. "I did it on the basis of my charts, so I know all about them."

August learned that his brother's sense of humor was probably equal to his own when Grady replied, *"Everything? Why, August, I'm surprised."* Laughter bubbled up in August's throat and he let it peal forth. Oh, the joy of laughing with his brother.

"Another naughty one, I see," Grace said, when she could control her cackling.

"I need to stop by and see Susan," August told Grace, who made the trip from La Guardia airport to Susan's office building in record time.

"You and Grady wait here; I shouldn't be long."

August strode into the lobby, glanced at the cold and uninviting white marbled columns and walls and stopped. The silent reception area, desolate but for the lone guard, a gray-haired old man in a gold braided blue coat, suggested the interior of a tomb. He resisted the urge to go back to the taxi and to his brother, whom he knew would welcome him, and walked slowly toward the elevator. He walked in, but couldn't force himself to push the button for the thirty-second floor. How far was he willing to go, and what was he willing to concede? Grady had implied that if he loved her, he'd better be prepared to make concessions. Maybe that was it. She'd been wedged deep inside of him almost from the minute he first saw her, and he needed her, wanted her badly; that was incontestable. Still . . . might as well be honest; he was crazy about her. He didn't know of a word for what he felt other than love and, if he gave her up, he didn't think he could accept another man's having a claim on her. He pushed the button with his fist and watched the floor numbers as the elevator quickly took him to her.

Susan hated that she'd had to announce to her staff that she wouldn't be taking a two-week vacation, wasn't getting married, and wasn't changing her ritzy Eightieth Street address. But she'd done it with head high, never once revealing the gut-searing pain that seemed to tear her into pieces when she thought of August. It didn't surprise her that, within an hour, Oscar Hicks and Craig Smallens, one of the senior partners, knocked on her office door. She could only describe Oscar's facial expression as a cross between a smirk and panic, while Craig wore the look of a man who had gambled and lost. She hadn't thought that Craig didn't want her as a partner and wondered what else she'd missed.

"To what do I owe this high-level visit?" she asked, looking at Craig who made it a policy to speak with subordinates in his office, never in theirs. Craig put both hands on her desk and leaned forward.

"Apart from competence, what we insist upon most in senior partners, Susan, is dependability." She got up, walked over to the window and relaxed against it. She couldn't tell him not to lean on her desk, but she didn't have to sit there while he did it.

"Why are you telling me that? I have a flawless record. There isn't a man working here who can say, as I can, that he's never fluffed or lost a case, never missed a day, and never arrived here late. In fact, I'm the most dependable person around here."

Craig's silence and careless shrug told her that it wasn't his war, that he was supporting Oscar, though she couldn't figure out why. Emboldened by Craig's presence, Oscar stepped forward and assumed the same stance as the senior partner at his side.

"You didn't really intend to marry Jackson, did you?" He bared his teeth and warmed up to his nastiness. "Or maybe it was the other way around." Susan's anger at their audacity dissipated. A couple of little bullies. She smiled and tossed her head disdainfully. If Craig knew how sickening his cologne was, maybe he'd switch to a cheaper brand. She let her nose tell him what she thought of it, as she gave his direction an unappreciative sniff and moved farther away. Thank God, August let his skin speak for itself. She couldn't imagine him applying a scent to his body. A giggle escaped her, bringing raised eyebrows and gestures of annoyance from the two men. August with that dreadful cologne . . . ? Laughter welled up in her and refused to be suppressed.

"You think we're amusing? Have you forgotten who I am?" Craig asked, as the vein in his neck expanded with the passing seconds and the pace of his breathing accelerated. A couple of months earlier, the scene would have distressed her, Susan reflected, and she couldn't figure out why she wasn't concerned.

"How could I?" she asked in a respectful tone, and added, "you aren't the kind of person that anyone forgets." Let him stew on that one. She knew that Oscar—why was she always tempted to call him Iago?—would point out the mischief in her seemingly innocuous remark.

"You think because you're tied to Jackson the rest of us will push your broom, do you?" Oscar sneered.

"I don't know what you're talking about, Oscar."

"Of course you do; you think you've got us across a barrel, because he hires some of the best criminal lawyers and criminologists in the state. You never intended to marry him; you just wanted us to know that you knew him and that you can count on him to get you whatever you want."

"Oh, she intended to marry him, alright," Craig said, "that is, as long as he didn't get in the way of the almighty partnership. But he didn't spring for it. He gave her the choice of being Mrs. Jackson or Miss Wall Street, and she took the latter. You surprised me, Susan. I was sure he'd win. Can't have your cake and eat it, too. And especially not with a man like August Jackson, or don't you know his reputation?"

"If any of this was your business, I would discuss it," Susan said, reaching within herself for the strength to maintain her poise, "but it isn't. Now would you please excuse me?"

August had heard more than enough as he'd stood at the door. He opened his palms, looked down at the deep creases embedded in them from the pressure of his nails and walked in, taking them all by surprise.

"Susan can have her cake and eat it too, Smallens," he said, standing toe to toe with the man. "Is there a stipulation in *your* partnership contract that prohibits your taking extended leave for any reason? Is there?"

"Oh my, August, I didn't see you," Susan said, her face aglow as she looked at him. He walked over to her, kissed her cheek and stood beside her.

"Is there?" he repeated, locking his gaze with Craig's until the man looked elsewhere.

"Well, no, but men don't get pregnant."

August shifted his stance. "I figured that was the reason for the illegal game you're playing, attempting to deprive her of her rights. You guys know the law. As vice president of Pine and Jackson, let me tell you that you're engaging in major discrimination here, fellows. You'll lose a bundle, and Susan will get that partnership *and* a leave of absence, if that's what she wants." He looked at Susan for confirmation. With her arms folded beneath her breasts and her head tilted away from him, she gazed in his eyes. He sucked in his breath and fought to control his reaction to her. Stunning. Beautiful. The center of his life. He smiled, but her eyes didn't light up, and he didn't see that crinkle at the side of her mouth. Susan was not pleased with him. He looked back in Craig Smallens' direction, but both men had left.

"Don't expect me to thank you, August. I can take care of Oscar and Craig."

He walked back and closed the door. "That's not what I heard and saw. They were doing a thorough job of intimidating you."

"They were trying, throwing their weight around, seeing how far they could go. You said yourself that the agreement Craig tried to impose on me was illegal."

He didn't like what he heard. "Then you knew that clause couldn't be enforced. So where was the conflict?"

"Don't get off of the subject. That's not the issue here. You shouldn't have interfered. I've been handling my affairs in this office for six years without difficulty. You were out of line." He wanted to shake her. Hug her. Love her. He took a few steps closer and glared at her.

"Out of line? I'm supposed to stand by and smile while two bullies crowd my woman."

"I'm not your woman." He took another step closer.

"You are. Period." If he'd made an impression, she didn't show it.

"You may protect me anywhere you like except on the thirty-second floor of this building. On this floor and in this office," she told him, poking her right index finger at his chest, "I fight my own battles. You might have meant well but, next time, please use some of your famous self-restraint."

"Well, I'm not sorry and I will not apologize." He couldn't help grinning at her cool office posture. He could see right through it, straight to the hot woman she was when he got her in his arms. "I'll bet Smallens drops that nonsense, and that six months from now, you'll be a full partner." She still hadn't softened.

"August, how would you react if I charged into your office and challenged your female colleagues? Wouldn't you be embarrassed?"

He knew it would aggravate her, but he couldn't help laughing. He wouldn't mind a bit if some of the women in his office accepted that he wasn't available.

"Not a bad idea." He paused for effect, hoping to jolt her. "You think I could get away with posting an office rule about skirt lengths, perfume, cleavage, and . . . Susan, can women find skirts that don't fit like bathing suits?"

"What? Are you serious?" He ran his hand over his hair, enjoying her look of consternation.

"Yeah. Some of those skirts can almost pass for a bathing

suit. I'm still getting used to it. You know, when I first came up here, I thought those women were coming on to me." She frowned, raised an eyebrow and slowly shook her head. Maybe he'd get a strong reaction to that.

"Didn't the girls at Duke University wear short skirts?"

"All I ever saw them in was jeans, unless they were going to a formal dance, and such occasions only arose once or twice a year. And back home in Wallace, well, to tell you the truth, nobody there bothers about fashion. Most people are just trying to make a living, barely getting by." She hadn't moved away from him and she looked agreeable, so maybe she'd forgiven him, though he didn't know why that was necessary. He pinched her nose, testing the water.

"Grady and Grace are downstairs, honey, so I'd better go. Can you have dinner with us this evening. I want the two of you to like each other." He watched in astonishment as her lips drooped in the most regal pout he'd ever seen.

"Don't jump to any conclusions, because we're not back together . . . I mean, we haven't solved anything."

"Aw, honey, don't be like this. I'm suffering. It's been weeks since you kissed me."

"You're exaggerating. It's been three days."

He laughed. "So you've been counting them. Come on, sweetheart, give in. You know we're going to get married; besides, if we don't, we'll spoil Grace's perfect record."

Her eyes widened and an expression of amazement blanketed her face. "You'd get married so that Grace can continue to say she's never been wrong?"

He saw that her thoughts had gone beyond their conversation to an issue of greater depth and substance, and he took her fingers in his own.

"Not by a long shot. I want you to be my wife, Susan. I want to laugh through life with you. Grow old with you. I want to see my babies at your breast." His hands moved to her shoulders and caressed her gently. "I don't want this with any other woman. Tell me what you want of me, and I'll do it. I won't give you up. Not now. Not ever."

"August, we're in my office. We can't talk or . . ."

"Or what?" he whispered. "Do you want to kiss me? Do you?"

"August, we can't . . . , I mean, people don't act like th . . ."

Her trembling lips invited his mouth and he gave it to her. Tasted her sweetness, reveled in her soft womanliness. He had needed her so badly. Her lips opened for his tongue and he knew he should ease off, but he needed more. He crushed her to him, and her every movement told him that, in seconds more, they'd both be out of control. He couldn't risk full arousal in her office, so he broke the kiss as gently as he could and stepped away from her.

"Can't you see that we belong together? That nothing we say, think, or do interferes with what we feel for each other?"

She moved close to him and buried her face in his neck, catching him off guard by the sudden vibration of her shoulders, and he realized, to his stunned amazement, that Susan had begun to cry.

"Sweetheart, what is it? Tell me," he pleaded with her, but she said nothing and her sobs increased.

"Alright. You're coming with me, if I have to carry you out of here in my arms." Lord knows, it wasn't comical, and he'd better not laugh, but he should have known that the idea of being taken out of her office in his arms would dry Susan's tears. She's the consummate professional, he thought with pride.

"Come on, baby, you've had enough stress for one day."

"You're not supposed to protect me in here," she grumbled, though she allowed him to tie her scarf around her neck and wrap her in her coat.

"I know," he agreed, "and I'm not doing that, either. I'm just speeding things up, since Grady and Grace have been waiting almost half an hour. You ready?"

She locked her desk, nodded and, to his delight, smiled

at him as she pushed the intercom and told Lila, "I'm leaving early. I have to do some shopping."

"May I see you for a second before you leave?" her secretary asked. Susan agreed, wiped her eyes carefully and led August to Lila's office rather than through her private door to the hallway.

"What did you want?" Susan asked her. To her amazement, Lila's gaze locked on August, and her swift glance from him to Susan suggested that what she wanted was an introduction. Summing it up quickly, Susan asked where she was when August entered her office unannounced while Craig and Oscar where there. An efficient secretary did not allow a man's easy smile to distract her from her duties and to give him special privileges. The young girl's obvious embarrassment was sufficient, and her answer cemented it.

"He said you knew him, so I didn't buzz." As gently as she could, Susan reminded her of the office rules. Then, she introduced them.

"Miss Benson, this is August Jackson, my fiancé." Empathy for her secretary flashed through her when the girl's face sagged and flushed with humiliation. She couldn't help wondering how often women were attracted to August's stunning good looks and charismatic personality only to have their hopes dashed upon learning that his regard held politeness, nothing more. She could have been in their shoes, because she, too, had fallen for him almost on sight.

When they reached the lobby, Grace walked toward them rapidly, a scowl on her face.

"Half an hour in that cab in this freezing weather could have been the death of me," she fumed.

"We were getting things straightened out," August explained. "Where's Grady?"

"In my car where he's probably got rigor mortis by now," she grumbled, walking toward the door.

"Not Grady. My brother is a survivor." Happiness for

August buoyed Susan's spirit, as she listened to the pride in his voice. She didn't think she'd ever get used to the brothers' striking resemblance, and when she remarked on it, Grady explained that they looked like their father as he remembered him.

"When is your sister, Ann, arriving," Grady asked her. "Grace tells me she sees her in my future."

"Of course, she's in your future," Susan told him, gainsaying what she figured would be Grace's next crusade. "She's supposed to be my maid-of-honor. Don't let Aunt Grace ordain your life."

"She was right on the beam with us," August defended Grace.

"Not yet, she wasn't," Susan interjected. "We haven't gotten things straightened out, and I don't want her working her charts on my sister."

"I don't work charts. It's already there, I just figure it out. And you'll see that I'm never wrong. No matter how many obstacles you two put in the way and how many excuses you give each other, you're getting married at the scheduled time."

"And your charts are never wrong," August added, winking at Susan.

She watched his lips begin to curve and tried to shift her glance, but couldn't. A warm bloom drifted up his cheeks until it reached his eyes and burst into a sparkling gleam. Without thinking, she reached for him, and her heart hammered wildly as he embraced her, pulling her into his strong arms, and nestling her head against his shoulder.

Grady, who had glanced to the back seat, whispered, as though not to disturb them. "I'm getting my tux pressed, Grace," he said.

"You go on and do that, you hear," Grace advised. "My charts ain't never before showed two people so well suited, and my second sense shows me what's going to happen. I tell you, Mr. Grady, they're a perfect match. And you mark my word and start off on the right foot with my other niece, Ann, 'cause she don't take no foolishness.''

Susan stirred against the haven of August's chest. She wanted them to reconcile, to find a way out of their dilemma. She didn't know what she'd do if he didn't relent. She felt the moisture on her cheeks and brushed it away against the fabric of his coat. When she'd joined the firm, that bastion of male chauvinism, the women who worked there, all in secretarial or clerical positions, had told her she wouldn't make it to the top. She'd worked twelve-hour days, sacrificed friendships, had no love life, had given herself completely to the job. And she'd done it, because her male colleagues had challenged her every move and decision, and the more they heaped on her, the more determined she was to succeed. She'd made it because she'd outshone them all. And all of them knew it. But would she have to sacrifice August in order to reap the rewards? She couldn't bear to think of his dropping out of her life. Their telepathic wires must have connected, she decided, because he gathered her closer and brushed his lips over her forehead.

"Grace, drop us off at Susan's place and take Grady on to my apartment." He handed Grady his door keys. "I'll be there eventually," he told him. "And don't worry about house security; if you speak and keep walking, Blake, he's the doorman, won't know the difference."

Susan primed herself for battle. August's voice had taken on a steel-like edge, and she knew he intended to bring to bear every argument he could muster in order to win his case. And her legal experience wouldn't help her, because he'd appeal to her emotions, to her heart rather than to her intellect. He moved in on her as soon as he'd closed her door and hung up their coats.

"What were you crying about?"

She would have moved past him into the living room, had he not blocked her way.

"Let me have my privacy, please, August. You don't have to know everything."

He moved closer, letting her sense his powerful male aura and smell the heat that leaped out to her. She backed away. If she was going to win him on her conditions or on their mutual terms, she couldn't allow him to take possession of her. She needed her wits.

"Why were you crying in your office, Susan? You sobbed in my arms, and I want to know why."

She hated lying, but he hadn't given her a reason to tell him why she'd suddenly hurt so badly, why the pain still stabbed at her, nearly drawing her into a depression. She raised her shoulders, stepped back, and looked into his eyes.

"I'm still mad at you for expecting me to play around with my career, maybe even give it up, after I've worked so hard for it." She wasn't angry, but how else could she deflect his interrogations?

"No such thing. I never said you had to give it up, I just said I didn't want our six-week-old babies to be left with a nanny."

She knew there were alternatives. She could leave her milk at home for the babies, or they could be bottle fed. Many mothers did that. She could bring them to work with her, too, though she could imagine the treatment that would get her from Craig and Oscar. But why should she have to do any of that? Most every time she and August had reached an impasse on a crucial issue, August had had his way. Not this time. They wouldn't stand a chance of living in peace unless he learned to compromise. And he could start learning right now.

"If I did what you want, I'd have to stay home," she said. She looked down at the floor, because he'd already started to go for the jugular with his jacket open and his hands in his pants pockets to display his perfect physique, and that curve had begun around his lips. She steeled herself.

"That's a supposition, honey. You just want to fight, when you ought to be kissing me. Come on, baby." His arm stole around her waist, his fingers caressed her, the smile reached his eyes, and he pulled her to him. Her breath caught in her throat when he tilted her chin up.

"Were you crying because you want to marry me, and you thought you'd have to give up your job?" His voice softened, dropped to a whisper. She wouldn't cry. She wouldn't.

"Honey, what is it?" He held her at arm's length. "Baby, you can't do this." He drew her back into his arms, took a crumpled handkerchief from his pants pocket and tried to dry her tears, but the more he wiped the more she cried.

"I . . . I'm . . . I hate m . . . m . . . myself when I cry." She fought to control the tears, ashamed of herself for that moment of weakness. "I'm s . . . s . . . sorry, August."

"For crying? Sweetheart, that proves just how unhappy you are. I know that crying isn't your style. Now, you're going to tell me why. Your partnership contract isn't the issue, and you know that. In the first place, it's against the law to deny parental leave, and second, that rider is flagrant discrimination against you as a woman. We only have to tell Craig that we'll go to court, and that would be the end of it. He's a lawyer, too. So what is the problem?"

Her gaze took in his gentle, caring visage. She had never emptied her soul to anyone, and that was what he asked. Frustrated, she turned away.

"Were you sad because you care for me? Can't you tell me?"

"Oh, August. August." She tried to stop the trembling of her lips, and he held her closer steadying her, and gazed into her eyes, weakening her knees.

"Do you care for me? Do you love me?"

She didn't notice the unsteadiness of his voice or hear

the uncertainty. Her mind focused on the question and his audacity in asking it.

"Why do you think you have the right to question me about that? You asked me to marry you; I don't remember hearing you say anything about love." She watched him brush his hand over his hair and frown, as if he couldn't understand what she was talking about.

"Love and marriage go together. At least, that's what I always thought."

"Well, you thought wrong," she huffed. "Just ask half of the married couples in this country."

He glared at her. "You're a genius at getting off of the subject. I'll stay here all night if necessary until you tell me why you've been crying. Now, Susan, don't start that again," he said, when laughter bubbled up in her throat.

"You're welcomed to spend the night; I've been telling you that since right after we met. You're . . ."

He threw his hands up. She exasperated him. But, Lord, he didn't see how he could live without her.

Grady's challenge to him flashed through his mind. Would he want to be away from his job for six months? In his mind's eye, he saw her heavy with his child, pictured her grappling with the pains of birth and shook his head slowly, as compassion enveloped him. After all that, why should responsibility for their babies' care rest on her? What had he been thinking about? An idea formed, and he knew he'd found a way out of their dilemma.

"If you cried about staying home from work 'til our babies are six months old, stop worrying. That's not a problem."

Susan could feel her eyes stretch their limit. "It's not?"

"You heard right. Tomorrow morning, I'm going to hire a consultant to plan a child care program at Pine and Jackson. We'll have to buy a car, which I'll hate, but our babies will go to work with me, and you can visit on your lunch hour or whenever it suits you. If they're sick, the one of us who doesn't have a court case or some other emergency will stay home with them, or we'll take turns. What could be fairer than—''

She flung herself into his arms. "August. Oh, darling. Love. I'm so happy." Joy filled her to overflowing, and she wondered if her pounding heart was out of control. She clung to him, sobbing and laughing. Her ribs ached from his tight hold on them, but she didn't care. She threw back her head and laughed.

"Look at me, Susan." Both the tenor of his voice and his somber gaze told her that he had never been more serious.

"Why have you been crying today? Before you answer, remember that when I asked you to marry me, I promised that I'd always be here for you, no matter what. I keep my promises. Can't you trust me?"

She looked at him and let him see all that she felt.

"When you were scolding Craig, I realized how much I love you, and it frightened me, because I knew that, if you refused to compromise, we'd never get married."

"What did you say?" August stared at Susan. He wanted her to love him, needed it as he needed water and air, and he couldn't count the times he'd told himself that she did love him. He'd prayed that she would. Was he dreaming, out of his mind, or . . .

"August, it isn't easy for me to stand here and pour my heart out when you—"

"Did you say you love me? Did you?" He heard the tremors in his voice and ignored them. He didn't care about pride. "Yes or no?"

She nodded, and he breathed. Breathed and lifted her from the floor and whirled around and around. He couldn't help shouting. He wanted to scream, to open the windows and tell east-side New York that his woman loved him. He felt her fingers ease down his cheeks and her thumb brush his bottom lip, and he rested her feet on the floor. Then, he asked her again.

"You really love me, honey?"

"Oh, yes," she whispered. He gazed into her eyes, saw the love shining in their depths, and dizzying currents of sensation bolted through him.

"Baby," he breathed and brushed her lips with his own. Her sweet mouth, pliant, submissive and eager, asked for more, and he crushed her to him. The feel of her soft breasts pressing against his chest and the quest of her parted lips for his loving sent his heart into a rapid trot, and he trembled violently against her. But her embrace tightened, and she pulled his tongue deeper into her mouth. In spite of his efforts at control, he rose against her in full readiness and shivered when she pressed his buttocks to her. Never had he wanted a woman so badly. His body told him to take her then and there, but his heart and head reminded him that it was not the time, that he'd promised her a trip to paradise. At the moment, he wouldn't be able to give her five minutes of careful attention. Slowly, he brought them out of their emotional high.

"You're an expert at criminal law," she said, pronouncing the words a little too distinctly, he thought. "What's the penalty for carefully premeditated murder?"

August laughed. Nothing she could have said would have reduced the tension quicker or made him laugh harder and longer.

"Capital punishment." To his amusement, she nodded slowly, as though weighing the pleasure against the consequence.

She looked up expectantly with an air of innocence. "What rights does a bride have? I mean, wouldn't the courts understand if she did something like that. Or, can she sue for . . ." He swallowed the end of her inquiry in a tender cherishing of her mouth.

"That's one question to which you don't need the answer. Thank God, it's all settled," he breathed, his relief palpable. "We're getting married in about two weeks; that ought to give you plenty of time to get a wedding dress. I want us to meet the minister of my church tomorrow night, if that suits you. The way things are going, we could sure use his blessings."

Susan backed away from him. "Get this in your head, August. I am not getting married in a church among a bunch of good sisters and brothers I never saw before, and the only reason I'll wear a bridal gown and veil will be because Mandrake the Magician waved his magic wand and got us a date in the Rainbow Room. He's long gone, so I'll meet you down at the marriage bureau."

August ran his hands over his hair, took a deep breath, and she could see that he had trouble summoning his famous smile. "Sweetheart," he began, almost haltingly. "You can't mean that. I refuse to say my vows to you at that marriage factory with couples lined up and the clerk squeezing as many ceremonies as possible between his coffee break and his lunch. A beautiful woman like you should be more romantic, and I'm disappointed that you're not."

She pulled air through her teeth and looked toward heaven, her patience ebbing. "Don't joke, August, we're having a fight. I'm sorry, but I don't see why I have to put on the symbols of purity—male dominance, actually—and hide my face behind a veil just to get married. And since I haven't been in a church since last Easter, it would be hypocritical to marry in one."

He spread his legs, folded his arms, and let a frown warn her of his answer. "And since I go to church every single Sunday, it would be out of character for me to get married any other place. I'm not giving in. I want to watch you walk toward me, your satin slippered feet crushing the rose petals I've strewn in your path. Just think how wonderful it will be when you approach me in a white satin gown and lacy veil, clutching the bouquet of white roses and lilies that I'll send you and the altar shimmering in white lilies and soft candlelight. I don't know if I can stand the wait."

She'd known he wouldn't give in easily, but she hadn't

thought he'd go for the jugular first thing. She took a deep breath and raised to her full height. "You're not going to win this one, August. Period. If you have your way about everything now, what will you be like when we're married? I always thought marriage would be liberating, that I'd be free." She thought for a second. "You know . . . like the Queen Bee, darting in and out of your arms as I pleased, but you've got too many fixed notions." Her voice darkened, and her words came out slowly as though floating from her lips. "I wouldn't mind standing beside you under a silvery sky with twinkling stars, a bold crescent moon and a snow-covered forest of glittering icicles all around us. The music would be soft and romantic. We'd create a special world. Beautiful. Spellbinding. Like that long ago New Year's Eve in the Rainbow Room. Just think, August, instead of bridesmaids and best men, sprites and wood nymphs would skip out of the woods, waving their magic wands and sprinkling precious stardust as they frolicked around us."

Her deep sigh and obvious melancholy pulled at him. He'd give it to her, if he could. But he couldn't and, anyway, the church was best. How was God going to make them one in something called a Rainbow Room? He doubted any angels knew where it was, and told her so.

She grinned at him, though he could see she'd rather he saved the jokes. "Then I'm not wearing a wedding dress."

"Now, honey, I've always dreamed of seeing my bride in one of those dresses." He didn't know what he'd do if she wouldn't change her mind, and he had begun to suspect that she wouldn't.

She looked at him for a long time, calculated her chances of changing his mind, and decided she didn't have any. And she wasn't going into that marriage handicapped by his notion that he could have anything he wanted.

She shrugged. "I'm sorry, August, but I won't do it. A

woman is supposed to have the kind of wedding she wants, and—"

His frown deepened. "You're not interested in a wedding. All you want is to get hitched. Honey, we hitch up horses." He looked steadily at her, the eyes she loved so much clouded with sadness. "I thought when we settled the matter of our babies, we were home free. Looks like we weren't so lucky after all. Well, I guess this is it, huh?"

She rubbed her arms, warming her suddenly cold flesh. "I suppose so. Let me know if you change your mind ... Oh, August, can't you give in just this once?"

With his sad smile for an answer, she turned her back so that she wouldn't see him leave her. "Give my regards to Grady."

"Sure." She heard him say just before the door closed.

August walked the two blocks over to Broadway, caught a taxi, and went home. Not even his joy in knowing that Grady awaited him banished his anguish. He stopped by his mailbox, collected his mail, and went up to his apartment.

"Who robbed you?" Grady asked. "Wait a minute. What happened between you and Susan? Anybody would think you'd been given a death sentence."

That analogy was too accurate; she'd killed his dream. "We broke up."

Grady grimaced. "Man, what's the matter with you two? Grace said—"

"I don't want to hear about Grace and her charts. Susan and I are perfect for each other until she gets stubborn." He glared at his brother. "And you can keep your amusement to yourself." He dropped the mail on the coffee table. "I'm damned if I'll let her get away with it." He'd like to wipe the grin from Grady's mouth.

"Get away with what?" Grady wanted to know. His bottom lip dropped and his eyes widened as August related his grievances. "That dame's wet," Grady told him. "If a man's going to do a woman the favor of marrying her, he should at least have things his way. Good riddance.''

August stared at his brother. ''Are you being a smartass?''

''Who me? Nah. I'm just telling it like *you* think it is.''

August looked hard at Grady's wicked twinkle, so like their father's, and decided not to take the bait. He sat down, flipped through the mail, and his glance rested on an envelope that bore ''Rainbow'' in the upper left corner. His shaking fingers ripped it open and his gaze fastened on the word, *Winner*.

''I don't believe this,'' August shouted, as he dashed to the telephone.

''Susan, honey, it's me, August. Get that dress, sweetheart, because we're getting married in the Rainbow Room on Valentine's Day.''

''How? What about the church and . . . ?''

''I'm compromising. You get the Rainbow Room, and I get to see my bride in a wedding gown. Do you hear me, Susan? You listening?''

''No. Yes. Of course I'm . . . Are you sure? Positive?''

He read the letter to her and explained what he'd done. ''I hoped, honey, but I didn't put much faith in it.''

He could feel her happiness. ''Oh, darling. I'm sorry I said you were pigheaded.''

A grin seemed to spread all over him. ''It's okay, sweetheart, I *am* sort of stubborn sometimes. When's Ann coming?'' He didn't wait for her answer before he asked, ''What kind of flowers do you want? Roses and lilies?''

Happiness seemed to spring from her to him through the wires. ''Any kind you send.''

August waited, Grady at his side, and the mayor in front of him, as Susan approached, a vision in a dusty rose gown and matching hat. A grin claimed his face when he saw her. Her teary smile tore at his heart and, as she came near, he reached out and took her hand to steady her.

Hang custom; she needed his strength. Minutes later they were husband and wife, and he lifted her veil, looked into her eyes and said, "I will always be here for you, no matter what and no matter where . . . through thick and thin. Do you understand?" She nodded, and he kissed her. And he thought that only she cried, until, with her white gloved finger, she brushed the tears from beneath his eyes.

Five minutes after their reception at the Waldorf began, August told Grady, "As soon as we cut the cake, we're leaving. Give everyone our thanks." As they left, he saw Grady lead Ann in a sultry dance and shook his head. Considering Grace's record, he wouldn't bet against them.

He had suggested to Susan that she pack what she'd need for the night separately from her honeymoon luggage, which he'd sent to the airport for their two-weeks in Honolulu. He took his bride to their bridal suite in the Waldorf where he'd ordered a cold supper and champagne.

"We have two bathrooms, in case you want privacy," he told her.

"Why do I need privacy? If you insist on giving it to me, watch out. I could claim wife abuse, extreme mental cruelty, even temporary insanity for my crime."

He grinned. She was wonderful, a challenge that made a man's blood heat up.

"Come here, Susan." He suppressed a laugh as she sashayed boldly toward him.

"Yes?"

"How do you get out of this thing?" She turned around, and he began the pleasure of making her his wife. He got as far as her bra and panties, and she folded her arms across her breast. It occurred to him then that she had been silent from the time he began to undress her, and he altered his approach, stopped and let his gaze drift over her. That seemed to embarrass her more, so he took her in his arms, and whispered words of encouragement.

"You're so beautiful, honey, I want to look at you. I've

waited so long." He let his fingers skim lightly over her flesh in the most sensual, arousing way, barely touching her, as he told her how much he wanted her and the pleasure he planned for her. He sensed that she relaxed, and kissed her lips fleetingly, but she clung as though not wanting to separate from him, and he offered her his tongue. Immediately, she took it, savoring it with gusto. Then he unhooked her bra and watched her beautiful breasts spill into his waiting hands. He stroked her nipples until her sighs told him that she needed more, and he bent his head and took her fully into his hungry mouth. Her undulations told him that dinner and the champagne would wait, and he carried her to their bed, careful not to make her anxious. As she lay there looking up at him, she covered her breasts again, and he had to hide his concern. He disrobed quickly and joined her.

"You seem tense, honey. Are you tired? Would you rather wait?" She shot up and leaned over him.

"Don't you dare. I wasn't kidding about psychological wife abuse. I'm just nervous."

He let out a long breath. Thank God, she didn't want him to wait another day. "What can I do to put you at ease?"

She buried her face in his neck.

"Just take it a little slow; I'm . . . I'm new at this."

Right then, he wished he had a bag of beetle nut, which was what many men in India chewed on to distract themselves at such times. He leaned over her and began gently to stroke her arms and to nuzzle her throat, but her impatience delighted him when she urged his head to her breast. So she'd liked that. He suckled her until she thrashed beneath him. Then he let his fingers skim her belly until they reached her secret treasure and began their talented assault.

"August, please. Can't you start now?"

"Soon as you're ready. You're not there, yet."

"Yes I am. I've got this awful ache. Please do something."

August raised his head. It was not a laughing matter. She seemed to have a built-in, automatic contentiousness machine, and he needed to set her straight.

"Honey, you'll have to be obedient tonight, otherwise, we'll have a fiasco. Your body will tell me when it's ready." He returned to his assault on her nipples and his devastating witchery at her lover's gate. Her low keening told him that she had neared completion, and he thrust quickly. Her scream tore at his heart, and he held her close, kissed her tears and waited for her to adjust to him, all the while encouraging her.

"Why are we waiting?" she asked eagerly. "I'm fine now."

Slowly, he reignited her fire, moving first gently and then with powerful thrusts. He bent to her breast and she cried out in ecstasy. "Darling. August, darling. I love you so."

He tried to assure himself that she'd been completely fulfilled, but the sound of her crying his name in passion precipitated his powerful release, and he gave her the essence of himself. Their passion subsided slowly as he brushed kisses over her face, cherishing her.

"Why did you pretend to be sophisticated?"

"I didn't pretend; I am. Well, about a lot of things, I am. Are you unhappy about me?" He rolled to his side, bringing her with him.

"I'd never given the amount of experience you'd had or hadn't had a single thought. You gave me something precious, and I wouldn't change you for anything. It did surprise me, though."

"It didn't happen by choice. When I watched some of my college classmates moving from one fellow to the next, it turned me off of the whole business, and I swore that if I never fell in love, I'd miss it. I fell in love with you, and I didn't want to wait a minute longer. But you had your own game plan. I'm not sorry, though." She rubbed her nose against his and let her fingers gently skim his forehead. "I may never say these words again, but this time you knew best."

He pulled her close to his side.

"Don't tell me things like that; I'll think I'm in bed with the wrong woman."

Susan lay beside August, uncertain as to what she had contributed to their lovemaking. He'd been right in insisting that they wait. He'd given her a chance to learn to love him, but if love had been his only criteria, he needn't have waited. She leaned over him and walked her fingers over his chest. Getting no response, she lifted the sheet and investigated his body. She hadn't realized that she licked her lips until he asked, "Look good to you?" Her eyes widened in astonishment.

"Where is . . . I mean . . ."

August grinned and pulled her over on top of him.

"Just resting. Ah, sweetheart, you're wonderful. I don't know how I ever lived without you. I love you so much, honey."

She braced herself with her hands on either side of him.

"You do? You really do? And you're happy with me after . . . well, you know?"

August stared at his bride of five and a half hours. "You didn't realize it? You're perfect for me in every way, Susan. I fell in love with you in Grace's taxi the day we met. Honey, Grace's charts had nothing to do with this. I was in for keeps before you'd barely gotten in that car. Couldn't you feel it? Why do you think I asked you to marry me?"

"That's funny. That's when I fell in love with you. Maybe Grace is right. Maybe we really are *a perfect match.*"

Dear Reader,

We think of Valentine's Day as a day of love, a day for sweethearts, wives and husbands, significant others. What we celebrate is our delight in having someone who cherishes us, makes us feel good about ourselves, and assures us that we are not alone. There are many kinds of love, relationships that kindle warmth and produce a happiness that glows within us. So, if you're without a significant other this Valentine's Day, call a friend, read to someone with impaired vision, help out at a soup kitchen or a center for the homeless, cross the street with that frail man or woman who fears doing it alone: you'll receive love in abundance that fills your emptiness, warms your heart, and lightens your steps.

Thank all of you for your wonderful response to *Ecstasy*, which Pinnacle Arabesque published last July, and to *Against All Odds*, which came out in September 1996. I value your letters of encouragement and promise to continue answering each one individually within three weeks of receiving them. My next novel, *Obsession*, will be published in April 1998, so don't forget to watch for it. You may write me at P.O. Box 45, New York, New York 10044-0045. You'll find my web page at http://www.infokart.com/forster/gwynne.html.

Sincerely yours,

Gwynne Forster

THE ENGAGEMENT

Shirley Hailstock

To the Ides of March Lunch Meeting (in which the main structure of this story was developed.)

Kim Lewis
Anne Medeiros
Lois Rosenthal
Candace Shuler
Donna Steinhorn

Chapter 1

Peter Lawrence's suitcase hit the floor with a thud. He hadn't heard a sweeter sound in five years. He was home. All he needed now was Serena. Checking his watch, he knew she wasn't due for another few hours. He had time. Tonight would be perfect. He'd make sure of it.

Back on U.S. soil for the past nine hours, he was tired but exhilarated. He had good news, such good news that if he were fifteen instead of thirty-three he'd dance a gig across the light gray carpeting covering the living room floor. As it was, he confined his exhilaration to shooting an imaginary basketball across the airy expanse and through the huge windows looking out on the most wonderful city in the world—New York.

Peter smiled and hummed "New York, New York" on his way to the shower. In twenty minutes he was refreshed, dressed in jeans and a sweatshirt, and rattling through the refrigerator knowing Serena would have enough food to feed the entire staff at WNYC after a tense news night. Well, he thought, there would be no news people here tonight, just him and the woman he loved, Serena Coleman.

Peter loved to cook. It had been years since he lived in a place where he could cook, but the brownstone house he shared with Serena had a wonderful kitchen. In minutes, the counters were filled with the makings of a romantic meal. The steaks marinated in a wide flat-bottom bowl, the salad was tossed and in the refrigerator, and the baking potatoes were making the kitchen smell as warm and cozy as the baking bread. Dessert, he thought, when everything was baking, simmering, or waiting for the right time to be put in the oven. Pulling one of the many cook books from the kitchen shelf, Peter opened his favorite one and looked up the recipe for Apple Brown Betty. With that done, he moved the newspaper and quickly set the table for two, adding candles and the flower he'd brought for Serena.

Wouldn't she be surprised to see him? he thought. And with the news he had to tell her. He picked up the paper. It was three days old. As he started to throw it out an article caught his eye. RAINBOW ROOM WEDDING CONTEST. The headline jumped out at him. What a wonderful place to get married, he thought. Reading further he discovered the rules required only a one-hundred-word essay on why he'd like to get married in the Rainbow Room.

Unconsciously, he reached for the pencil and pad that sat next to the phone. He thought of Serena and their years together. Fourteen wonderful years. Love poured into him and the words came through his pencil without effort. Years of knowing her, seeing her smile, talking to her, making love with her, garnered feelings inside him that were hard to control. Stopping at only one hundred words was difficult. He could describe Serena for at least a thousand more.

Reviewing the paragraph he sat back, wondering if he should really enter the contest. His chances of winning had to be small. Millions of New Yorkers read the *Times* every day. His entry couldn't have much of a chance. Yet

Peter found himself addressing an envelope and walking to the mailbox on the corner.

Gripping the blue door, he pulled it open and watched the white envelope fly downward toward the dark unknown. He'd often told Serena he loved her, but never had he put as much into words as he had in the letter he'd just delivered to the U.S. Postal Service and to some stranger at the Rainbow Room.

Nothing he'd written was a lie. He'd loved Serena Coleman since seeing her across the main campus at Howard University on his first day at college. He knew then and there he wanted her and he felt the same now.

Returning to the house, he checked the meal and the time. Serena should be home soon. He imagined how surprised she'd be to find him here a day early and with news that would change their lives.

"So, rumor has it Mr. Right will actually be in the country this weekend."

Serena Coleman looked over her reading glasses at her vice president and long-time friend, Chase Roberts. "Don't call him that," she said, her tone low and serious.

Chase crossed the floor of Serena's office and flopped into a chair in front of the desk. "I ought to call him Nathan Detroit and you Miss Adelaide."

"Nathan Detroit!" Serena repeated.

"Serena, anyone who's been engaged as long as you two could only be Nathan and Miss Adelaide."

Closing the file she'd been reading, Serena thought Peter was nothing like Nathan Detroit. He was dependable and loving and would never skate around getting married.

Serena couldn't help being anxious about him coming home. This was his third attempt. Each time he'd called to say he was coming, something always came up before he made it back to New York. He'd be here tomorrow if everything went right. If no world crisis happened, no plane crashed, or no government toppled to send him running toward disaster, the two of them would be together in twenty-four hours. She could feel herself shivering at the thought that something might spoil their plans.

Trying to avoid thoughts of these mishaps, Serena had delved into work. It had only made her day worse. Her newest client, Athena, an up and coming actress, wanted S. M. Coleman & Associates to turn her into the next Madonna. If they could do it overnight, they'd get a bonus. If not overnight, their deadline was the weekend. Serena had been looking for ideas and ways to get the starlet's name and face in print. Obviously, the woman had financial backing. S. M. Coleman didn't come cheap and this woman wanted results, and she wanted them fast.

Giving her full attention to Chase, she asked, ''Why don't we get out of here early for a change? If I look at this folder again I'll . . .'' She left the sentence hanging and stood up. Chase stood, too.

As the two women left the mile-high building in midtown Manhattan, the cold January wind gusted around them. Serena pulled her coat collar closer to her neck. Chase's comments bothered Serena. She and Peter had been engaged a long time, since they were in college. Actually, they'd become engaged as sophomores but didn't tell their parents until graduation. That was nearly fifteen years ago. She'd never thought they'd be engaged this long, yet getting married had never been convenient.

Peter returned for graduate studies in journalism after undergraduate school. She went to work for a public relations firm. After their two-year separation, he was assigned to the Middle East, a place that wasn't safe for a family man. They postponed marrying until he returned home. Then she began her own business and worked night and day to get it off the ground. She had no time for marriage then and Peter was reassigned to Paris and later Japan. He'd spent a few years at a local TV station in New Jersey. At that time he'd asked her to come and live with him. It was the only time in their relationship when she thought she might lose him. S. M. Coleman & Associates had just begun to turn a profit. Marrying was inconvenient then and it wasn't any better now.

Serena walked silently with Chase toward the curb. She suddenly didn't want to go home. Tonight she didn't want to be alone, didn't want to sit next to a phone that could ring and destroy her one weekend with Peter. She was sure it would be short. If he made it home, it would only be to tell her where he was being assigned this time.

"Let's go get something to eat," Serena suggested as they reached the street and a taxi stood before them.

"Sorry," Chase smiled. "I have a date." She slipped into the back seat of the cab and pulled her briefcase and the ends of her coat with her. "He'll be here this time, Serena. Go home and get a good night's sleep. It's only one more day."

The cab swept away from the curb leaving her alone. Tomorrow, Serena thought. The wind grabbed at her, tearing her hair and reminding her she was standing on a street corner. Quickly she hailed a cab and headed for home.

Serena sat forward in the taxi the moment it turned onto East Eighty-Eighth Street. The light in her window was on. Her brain registering the fact that Peter was home and the hammering of her heart occurred simultaneously. She was out the door, throwing the fare at the driver, and rushing up the five steps to the front door in record time. She didn't even know if Peter knew he always turned the light in the upstairs hall on when he came in. It reflected through the windows and Serena found it a welcoming beacon.

"Peter!" she called, closing the door and dropping her briefcase. She was afraid she may be wrong and he wasn't there.

"In the kitchen," he said.

Serena's heart soared. Peter stepped through the

kitchen door into the hallway. She wanted to run to him, but fear kept her in place. Suppose she was dreaming? Suppose he was only an apparition and those broad shoulders and slim waist, that athletic build and dark skin would dissolve into thin air.

"I'm real," Peter said, as if he'd read her mind.

He was here. He was really here. He moved toward her. She was sure it was him. He wasn't the small figure on her television screen, or the static photograph she saw each morning when she woke. He was real. He could walk and talk and hold her close.

Suddenly Serena heard her own footsteps. She ran, her heels clicking a rapid staccato against the polished hardwood floor. Peter opened his arms and she flew into them. He caught her, whirling her around like a human cyclone. When he stopped, he set her on the floor and gazed into her eyes. She saw passion there, raw, powerful, exciting.

"God, I've missed you." Emotion laced his deep-throated speech pattern and made her insides dance. His mouth touched hers softly, with such tenderness that she thought she would cry. Then the kiss changed, deepened, he was devouring her mouth as if he'd found the fountain he'd been looking for. His tongue pushed past her lips mating with hers like a long-lost lover. Serena met his mouth with the same earth-shaking passion that had rocked her foundation as a sophomore in college and still reduced her to Jell-O fourteen years later. Her arms circled his neck as she raised her heels in an effort to get closer to him. His hands spanned her waist, caressed her back and smoothing the length of her until they cupped her bottom. Pulling her body into his, he groaned deeply and slipped his mouth from hers. Serena stood in his embrace feeling as if she'd burst with the love that flowed through her.

"You're home early," she spoke into his neck. She could smell his soap and that indefinable scent that was only his.

"I couldn't wait to get to you."

Serena's knees would surely have buckled if Peter hadn't been holding her. She wondered how long he could stay. How much time did they have together this time. She wouldn't ask. Not now. Not yet.

Then she became aware of her surroundings. "What's that smell?" she asked.

"Dinner," he said. "I believe it's my turn."

The dining room table was set for two and candles were burning on it. The house smelled of baking bread, beef, and something sweet she could not place. Serena was suddenly famished.

"Why don't you sit down and I'll get the food?"

She smiled, not wanting to leave his embrace, but feeling the sudden pangs of hunger.

"I'll go change," she said and tiptoed to kiss him on the mouth.

Serena went to the bedroom. Peter's suitcase sat open on the bed. Most of his clothes has been unpacked. She went to it, running her hands along the zipper edges. She pulled a shirt from the inside and hugged it to her. "Thank God," she prayed, then put the shirt in the drawer.

Trading her business suit for gray slacks and a fisherman-knit sweater that hung to her knees, she stopped on her way down the stairs. Peter stood in the dining room putting the finishing touches on the table. Serena had a moment to study him without his knowledge. He had an easy, comfortable stance. He looked as natural in the kitchen as he did reporting a story from the other side of the ocean or in the bedroom. Her ears warmed at thoughts of them between the sheets.

How had she been so lucky? Peter cut such a good-looking figure at nineteen, with his deep, dark skin and black eyes. His body, honed to perfection on a high school basketball team and a summer of working construction to help pay his way through school, had every girl in the dorm hanging out the windows just to stare at him. Yet she had been the one to snag him and she hadn't regretted one minute of it.

His body had a chiseled quality to it. Definition could be seen even through his jeans and shirt. Often she'd run her hands over his contours as if she were a sculpturer fashioning him into flesh and bone.

"Just in time," Peter said, snapping her dream and bringing her back to the present. Serena went forward and into his arms. She snuggled against him and rested her head against his beating heart. Closing her eyes she breathed in the essence of him. Her body warmed as it always did when he held her. Her hands caressed his back, slipping under his sweatshirt and fondling the hard texture of his bare skin. Sound caught in her throat as she pulled herself closer to him.

"Peter, I missed you so much." The gravelly sound of her voice spoke the volume of feelings that struggled to burst from her breast. Peter raised her chin until she looked into his eyes. They were bright, filled with love and a little uncertainty. She liked that. For a long moment he only stared at her. Then slowly, his head moved down and his lips touched hers. Serena's mouth opened to accept his wanted invasion. His tongue swept inside her mouth, joining hers and sealing them together as if their two individual persons had merged into one.

Looping his arms over her, Peter leaned into her, running his hands down the length of her back over her sides until his hands touched the plumpness of her breasts. She did things to him, things he remembered but couldn't control. He wanted her, wanted her now, this minute. Her mouth was hot and wet and sweeter than he thought any refreshment could be. How could he have been away so long? How could he have missed this precious torture for such a long period? He pushed himself even closer to her, and Serena moved one leg accommodating his arousal and making him want to lower her to the floor and make mad, wild love to her on the carpet.

Inside Serena was melting, becoming unglued at the simple and complex nature of Peter and the power he held over her. She let her hands roam over him, trying to touch all of him at once. She'd yearned for his touch, the feel of him in her arms, the way his body pressed into hers, the way he could make her feel with his mouth and his hands and his harder-than-steel body. She continued her perusal making him tremble and quake.

Peter pulled his mouth away as if the effort took all his strength. "If we don't cut this out," he whispered raggedly, "we'll never get to dinner." She felt his labored breathing in her ear and over her throat. His lips nibbled along the column of her neck.

Serena groaned. Right now she could skip dinner. Her body was hot and weak and hungry, but it craved Peter more than the meal he'd prepared. Sagging against him she took long, exhausting breaths. Peter held her, until they could both breathe easily. Sanity returned and she could again distinguish the delicious smells of Peter's cooking.

Her mouth watered at the thought of food. Peter had put a lot of work into the meal. It was his first night home and he wanted it to be perfect. Her stomach suddenly grumbled letting her know she *was* hungry. Backing out of his embrace she walked to her seat but her eyes never left him.

Peter couldn't take his off her. She was as delicious looking as any of the food he'd spent the afternoon cooking. Peter backed into the kitchen, thanking God they'd installed the louver doors. He needed a moment to compose himself. Serena had turned him into an inferno and had him ready to abandon his plans for the evening and take her straight to bed.

For a moment he stood still, opening the refrigerator and allowing the cooled air to flow over his heated skin. Then he opened the oven and took the burst of heat, which did nothing to reduce his own heat level. He spent extra time ladling the food onto a tray and unnecessarily cleaning up counters before returning to the dining room.

"I feel like I should be wearing an evening gown."

"You never looked more beautiful," he told her.

Blushing, she lifted her napkin. Peter had fashioned it into the shape of a single long-stemmed rose and laid it across her plate like a delicate bud.

"It's beautiful," she said, raising it to her face and smelling it as if it had a fragrance. "When did you learn to do this?"

"Long nights in my hotel room with too much room service," he said.

Serena thought of her own long nights. She'd had plenty of time alone while he'd been away, but tonight would be theirs. She would not think about him going away again. She knew the heartbreak it caused and she didn't want that to cloud his homecoming.

Peter slid into the chair opposite her and poured champagne into two crystal glasses. "To us," he said, lifting his glass and saluting her. Serena clinked the delicate glassware against Peter's. It produced a beautiful bell-like note. They drank. And ate. The first morsel of food that touched Serena's tongue tasted like the best food she'd ever eaten. Her steak was perfect, her potatoes seasoned and hot, and her broccoli covered with melted cheese and steamed to the degree of crunch that enhanced her palate.

"We haven't drank champagne in a long time," Serena said, draining her glass.

Peter refilled it. "We have something to celebrate."

"What?" she asked.

"I'll tell you after dessert." Peter gave her a wicked smile that said I know something you don't. Serena was curious, but she didn't press him.

"What are we having for dessert?" She'd just finished her meal. Glancing toward the kitchen, she tried to isolate the sweet smell, but there were so many appetizing smells that came from there she couldn't distinguish anything more than sugar.

"Apple Brown Betty," he replied.

"You made Apple Brown Betty?" It was her favorite next to sweet potato pie.

"Only for you, honey. Only for you."

Peter got up and took the plates. In moments he was back with the dessert and coffee. Both were delicious. Serena couldn't help the satisfying sounds that came from her at the taste.

"You know I keep you around because you can cook," she teased.

"Yeah," he laughed, then his eyes turned piercingly serious. "Ask me why I keep you around?"

Peter settled Serena closer to him. They sat on the sofa, her head on his shoulder. Her eyes were half closed and she was pleasantly drowsy. Peter felt wired, exhilarated. He sipped his second cup of coffee. Tonight, however, he would need no stimuli.

"Serena, I have a job," he said.

"That's nice." She yawned.

"I mean I have a new assignment . . . here in New York."

Peter could feel the stillness in her. She hadn't been moving next to him, but the cessation of all vibration was tangible. She lifted her head and looked at him. She hesitated a long time, confusion taking control of her features. Peter thought she was trying to formulate a question.

"Where?" was all she said.

"I had the final interview today. Next month I begin as anchor on the evening news at WNYC."

"Is . . . is it . . ."

"Permanent?" he helped her. "Yes, I signed a five-year contract that lets me stay here and do the news, plus four special interviews of my choosing throughout the year, and two news magazine programs." He smiled, remembering the negotiation and thinking how happy she was going to be when he told her they were finally both going to be in the same city at the same time.

She didn't disappoint him. Serena raised herself up on her knees and hugged him.

"You're sure?" she questioned. "You wouldn't tease me?" Her eyes were serious. "Peter, if this is a joke, it's not funny."

"It's true. I start next month. They're going to do a commercial campaign to build up interest and then I'll begin right after Valentine's Day."

Serena lunged for him, raining kisses over his face and neck. She was thrilled. Finally, after fourteen years, they were going to be able to bump into each other in the bathroom, meet at the breakfast table each morning and the dinner table each night without Peter running off to catch a plane. She could hardly believe it was real. She wanted to pinch herself to make sure she wasn't dreaming or that this wasn't an elaborate practical joke.

Peter fell over from Serena's excited enthusiasm. He caught hold of her and pulled her with him. They laughed like they hadn't done since they were college students. He loved Serena, had loved her all these years and now he wanted to finally marry her. They did have something to celebrate. He remembered the words he'd written on the contest entry form.

"Serena, stop," he said, laughing. She tickled him. Knowing turnabout was fair play, he grabbed her around the waist and tickled her. She squirmed and twisted in his arms until they both fell on the floor, Peter on top. "Now I have you," he said, his legs straddling hers in the small space.

She continued to laugh.

"You'd better stop," he warned. She shook her head apparently up for the challenge. Peter gave her a mock frown and lowered himself onto her. She was soft and warm and his body tightened and strained against his jeans.

Serena immediately stopped laughing and lifted her arms to his shoulders.

Peter could feel the heat of her touch. Her eyes grew dark and sexy and Peter trembled at the passion reflected there. He settled closer to her, his body fitting the familiar space, yet he felt the primal excitement of their first time. They had to be the luckiest couple on earth. They'd found each other, found the best kind of loving. The enduring kind. The happily ever after kind.

Heat coursed through him as his mouth lowered and took hers. Passion gripped him and he immediately deepened the kiss, taking her mouth as if only her special kind of nourishment could satisfy his need. The heat around them burned into a soft glow, then intensified until Peter thought his skin would melt. Serena's arms tightened around his neck and pulled him closer. Her body, which was toned from constant exercise, softened beneath him, her hips rotating into disturbing rhythms that had him as hard as granite.

They'd been separated for months, long lonely months, and he'd wanted to take it slow, savor their time together, make it lasting and memorable, but he was long past that now. The moment she walked through the door, he wanted to scoop her up and take her to bed. He'd forced himself to wait. The waiting was over now—for both of them. He couldn't do it any longer, his body was too tight, too in need of her kind of fulfillment.

With a strength that surprised him, he broke the kiss and stood up, pulling her with him. Slipping his arm around her waist he led her to the bedroom. The light was off and winter moonlight shown through the curtains, bathing the room in a silvery glow. He stopped by the bed and turned to face Serena. Her eyes were large and luminous in the half light. Cupping her face he stared into her eyes.

"I love you," he whispered, his voice almost a prayer. Then he kissed her, softly, tenderly, reverently.

Serena's senses went into overdrive. Emotion welled up inside her, threatening to burst at the flow of love she felt for Peter. Lifting herself on her toes and pulling herself up, she tried to match Peter's six foot plus height as she leaned into the kiss. Her stomach rubbed against his arousal and she felt more than heard him groan into her mouth. Her feet left the floor as Peter's powerful arms pulled her up and down, increasing the pressure between their bodies and making Serena aware of her body's natural flows. Juices pooled at her center, calling to him to take her, fill her with his love, satisfy her as only he could do.

Serena felt a scream coming at the sheer pleasure that rocketed through her. Then Peter set her on her feet, his hands finding the sweater's edge and going under it until he touched skin.

His hands caressed her, drawing patterns over her smooth veneer that had her fighting her rising passion. Then the sweater was gone and Peter unhooked her bra. Her small breasts spilled into his hands as the coolness around them gave her momentary relief. Then his thumbs raked over her swollen nipples and she sucked in the air.

"Peter," she called when his mouth replaced his hands and she felt the wetness against her searing skin. Her knees threatened to buckle. She grabbed Peter's arms for support, her back arching at the same time. Sensation racked her, overwhelming her as life poured into her loins and she felt a wetness between her legs.

Her fingers found the snap of his jeans and she pulled it free, then unzipped his pants and slipped her hand inside the fabric. Peter's reaction tumbled them onto the bed. He kicked his suitcase to the floor and took her mouth in a soul-dying kiss that told her he was far over the edge.

With lightning speed they took each other's clothes off until their only covering was the moonlight streaming into the bedroom. Peter hesitated a moment, his eyes taking in her nakedness. Serena felt no shame. His eyes worshiped her as hers did him. Then his knee parted her legs and he entered her smoothly, but with an impact that had her crying out at the ecstasy that took hold of her. Peter's movements began slowly, but quickly changed to a frenzied pace. Her fingers dug into his shoulders at their much overdue flight. Being in Peter's arms brought back, with blinding familiarity, an awareness Serena thought she'd forgotten. She matched his rhythm, abandoning any attempt to rein in her feelings.

The lifetime that had separated them evaporated into the present and Serena arched up to meet Peter's thrust. Each time he entered her a shocking passion filled her until she felt that unstoppable force, the invisible wave that would explode around them, producing the greatest sensation any two people could experience.

Serena felt her scream again. It gained speed and force with the wave and as the climax gripped her she called out Peter's name over and over.

His weight fell on her, heavy and welcoming. Bathed in sweat she'd never felt more alive, more vibrant, and more in love. She wanted this to go on for the rest of their lives. Now that he was going to be in New York, they had every chance of that happening. Serena hugged him to her and took a deep breath. She inhaled the love in the air, a love they had created, a smell so sweet, so eternally primal that it astonished her.

Peter raised himself up and moved his weight to the space next to Serena. He pulled her to him, keeping their warmth and fitting her against him spoon-style. Propping his chin on her head, he cupped one of her breasts and squeezed it gently.

"Serena," he whispered.

"Yes." Her voice purred like a satisfied cat.

"We've been together a long time."

"Yeah," she said. "Chase is calling us Miss Adelaide and Nathan Detroit."

Peter laughed.

Serena pushed herself away from him and looked over her shoulder. "You think that's funny?"

"She's right."

Serena made a sound of disgust.

"We never intended to be engaged this long. Time just sort of got away from us. But—" He took her shoulders and turned her to face him. The moonlight cut across her features making shadows on parts of her face. "We can rectify that. Let's get married on Valentine's Day?"

Serena stiffened in his arms. Her breath stopped and she went still. The fact that something was wrong reached every single one of his nerve endings. He loved her. She loved him. He had no illusion about that. They had been engaged for fourteen years. Why wasn't Serena reacting the way he expected her to, the way she'd done when he told her he would be permanently stationed in New York?

"Serena, is something wrong?"

She hesitated. Peter could feel her struggling, trembling.

"Serena?"

"Yes." Her voice was a hoarse whisper.

"What is it?" Thoughts that she might be sick filled his mind.

"I don't want to get married."

Chapter 2

The basketball bouncing against the wood floor in the empty gym sounded like water splattering, then echoing. Peter put his hands up and his brother, Michael, passed him the ball. He turned and jumped for the easy lay-up. The ball hit the rim, popped up, and arced toward the floor.

Michael grabbed the ball and tucked it under his left arm. They'd been playing for an hour and sweat poured off the two brothers. Peter's T-shirt showed a huge wet stain that ran into a V from his neck to the middle of his chest. Michael's looked the same.

"All right, Peter," Michael said. "What's going on? I've already given you the benefit of possible jet lag, but your game has never been off this far."

Peter bent over and placed his hands on his knees. His breath came in hard gasps as sweat poured off his lean body. He knew he wanted to talk to Michael when he'd called, but now he wasn't sure he didn't first want to try to work things out with Serena.

A picture of her crowded in on him. Serena's brown

skin, dark and rich, the color of the nut brown powder they dabbed on him before going before the cameras. Her body was tight, slim, standing five feet four to his six feet two inch frame. Her hair just touched her shoulders and she wore it straight with only the slightest turning of the bottom. It made a perfect frame for her face.

Peter kept her image with him always. He laughed, remembering a photo of her he carried with him when he traveled. When he'd first seen her picture in the campus newspaper among the candidates running for student council, he'd thought how beautiful she was even in black and white.

Michael walked over to him. Peter still had his hands on his knees. "Why don't we get something to drink and you can tell me what's wrong?"

Peter stood up nodding. The gym was empty at this time of day and the two brothers left the floor of the WNYC gymnasium and walked to the tables along the edge of the basketball court. Peter grabbed his towel and wiped the sweat away. Michael got bottles of spring water from the refrigerator and handed two to Peter. Turning the chair around Michael straddled it and waited for Peter to begin talking.

Peter emptied the first bottle in one long swallow, then set it on the table. "Last night I asked Serena to marry me on Valentine's Day."

"That's wonderful!" Michael was out of his chair slapping Peter on the back and pumping his hand. He stopped suddenly. "For a bridegroom you don't look very happy about it."

"She said no."

The look on Michael's face was incredulous. It must have mirrored his own twelve hours earlier when Serena told him she didn't want to get married.

"But you've been engaged for . . ."

"Fourteen years," Peter finished.

Michael resumed his seat and took a drink of his water.

"Has she found someone else?" he asked in a voice that showed concern.

"It's not that." Peter shook his head. "She says we have no need to get married, that our relationship is fine the way it is."

"And you feel differently?"

Peter looked directly into his brother's eyes. "You bet I do."

"Then why haven't you married her before?"

Peter felt uneasy. The question had never seemed to matter before. Now it felt like a dagger piercing his heart. Had he married Serena when they'd graduated, it would be their fifteenth anniversary they were looking forward to. Instead it was only the anniversary of their engagement.

"We always intended to marry. I don't know where the time went. Suddenly it's fourteen years later."

When had Serena changed? Why hadn't he noticed? He'd been too busy conquering the world to think that Serena would change without discussing it with him.

"She said all our friends have married and divorced. People whose weddings she's been in or attended are no longer married. Chase, her best friend, has married and divorced while we're still together. She says our relationship has already survived longer than some marriages."

"Then what's wrong with taking the step?"

"Serena believes our relationship would change. That living together is one thing, but when people marry they somehow change and she doesn't want that to happen to us. She says we have the better relationship right now and it could be working because of the distances that have separated us."

"Do you believe that?"

"Part of it. I also believe she's afraid that things will be different."

"She's right."

Peter's head came up and he stared at his brother. "You're supposed to be on my side."

"I am on your side. Remember I'm also married and I lived with Erika before we got married."

"I know." Peter remembered Michael and Erika's wedding. Their circumstances had been different from Peter and Serena's. They didn't meet in college and hadn't had years of history together and the number of years of separation due to their jobs. The love Michael and Erika shared was so tangible it could be seen. Peter thought he and Serena had that kind of love.

"I mean, married life is different," Michael broke into his thoughts. "I feel more relaxed now, like Erika will always be there for me. That no matter what happens the two of us stand as a team."

"Erika is very special," Peter said. "I liked her the moment we met."

Michael grinned. He probably didn't realize the silly way he looked whenever Erika's name was mentioned. Then maybe it wasn't silly. Maybe it was that glow of love that showed in his face and body.

"You and Serena have technically *been* married for fourteen years."

"I told her that, but she says we've been together, but we haven't been *together* since I was always heading for an airport or some late-breaking story. We could have grown apart and no longer have the same outlook on life."

"That could be the truth." Michael spoke slowly allowing each word to set in. "You have been experiencing all sorts of things and she's been here."

"Michael, this is New York, a microcosm of the world. It's not like she's been living in a cave." Peter grabbed the second water bottle and drained it. "I just don't know what to do."

"Why don't you eliminate her arguments."

Peter stared at his lawyer brother. Even though Michael no longer practiced law, his instincts were still there.

"What do you mean?"

"Show her that the two of you can compromise on the

issues between you. For want of a better word, court her again. Let her see how much you love her and how much she loves you. You're already assigned here, so distance won't be a factor much longer. Just take it slow and your love will guide you."

"I'll give it a try."

"If that fails," Michael smiled. "Tell her you're pregnant."

Fifth Avenue used to be called the Lady's Mile. On Sunday afternoons women of the early 1900s would dress in their broad hats and long dresses and walk the mile window shopping and enjoying the summer breeze. It wasn't summer, yet Serena didn't feel the cold. The streets were filled with people hurrying one way or the other, trying to get to where they were going and out of the elements. Serena strolled as if she were a ghost from the 1900s taking in the morning air.

She stopped, looking in the window of one of the stores although she saw nothing. She had no idea where she was. The only normal thing she'd done that morning was call Chase and tell her she'd be late. She didn't offer an explanation or say how late she'd be.

She thought about Peter and his absurd proposal. Valentine's Day was barely a month away. They couldn't get married that fast even if they wanted to. He had commercials to shoot and preparation work to do before he actually took the anchor's chair. She had a new client and others who needed her services. Why did he want to get married now?

Serena looked up at the window. A blond mannequin stared lifelessly out at the busy avenue. She wore a captain's outfit of white pants and a navy blue jacket with gold buttons. Cruise clothes, Serena thought. Christmas was over, it was time for cruise wear before the windows turned to red hearts and Valentine slogans. She smiled abruptly.

A Valentine wedding would be pretty, she thought. Then the frown took over her features. She saw herself reflected in the store window.

None of the marriages had worked. Not her parents', not Chase's, not any of her friends'. They'd all gone through so much pain when they were over. How many times had she been the shoulder someone was crying on? How many times had she counted her blessings that she and Peter had the perfect relationship? And now he wanted to change things. He wanted to get married. If she did that, how soon would it be before the routine of married life had them growing in separate directions and finding separate goals?

Suddenly someone jostled her. She looked around. Cold swept through Serena. Startled she again looked in the window, then promptly went into the store. It wasn't crowded and she moved easily from counter to counter. When she found herself in front of the jewelry counter a clerk came over.

"May I show you something?" she asked, her customer-service smile in place. Serena looked down. Wedding rings twinkled under the lights. How had she come to be here? Was her own subconscious mind working against her, too?

"Where are the bridal gowns?" Serena heard herself asking.

"Fifth floor."

She turned toward the elevators and in seconds stepped out onto the fifth floor. The gowns were in the back of the store and she walked toward them like she had a homing beacon directing her. Why she was looking, she didn't know. The bridal area was large for a New York department store. A pedestal covered with dark gray carpeting stood in the center of the room. Along one wall gowns hung in plastic bags. Another wall held a smaller pedestal with three mirrors so the bride-to-be could see herself from all angles. Head pieces and veils were displayed with arrangements of silk flowers. A desk held books that had samples of everything from invitations to tuxedos.

Serena took a tentative step into the area that looked sacred. At the same time, a woman came out of the dressing room in a white lacy gown and approached the large pedestal. Serena stopped. The woman looked beautiful. She smiled broadly, looking forward to the wedding and the marriage. Serena wanted to turn and leave but she couldn't. She stared at the woman with her glowing face and happy smile. Another woman, with a tape measure hanging around her neck, came out. The mother of the bride stood up from a chair Serena had not seen and admired her daughter. Tears gathered in Serena's eyes. She turned and left.

By the time she got to her office she was composed and in control of her emotions. As she passed secretaries they spoke then turned and whispered to each other behind her back. Serena knew something had happened and she had the feeling she was the only one who didn't know what it was.

At the door to her personal office she turned the knob and pushed it in. The smell of roses overwhelmed her. She could hardly believe her eyes. The room was full of them. Every space, every table, every bit of the floor, her desk, her conference table, even her computer had a vase of long-stemmed American Beauty roses on top of it. The scent was as strong as a florist's shop.

Everyone in the office seemed to gather around her. "Serena, there was only one card." She heard her secretary's voice.

Tears filled her eyes. "Peter," she whispered. Her chest became tight and she fought not to embarrass herself by breaking into racking sobs. The most she could do was remain quiet and stare.

"Sure looks like it's going to be a *good* night," Chase said next to her.

Serena turned and looked at her friend. Chase didn't

know Peter had arrived a day earlier than planned. That he'd been home last night and that the flowers had nothing to do with a planned tryst, but with the aftermath of an argument.

"As near as we can estimate," someone said from behind her. "There are over twenty dozen flowers."

"And only one card," someone else said.

Serena went into the room. The crowd moved in after her like flowing water filling a suddenly open space. She only had a few steps she could take without knocking something over. Red roses, yellow roses, tea roses, pink, white, even orange roses surrounded her in a garden office. On the edge of her desk was the vase with the only card. The vase was clear blue and no water clung to the stems of fourteen linen roses. One for every year, Serena thought. Pulling the card free she opened it. The words *I love you* written in Peter's strong handwriting swam before her eyes.

"Serena."

Her head came up and she looked straight ahead. Her back stiffened. She'd heard Peter's voice. Turning around, the crowd in her doorway parted like the Red Sea. At the end of the column Peter stood. He walked toward the open door.

"I came to ask you to lunch," he said.

Serena hesitated. Her throat was still closed from the overwhelming amount of roses in the room. From the love that sent them to her and from the man standing in front of her.

"Peter, this is so unfair." She glanced about the room before her gaze came back to him. She hesitated a moment then flew into his arms.

Vaguely she heard the door close and knew Chase was ushering people back to work and giving them some privacy.

"I'm sorry about last night," she said.

"Me, too." Peter kissed her. Instantly fire burned through her system and her body seemed to liquify. She pushed her hands up his chest and around his neck. Serena poured herself into the kiss. Standing five feet four inches, Peter outdistanced her by another ten inches. She pushed herself up on her toes to reach him, making sure there wasn't enough distance between for air to past. Peter's mouth was hard and sweet and hot and she wanted him more now than she had after a several-year absence.

She wanted to talk to him, tell him her fears, explain everything away until there were no secrets between them. She tried it with her mouth, opening to him, tasting him and giving her all, telling him with her mouth how much she loved him and how she was sure of her love.

Just as she thought she couldn't stand it any longer Peter changed the kiss. It became tender and soft and disturbingly gentle. Serena felt its touch deep inside her. So deep that it brought tears to her eyes.

"Why are you crying?" Peter asked when he felt water on his face and pushed himself back. He wiped her tears away with his fingertips.

"Rose fever," she said, trying to laugh. "Where did you find so many? Come Valentine's Day—" She stopped, dropping her head as she realized what she'd said. She'd never had to caution herself when talking to Peter.

"Go on," he prompted. "Come Valentine's Day . . ."

Serena looked up at him. "There won't be enough roses to go around."

"Don't worry. I'll fill the room even if I have to have them flown in from Asia."

Serena knew he'd do it. His eyes were filled with love. At this moment she had no argument for not marrying him. She knew she'd never love anyone the way she loved Peter. That no one could take her breath away, make her feel like she was about to jump off a high cliff but him.

"How about some lunch?" he asked.

"Peter, I just got here." She took her coat off and looked around for some place to put it. Turning completely around she searched for a small amount of free space.

Finding none she hooked it over her arm. Peter took it from her and hung it on the back of the door.

"I didn't know you had a meeting?"

"I didn't," she said a little too quickly. "I—" she started, then stopped. The flushed face of the smiling bride came unbidden to mind. "I just kind of walked around for a while."

Peter glanced at his watch. Serena wanted to look at her own. If he were inviting her to lunch it must be close to noon. She'd left the house at eight-thirty. Had she been walking for three hours?

"Why?" Peter asked.

"Thinking," she told him. She wished she had more space. She wanted to put some distance between them. Yet the roses kept them within the heat of each other's bodies.

"What were you thinking about?"

The department store bridal area entered her conscious again, but this time it wasn't the woman she'd seen in the gown on the pedestal who congealed in her memory. It was her—Serena, standing in a white gown full of lace and smiling at her mother.

"Us," Serena finally answered him. "What you said last night about . . ."

"Getting married," he helped her.

"Yes," she nodded. "I've been thinking about it."

Peter waited. Serena knew he was holding his breath. Never had it been hard to talk to him, but she found it extremely difficult to formulate her words.

"I need some time, Peter." She copped out.

"Time?" Peter exploded. "We've been engaged for fourteen years. How much time do you need?"

Her argument sounded weak but she was angry now. "Why are we in such a rush? Valentine's Day is only a month away. You only came home yesterday. I don't get it."

"Tell me the real reason, Serena? Either you don't love me or there's someone else."

She recoiled as if he'd struck her. "There isn't anyone else." Her voice was menacingly quiet.

"Then if you love me, why won't you marry me?"

Serena couldn't say it.

"Tell me, Serena," he shouted, taking her arm. "I need to know."

Serena snatched her arm away. "All right," she screamed. "I'm scared." She paced the tiny area that only allowed for two steps. "Everybody I know who got married is now divorced. I've walked down that aisle seven or eight times and witnessed happy couples take the vow, only to have the bride and groom hating each other several years later. Marriage just doesn't work, not for them, not for us, no even for my parents."

She snapped around turning her back to him, wrapping her arms about herself, visibly holding her anger in. Her heart pounded and her breathing was long and uncontrolled.

Peter wanted to touch her. He could see her shaking. She stood only a foot away, yet a chasm of distance separated them. For the first time in their relationship he couldn't comfort her. He'd had no idea her fear of marriage went this deep. Her parents had divorced right after they'd graduated from college. Serena appeared to take it well. He'd been in graduate school in D.C. and she'd been working in New York City. The ensuing years with her friends marrying and divorcing only reinforced her fear. Peter wanted to kick himself for not seeing it, for not being there when she needed him.

His own family life had been stable. His parents had been happy until his father died. Their home was always a happy place for him and his two brothers, both of whom had happy marriages.

Peter took the step that brought him directly behind Serena. He put his hands up to touch her, then dropped them. He could feel her pain and he wanted so much to take it away.

"Serena, I love you," he said softly. "I want you to be my wife. I've always wanted it. I can only say I'm sorry we didn't marry fourteen years ago. If we had, you'd know our marriage will be nothing like your parents' and any of our friends'. I can't say why I know this. Certainly experience and statistics won't bear me out, but I've never been more sure of anything in my life."

Serena turned around. Her eyes were bright but she wasn't crying. Peter took her arms and pulled her against him. Her arms went around his waist and she rested her head on his chest.

"If you need time, take it," he said. "We've waited fourteen years. We can wait a little longer."

Chapter 3

"Good night, Serena. Thanks for the flowers."

Serena looked up at Annette Robinson, her secretary, and smiled. "Enjoy them." Her office was almost back to normal. Only three of the twenty dozen roses remained, along with the vase of fourteen linen buds.

It was nearly time for her to leave, almost time to meet Peter. The office, quiet and empty, was a time she loved. Most of her creativity and ideas came in the easy darkness. Today it had come earlier, after Peter left and she'd begun clearing her office of the flowers. She didn't think the smell would ever come out of the carpet or the walls. A slow grin tipped her lips upward. Coming in to the scent of roses everyday wasn't too bad and they would always remind her of the man she loved. Beginning her day like that could only be good.

Serena got up and checked her makeup. She and Peter were going to a play tonight. Being in television had its advantages. He'd managed to get tickets to the best play in town. Serena removed her suit jacket and blouse, then replaced the jacket. The effect gave her a more sexy, evening look. She refreshed her lipstick and eye makeup before adding long earrings and a necklace. She liked the effect and left the small bathroom.

The door to her office opened at the same time.

"Serena, I'm glad you're still here."

Athena, the only-one-name starlet advanced into the room. It was always shocking to see the twenty-three-year-old who took off her coat and dropped into one of the chairs in front of Serena's desk. Tonight she wore an off-the-shoulder gown of black sequins that molded to her body as if she'd been born wearing it. Her jewels were big and gaudy and she wanted to make them her trademark.

"I didn't expect you, Athena," she said. "I was going to call you tomorrow."

"It's all right. I heard the great news from my agent. How did you manage to get me the interviews so fast. I can't thank you enough."

Athena rattled on, not letting Serena say anything. This afternoon Serena had called several talk show hosts she knew. Her timing must have been on the money for she got Athena booked on two programs. Then one of her contacts at a glitzy magazine called and she'd set up an interview for the starlet.

"Oh, let me tell you what else happened," Athena was speaking. "I got a part on a soap." She spoke as if she'd received an Academy Award nomination.

"Wonderful!" Serena said. She really felt glad for the young woman.

"I can't thank you enough," she said. "You can be sure I'll recommend you to all my friends."

"Thank you, Athena." Serena wasn't quite sure she could handle too many people like Athena.

Then the flighty young woman jumped up and repositioned her coat.

"I have to leave now. I'm having dinner with Bill DuBois."

Serena's eyebrows went up. She was impressed. Bill

DuBois was one of the hottest properties in Hollywood. She hadn't seen him, but the papers said he was in town to attend a benefit fund raiser for the National AIDS Research Project of which he was chairman.

"Can I ask your opinion on something?" Athena whispered as if the office were full of people and she didn't want to be overheard.

"Of course." Serena looked her directly in the face.

"It's about getting married."

Serena stiffened just a little bit. She was sure the woman didn't see it. Athena was too much concerned about herself to notice other people.

"I'm thinking of marrying Bill."

Air caught in Serena's throat, but she held it back and didn't make a sound. "I hadn't heard you two were engaged." That tidbit hadn't even hit the supermarket tabloids.

"We're not. At least not yet." She paused a moment. "I'm thinking it would be good for my career."

Serena frowned.

"Bill is a pretty good actor . . ."

Pretty good, Serena thought. He's won several Oscars and had a collection of every other awards given for performances on the screen. Serena admitted his performances were riveting. He was the kind of man who could jumpstart a woman's heart, but she couldn't imagine him married to Athena.

"He could certainly help my career," she was saying when Serena came back to listening.

"Athena," Serena said loud enough to arrest the woman's attention. "Are you in love with Bill DuBois?"

"Well . . ." she hesitated. "You have to admit he is a good-looking guy."

"I'll admit that."

"And he's a good actor . . . with a fine reputation," she rushed on.

Serena nodded.

"I like being with him. He always makes me feel comfortable."

He would, Serena thought. From firsthand experience she knew Bill made a point of making everyone feel comfortable and easy.

"But do you love him, Athena? Is he the man of your dreams? The one you'd like to spend the rest of your life with?"

"The rest of my life?" Athena said it like she'd been sentenced to hard labor.

"That's what marriage means. Working together, sharing, being there for each other during the good times and the bad. You take vows, Athena. They should mean something."

Athena stared at her and Serena stood up.

"I don't know if I want to—" She groped for a word.

Serena refused to help her. Marrying someone because it could help her career was the wrong reason for getting married. They'd be slated for a divorce before they finished the marriage ceremony. And Bill. She was so disappointed to think that he could even be a part of something like this.

"Serena, look who I found downstairs hanging out in a lonely limousine." Peter came into her office with a wide smile on his face. Bill DuBois followed him. "I'm sorry," he said when he saw Athena. "I thought you were alone."

"It's all right. Athena already knows Bill." Serena introduced Athena to Peter. "Hi, Bill," she said coming around her desk with her arms extended. She hugged him. "It's been too long. You should really come to town more often, or at least call your old friends."

"You know each other?" Athena asked, staring at the three of them.

Serena turned back and nodded. Bill stood a head taller than Peter and he looked like a movie star. His skin was clear and unlike Peter, who sported a mustache, Bill wore nothing above his lip. He had strong shoulders and a winning smile. Serena knew exactly why casting directors would pull him out of a line and have him read. Of course, reading for parts was a long way back in his career. Now he commanded roles and never failed to thrill the audience by giving them exactly what they wanted. She glanced at Athena and wondered if Bill knew what she wanted.

"Bill and I met at our first interview for a job in television," Peter explained.

"Yeah," Bill said, pointing toward Peter, *"he* got it."

"So Bill went to Hollywood and conquered the silver screen and I went to cover a war in the Middle East."

Athena came to stand next to Bill. She took his arm and turned on a smile that could light the World Trade Center. Serena got her coat from the door and Peter helped her with it.

"Athena tells me you two are having dinner," Serena said to Bill. "Peter got tickets for a play so we need to hurry."

They turned toward the door and headed for the hallway. Serena locked the offices and they all stopped in front of the elevators.

"How long are you going to be in town?" Peter asked. "Maybe we can get together and catch each other up on what's been happening."

"Sorry, I'm flying out in the morning. I'm in the middle of a production."

Serena knew he was starring in an updated version of *The Long Hot Summer.*

The elevator opened and Chase stood there. She looked up, surprise evident on her face. Obviously she'd expected the floor to be empty.

"Chase, what are you doing here?" Serena asked. Chase had gone home hours ago. She didn't appear to have heard her. She stared in open-mouth amazement at Bill.

"Chase," Serena tried again. Still Chase did not react. Serena took her arm and pulled her from the car before the door closed.

Chase knew everybody except Bill, although in her state, she probably wouldn't recognize her own reflection in a mirror.

"Bill," she said. "This is Chase Roberts. During normal hours, she's vice president here, but at the moment she appears to have lost her power of speech."

"It's Bill," Athena said. "He had the same effect on me when I met him."

Bill took Chase's hand and shook it. "I'm pleased to meet you." His voice was so sexy even Serena reacted to it. So did Chase. Her trancelike state disappeared and she was the old Chase again, a little embarrassed, but the same.

"Excuse me," she said. "I forgot something." Chase pushed past them and went toward her office, but Serena noticed she looked over her shoulder at Bill. And Bill returned her gaze.

"I think she was a little surprised," Peter said.

"I think she was bowled over," Athena corrected, tightening her grip on Bill's arm.

Serena pushed the call button and the elevator immediately opened. The foursome got inside.

"Peter, you and Serena are engaged, is that right?" Athena asked.

Peter nodded.

"We were talking about marriage before you came in."

Peter looked at Serena, but she wouldn't make eye contact with him. She knew he wanted to know what they had said. He interpreted her remarks to mean they had spoken of Serena and Peter's engagement, while the conversation had been centered on Athena alone.

Serena felt Peter's arm slip around her waist. He pulled her into his side. She was forced to look at him or make it appear that she was avoiding his gaze. The smile in his eyes eased her mind and made her wish they were alone.

She wanted to turn in his arms and feel his mouth on hers. She wanted them to return to the house and spend the evening in each other's arms.

The elevator doors slid silently open and the four of them exited it. On the street, Bill asked if they could drop them anywhere. Peter looked questioningly at Serena. "It isn't very cold for January," Peter said. "I think we'll walk. You and Athena go on and have your dinner."

They shook hands. Serena hugged and kissed Bill on the cheek and told Athena she'd talk to her tomorrow. As Bill got in the limo, Peter took Serena's hand and turned toward Sixth Avenue.

"What did you and Athena talk about?"

She knew he was going to ask. As soon as Athena mentioned the word marriage, Peter had picked up on it like a television camera zooming in for the close-up.

"She's deciding if she should marry Bill."

Peter stopped and turned to face her. "She's not his type."

"She doesn't know that. She believes marrying him will provide her with an upward surge to her career goals."

"No doubt it will, but Bill would never marry for that reason. He's been married before and it . . . ." Peter trailed off.

"It didn't work out," Serena said. She remembered Bill's heartache over the breakup of his marriage. Since then he'd been seen with many of Hollywood's most beautiful women, but his name was never linked with them for more than a few weeks.

"Serena, I didn't mean to bring—"

"It's all right," she interrupted Peter. "I know all about Bill and Audra."

They started walking again. "What happened to them won't happen to us," Peter assured her.

"Peter." She yanked on his arm and he stopped again. "You're working too hard. We agreed this afternoon to take our time. Let's enjoy the play and not think about marriage tonight."

Peter agreed, but he couldn't keep his mind off of it. He'd intentionally chosen a play that had a strong love story in it. He wanted to keep marriage on Serena's mind even if it was subliminal. He wanted her to see positive images of marriage so that she would know he would love her the best he could and for the rest of their lives.

Peter thought about their time apart. He'd spent a lot of time overseas, on one assignment or another. He'd missed her terribly and wanted her to join him. He'd fantasized that he'd look up from a table at an outdoor cafe and she'd be walking toward him. That her love would force her to fly thousands of miles to reach him. He was sure Serena loved him, but he'd wanted that one fantasy to come true. He wanted her to choose him over everything and everyone else.

Yet it had never happened. She'd never come without an invitation. Her time was always spent making her company succeed. Now that she had it on solid foundation, did she need anything else. Was it really that she was scared of marriage or had she somehow begun to question her love for him?

Peter found himself sweating in the air-controlled room. Had they grown apart? Had Serena decided she no longer wanted her future tied to his; with the one they'd talked about all those years ago? Then he thought of them making love last night and he knew better. The sex was better than it had ever been and it started out on a fantastic level fourteen years ago.

Glancing at Serena, he found her gaze fixed on the stage. She was totally engrossed in the play. He could only hope Michael's suggestion was working and that the foundation of her arguments against marriage had begun to crumble.

* * *

"Serena Coleman, how could you be personally acquainted with the best looking guy on the face of the earth and never say a word about it?"

Chase didn't bother with good morning. She launched straight into conversation.

"Peter?" Serena raised her eyebrows.

"Serena," she said it through clenched teeth. "You know who I mean, Bill DuBois. How long have you known him?"

Serena set her briefcase on the desk and took off her coat. "Since before he was Bill DuBois." She shook her head in an exaggerated gesture. "What happened to you last night? You got off that elevator looking like a zombie."

"I don't know. The doors opened and there he was. I'd never been so . . . overwhelmed in my life."

"You lost control," Serena teased. "The Miss-Sure-of-Herself attitude was gone and you were lost; caught in the beam of a pair of brown eyes."

Chase dropped her eyes and Serena stopped the teasing.

"I would arrange something for you, Chase, but Bill is returning to California today. He's in the middle of a picture."

"It doesn't matter," Chase said, but Serena knew better. The three words revealed something about her friend she hadn't seen before. Chase's vulnerable streak was closer to the surface than she'd realized, but falling for Bill was not a good idea. His marriage had left him sour on relationships. Serena knew Chase wanted a solid relationship. She'd never said it, but her comments to Serena on the state of her engagement and Chase's constant dates told her Chase was searching. In Bill she'd found that instant chemistry that makes your heart beat and robs you of breath, but Bill didn't want to be married and Serena knew Chase did.

Why couldn't she feel like Chase? That would make everyone happy; Peter, herself, and Chase in a vicarious sort of way. But she wasn't Chase. She was Serena, scared, petrified that her decision not to marry Peter would be as bad as a decision to marry him. How long would he keep up his offers? When would he tire of her refusals and find someone willing to play the role he wanted? The thought terrified her.

Chapter 4

Backstage at a television studio was a maze of wires, cameras, sound equipment, light fixtures, and the paraphernalia of dreams. The kinds of things that bring fantasy to the screen. Even the newsroom wasn't totally real. The desk set had a photo behind it, not the real lights of New York City. In order for him to sit in front of that kind of scenery and in that place, Peter would have to be hanging out of a helicopter over midtown Manhattan. In a few weeks time he would sit before this make-believe world twice a day and read the events of the nation and the world.

Peter stared at the anchor's chair, but he didn't sit in it. He had a superstition about doing it before the time was right. He'd been in this room many times before and after his return from Europe, but he avoided that particular chair. It was as if there was a fantasy world existing here and if he didn't play strictly by the rules something would happen to destroy his future. He didn't want that to happen. He was home now and here was where he wanted to stay. Checking his watch, he noted the time. Serena would be here soon and he wanted to check something before she arrived.

Leaving the area he went to see Eddie Davis in the film room. Eddie sat in front of a console with enough switches to confuse an airline pilot. Four television sets sat on a shelf over his head. Everyone of them reflected a picture of Serena.

"Man, you sure you want to do this," Eddie asked.

"I'm sure," Peter told him.

" 'Cause if someone did this to me, I'd be a mad SOB. You hear what I'm saying?" Eddie talked out of the side of his mouth, lowering his voice as if he were a co-conspirator and using street language. He looked like a street person, with dread locks and clothes that didn't really fit, but Edward Isaac Davis held a master's degree in fine arts and had garnered three Emmy Awards in the past three years catapulting WNYC's evening news to the number one spot in the ratings. He taught a course at the City College and was the best sound man in the business.

"Is everything set up?" Peter asked.

"It is." Eddie froze the image of Serena on the screens and looked up at him. "All we need is word from you and they roll."

"You got it," Peter said. "I have to go now. I'm meeting her for lunch."

"She's a real looker, my man," Eddie said, looking over his shoulder. "I sure hope you know how to handle anger."

The offices of WNYC sat on Sixth Avenue not far from Radio City Music Hall and only a hop from Serena's office. The entrance was high and made completely of glass. A huge square chandelier dominated the entrance as it hung over the receptionist's desk a story below. Traffic outside was always busy. At this time of day it was frenzied. Cabs darting in and out of lanes, police cars with flashing lights and blaring sirens and irate motorists were all a muffled hum behind the thick glass. Peter stood on the mezzanine level. From his position he'd be able to see her coming. Checking his watch again, he noted the time. She was late.

Half an hour passed and she had not appeared. This was unlike Serena. She was notoriously punctual. Even if something had her attention at the office she would still make her appointments.

Returning to his office, Peter called her. Her secretary told him she'd already gone. He hung up and called the reception desk. "This is Peter Lawrence. When Serena Howard arrives would you please call me."

The efficient voice on the phone said she would let him know. Peter picked up the remote control and turned the television on. The noon news was on and he listened to the anchor's delivery. He envisioned the set beyond that which could be seen by the viewing audience. He knew the area was smaller than it looked on the tiny screen, that the two people at the desk had been at the station since early morning and that they had read and reread the news before air time and the teleprompter rolled.

At twelve thirty the news ended. Peter checked the time. Serena was over an hour late. He reached for the phone to call her again, but it rang in his hand.

"Mr. Peter Lawrence?" an unfamiliar voice said.

"This is Peter Lawrence," he confirmed.

"Mr. Lawrence, this is Allie Wishorne at Manhattan Hospital." She paused and a heavy fear sat on Peter's heart. "Mr. Lawrence are you there?"

Peter cleared his throat. "I'm here."

"There's been an accident, Mr. Lawrence. We have . . ."

Don't say it, Peter prayed. *Don't tell me you have—.*

". . . Ms. Serena Coleman in the Emergency Room," the soft voice confirmed his worst fear.

"Is . . . is she all right?"

"The doctors haven't finished with their diagnosis, but she's calling for you."

"I'll be right there."

Peter didn't wait to say goodbye. He dropped the phone

in its cradle and grabbed his coat on the way to the ground floor. Outside he jumped into the first available taxi and headed for the hospital. His heart thumped hard and heavy in his chest. *She's going to be all right, she's going to be all right,* he chanted over and over on the ride that seemed more like a crawl over the few blocks to the hospital.

She's got to be all right, he told himself. I can't live without her. Doesn't she know that? Doesn't she know that without her I have no reason to go on? Peter talked to himself, to Serena, all the way to the hospital, asking her questions, telling her his concerns, but getting no answers.

Finally they were there. He paid the driver, not taking time to get his change, before springing from the yellow cab and rushing through the double doors.

Twenty feet inside the door sat a nurses' station. Peter went straight to it. Only one woman, wearing a uniform of white pants, an overblouse, and Nike sneakers stood in the center of the area. She looked at him.

"I'm here to find Serena Coleman," he said. His heart still raced and his hands drummed on the counter. "Is she all right?"

The woman, wearing a name tag that identified her as Allie Wishorne, RN, came toward her side of the counter.

"Are you a relative?" she asked.

"I'm her fiancé."

"I believe," she began, then sat down and started to punch letters on a concealed computer keyboard.

Peter's heart raced, sweat beaded on his forehead, and his legs felt like rubber. She had to be all right. She just had to.

"Ms. Coleman is being released. I'll let her know you're here." The nurse walked toward the curtained cubicles. Peter collapsed into a chair opposite the station. He was cold with relief, unable to stand any longer. He'd have fallen if the chair hadn't been there. Taking deep breaths, Peter tried to calm his heart. It galloped like a thudding horse, flying faster and faster until he thought it would burst. Wiping his face, his hand came away wet and sticky.

"Are you Mr. Lawrence?" The RN stood before him.

"Yes," he said, springing to his feet.

"Ms. Coleman is in room four." She pointed toward a partially open surgical curtain. Peter went toward it. Serena sat on the hospital bed with her arm in a sling. Her hair was mussed and she looked pale and scared.

"Serena!" Peter rushed to her but stopped short of touching her. He didn't want to hurt her more than she was already. She slipped off the bed and he put his arm around her.

"I didn't see the car," she started. "When I looked it was there, too close for me to do anything. Thank God my arm was only bruised and not broken."

"Shh," he said. "You're going to be fine. That's all that counts."

"It was stupid," she went on as if he'd said nothing. "Walking in front of a cab in New York. They're as unpredictable as animals, darting this way and that. You'd think I'd grown up in Kansas or something."

Peter kissed her cheek. He didn't care where she'd grown up. It felt so good to just hold her, even if he did have to be careful of her arm. He was glad her accident had been minor. He didn't know how he could live if something happened to her.

They turned to leave when a doctor came in and gave Peter instructions on possible symptoms that might occur in Serena. If any of them persisted he was to take her to a doctor immediately. Peter took the prescriptions for pain pills and escorted Serena to the door.

A waiting taxi took them to the house where Peter insisted Serena go to bed. She didn't argue with him, but got in the queen-size bed and took the pill he gave her. Within minutes she was asleep. Peter took a chair and watched her for a long time. God, he prayed, what would he have done if something did happen to her?

* * *

The End appeared on the big screen TV and the theme song began its final version of the song that had underlined the love story for the last two hours. Serena lay comfortably in Peter's embrace, where she'd watched Cary Grant and Deborah Kerr fall in love in *An Affair to Remember*.

Peter hadn't left her for more than an hour in the three days since the accident. When he suggested they rent a movie she should have known he'd come back with something that had to do with marriage. He was inundating her with love. Her accident had only played into his scheme. She was more in control of herself now than she had been the day they returned from the hospital. Fear of dying and losing him had been uppermost in her mind. If Peter had asked her to marry him then, she couldn't possibly have refused. In the past three days, he'd catered to her like a hired maid; cooking her meals, making sure she took her medicine, relieving her of all jobs that could cause any stress and prevent her from healing.

She felt better. Her arm was a little stiff and the grazed flesh had scabbed over, but there was no reason why she shouldn't return to work tomorrow. So Peter had rented the tape and they'd watched it.

"It's not like I don't know what you're trying to do," Serena said, shifting in Peter's lap so she could see his face.

"Excuse me," he hedged, throwing an innocent look at her.

"You're parading an array of people and situations by me so I'll change my mind about getting married. First the flowers, then the play. Now this film." She pointed at the television. "And this weekend we're to go to your brother's house in New Jersey so I can see how two truly in love people live after marriage."

"Is it working?" Peter grinned, glancing at her.

"No," she told him, then snuggled against him so he couldn't see her smile.

"Well, I suppose I'll have to try something else," Peter said, bending to nibble on her ear.

"What?" she purred.

"I'm not sure. Maybe I'll hire an advertising and promotions agency to help me."

Serena laughed out loud. She had to admit she loved the attention. Not that Peter had ever taken her for granted, but she felt like she did fourteen years ago when they'd first met and he'd come by the dorm to pick her up. She was breathless waiting for him to arrive and her heart beat wildly when she finally saw him. Exactly like now. She couldn't be happier that he was home, finally. There would be no planes taking him to war zones, disease outbreaks, or palatial weddings. Wedding! She must have heard that word a million times in the last week. Chase worked it into every conversation and Peter's avoidance of its use made it even more vocal.

"You know S. M. Coleman & Associates is not available for that kind of work."

"There are other agencies." Peter's nibbling increased. It was hard for her to concentrate on anything when his tongue was searching the contours of her ear. She shifted, turning on her back and hugging him as his mouth sought hers.

"How do you feel?" he asked.

She nodded. "I feel fine."

"No pain in your arm?"

"None." She lifted it up and down demonstrating its flexibility and motor capability.

Peter's eyes darkened as he looked down into her eyes. If she'd had any pain he would have eradicated it with that look. Her mind went on vacation whenever he came near her and right now, lying in his arms, with the remnants of the movie song floating through her mind she reached around his neck and pulled herself up to him.

His rock-hard chest pressed against her breasts as his hands slipped around her back and pulled her into position. His mouth touched hers wet and hot as a heat-seeking missile. He kissed her hard, passionately, his hands running a trail of fire down her body, under her sweater, probing until he found flesh. Serena squirmed in his arms, her mouth fastened to his, their tongues mating as they had for fourteen glorious and wonderful years. She shuddered as his hands wrapped around her, circling her heated skin all the while his mouth was causing a major meltdown inside her.

Peter groaned pulling his mouth from hers but keeping their bodies close, heart-to-heart beating with the thunder of a rolling storm. He pushed her up and stood. The action didn't ease the pain in his jeans any. Serena stared at him from her position on the sofa. She surprised him every time he saw her. Her expression was tender and soft, laced with sex and begging him to return for a small taste of paradise.

Extending his hand, Serena placed hers inside it and he pulled her to her feet. Her body came up against his. Every part of them touched except their lips. Peter caressed her with slow even strokes down the sweater she wore, over her jeans, to cup her bottom. It fit his hands like twin melons. He pulled her into a secure position against him. His body was hard enough to break if he didn't relieve it soon. But he wasn't ready. He'd prolong this exquisite torture as long as he could stand it, as long as Serena could stand it.

One of Serena's hands moved up his chest and circled his neck. Then the other one followed a similar path. Her breasts teased him. His body shuddered, increasing the pressure in his pants while it threatened to melt him in every other part of his body. Her lips feathered against his like butterflies teasing the air. He groaned, pulling her closer. His hands worked their way under her sweater and he found the hook of her bra and released it. He felt the weight of her breasts spill against him. Serena's hands moved around and slipped the first button of his shirt through its opening. Her eyes stared into his as she worked the shirt apart. Peter felt her trembling as she pressed her lips to his naked chest. Shockwaves rocketed through him. She pushed the shirt over his shoulders and down his arms. Her movement, slow and unhurried, set fire to the room and to him.

Her mouth closing over his nipple had his knees giving way. He clutched her, pulling her head up and devouring her mouth. He plunged it with his, sweeping his tongue deep in her mouth and tasting her, drinking in the nectar of her being, making up for years of want and thirst. Her hands raked over his nakedness, finding the snap of his jeans and opening them. Peter could barely stand alone. Soon he'd collapse on top of her. He scooped her up and walked to the bedroom. He lay her on the bed as gently as if she were a wounded dove. The only light in the room spilled from the open doorway.

Peter sat on the edge of the bed and took her in his arms. He pulled her sweater over her head and dropped it on the floor. Her brown body gleamed in the half light. Would he ever get enough of her? His thumb pads teased her nipples which sprang to life as if they needed him to complete their sole purpose. Peter felt a surge of love flood through him. Serena closed her eyes, her head went back and her mouth opened slightly. He could see the pleasure she was feeling in the rapture on her face, hear it in the small sounds that escaped her throat.

They helped each other remove their remaining clothing. Peter lay her back and joined her. He settled himself on her, holding his weight on his elbows on either side of her head. His body sank in the juncture of her legs, his arousal pressing against her. He held back, refusing to let his body have the sanctity it craved. He didn't want to join them until they were both crazy with need and he was getting there fast.

He rubbed against her, baiting that one spot on her body that he knew made her his. He could mold her, do anything he wanted as long as he continued to entice that one area. It also drove him crazy. Her hands reached for him. Her legs opened to him. She was wet, hot, ready. He drove into her, knowing she'd gasp at the intrusion, knowing the sound didn't mean pain but signified rapture.

It was his pleasure, too. She was warm and tight and clutched him with her thighs as if she could draw him into her, make him a part of her anatomy. After fourteen years, Peter couldn't describe the pleasure she invoked in him. He felt her through and through, thrusting so deeply he thought she'd be hurt, but she took him in whole, took his body into hers and together they became a single life form. Peter controlled the rhythm, thrusting in and out until he felt the wave, the avalanche of feeling that swept through him and drove him harder and faster toward the goal of pure paradise.

Serena chanted Peter's name over and over. His body was powerful and he filled her with intimate pleasure. She didn't know how a person could endure it, a pleasure so beautiful, so exquisite it bordered on pain. She hugged Peter to her, her hands slipping up and down his back, over his shoulders, his arms, she wanted to touch every inch of him. She wanted to caress him, kiss him, tell him with her body that she wanted him and would always want him.

Then she felt it. Her body burned, incinerator-level heat poured over them, joining with them, wrapping them in a web containing only light and feeling and love, a place where the world ended, love endured, and paradise burst into a flash of white-hot color.

Peter collapsed onto Serena. She took his full weight, breathing heavily and loving it. She brushed her hands down his body, feeling the silkiness of his smooth skin. God he felt good.

"God," she said breathlessly, "I can't believe every time we make love it's better than the last time."

Peter raised himself and looked at her. She felt the cold steal into the place where his body used to be. He kissed her lightly and moved to the space beside her. Serena turned to face him. Peter's arms came around her, dragging her close and entwining his legs around hers.

Humming the theme song from *An Affair to Remember* she ran her hands over his body and reveled in the aftermath of a hot zone.

Chapter 5

Peter had no real hours until the day came for him to take the anchor's position. Yet there was plenty he needed to do in the office. Since Serena returned to work last week, he'd taken to going in every day and familiarizing himself with the operation then picking up a game of basketball before returning to catch the news. He especially liked to sit on the camera side of the table during the newscasts that came on at noon and six.

In a matter of weeks he'd be taking the chair and reading the teleprompter at six and eleven. Commercials had been running for over a month announcing his placement. Footage of him dressed in army fatigues in the Middle East and wearing a space suit while he covered the possible outbreak of a new virus were flashed across the screen several times a day.

Today he'd arrived later than usual. The night with Serena had been especially rewarding and he'd lounged in bed longer than normal. On his way out he'd met the mailman and took the mail which he stuffed in his briefcase as the car arrived that would take him to WNYC. Peter got there in time for the noon news. He watched from the darkened foreground while the two anchors read the top news stories of the day.

He liked what he saw at WNYC and it confirmed his decision to take this job. In addition to it fitting in with this period in his life when he was tired of being the man on the go, running to every crisis center in the world, it was a professional operation. Some of his best friends worked here and Serena was only a few blocks away.

Returning to his desk, he remembered the mail and pulled it out. There were the usual junk mail envelopes, flyers for the supermarket sale of the week, and a credit card bill. Then Peter saw the envelope with a return address of the Rainbow Room. He dropped the other letters and picked up his letter opener. Slitting the top he pulled out the single page letter. A moment later he sat down. He could hardly believe his eyes. He read the letter again. The second time through the words remained unchanged.

He'd won.

"Will you marry me?"

Serena sat wrapped in an afghan on the sofa. She held a glass of wine in one hand and had been looking out on the window when Peter entered the room. He turned off the light in the kitchen. The living room had only one small lamp lit. Soft music played in the background. If they'd had a fake moon and a breeze it would have been a Hollywood-perfect setting.

"What did you say?" Serena asked.

"I asked you to marry me. I know I promised to give you time, but I don't want to wait any longer."

"Why not? Has something happened?"

Peter thought of the letter from the Rainbow Room. He wanted to tell her about it. When she agreed to marry him, he'd tell her. Valentine's Day was three weeks away and he could think of nothing more than seeing her dressed in a long white gown coming down an aisle.

"Nothing has happened. It's been a few weeks. I thought you might have made up your mind by now."

She should have made it up years ago, he thought, but didn't want to push her or instigate an argument that would send them off on a tangent.

"Nothing has changed, Peter. I still feel we already have the best relationship we could possibly ask for. We live together, we share everything. What more could marriage afford us we don't already have?"

Peter sat on the coffee table in front of her. "What about children?"

The wineglass Serena was carrying to her mouth stopped in midair. "We've never talked about children."

"We did a long time ago." Serena frowned at him. Could it be she really didn't remember? "When we got engaged. We wanted to have a big family. You didn't want to have an only child since you'd been one."

"I remember," she said. "It was such a long time ago. So much has changed."

"I haven't," Peter said. "Have you?"

It was one of the most frightening questions he'd ever asked. He'd been away. They'd been separated for years at a time, yet he'd been faithful to her, not just sexually faithful, but true in his mind. He'd known from that day on the main campus so many years ago that Serena was the woman for him and nothing would ever change that. Fourteen years later, he could still make that statement.

Serena thought about that question. She'd been so concerned that Peter would change, that he would want things in life that she did not, that the thought of herself changing had not occurred. But that was the absolute truth. She *had* changed. She couldn't say when it happened or what was the event that brought about the change, but in the last fourteen years, she was the one who wanted different things.

Children! She hadn't been around any children in years. Some of the people in her office had them, but her only association with them was scattered photographs on their desks or conversations when one of them had a skinned knee or competed in some sporting event.

Selena couldn't imagine herself pregnant or even holding a child. Once she had wanted that. When had she changed?

Tears rolled from her eyes. Peter took her wineglass and pulled her into his arms. He sat with her cradled against him.

"I don't know how it happened, Peter," she sobbed. "I am different."

"We're both different, Serena. We're older, life has given us more experience and more insight, but deep down I know I'll never love anyone the way I love you."

"I know that, too," she said.

"I can't promise you we won't continue to grow and change. That in ten years or twenty years we won't divorce the way your parents did, but I can promise you I'll try my best to make sure we beat the odds. If you do the same, we should celebrate a golden wedding anniversary."

Serena buried her face in Peter's chest. "I'm still scared."

"There's no shame in being scared. I am, too."

Her head came up quickly and she looked at him. "I thought you were so positive about this."

"I am positive, but the future is an unknown and by nature we're afraid of the unknown. All we have to do is take it as it comes and work together to get over whatever comes our way. If we do that, I know we can have a successful marriage."

"But, Peter, look at Bill's and Chase's and—"

"I can look at hundreds of them, Serena, but while we're concerned that fifty percent of them fail, remember the other fifty percent succeed."

That was true. She'd forgotten that side of the equation. It was worth giving some thought.

"I'll truly think about it," she said.

Peter smiled. "Michael said I should tell you I'm pregnant. Then you'll have to marry me."

She smiled at that. Peter took her chin between his fingers. When he spoke his voice was quiet, so much so that his words had serious intent. "Maybe I should just take you to bed and make love to you until you're pregnant, then you'll have to marry me."

He finished by sealing her mouth with his. Thoughts of children with miniature versions of their faces pushed him over the edge. He pressed Serena back into the sofa and kissed her until he thought he'd lose his mind. Passion flared around them so hot he thought they'd spontaneously combust. In seconds they were tearing at each other's clothes, undressing each other in a frenzy to join and become one. Peter thrust himself inside of her, holding her hips and rocking her to fit his cadence. He'd never taken her this fast or wanted her this badly before. The sensation between them had never been this intense or this lethal. He pumped himself inside her, pushing into her warm juices, exiting to the tip before returning to find a new warmth, a new space marked only for him, riding her until he thought the world would end at any second. He screamed her name in the moment of climax and fell back to earth, out of breath and too spent to talk.

For the first time since they'd walked across the same campus and found each other, they made love without a condom.

Peter wasn't sorry.

The telltale smell of roses filled the air of Serena's office. It was a nice hint of floral, not overwhelming and not enough to make working there uncomfortable. The roses reminded her of Peter. She slipped out of her coat and hung it behind the door. The long-stemmed American Beauties she'd left in the office had been removed. She knew they'd withered and died in her absence and she knew she could thank Chase for not allowing her to return to dead flowers.

Chase came in on the heels of her thoughts. "Have you seen them?" she asked. She handed Serena a cup of coffee.

"Seen what?" Serena took a drink of the hot liquid.

"The billboards, advertisements on the buses and they're all over the subways."

Serena sat down. "Chase, what are you talking about?"

"How did you get to work this morning?"

The question made Serena frown. What did that have to do with anything? "I took a taxi, why?"

"What did the ad on the top say?"

Serena thought a moment. She hadn't really looked at the ad space. Usually she did. In her business they needed to notice every form of advertising. They needed to understand what worked and where a client could get the greatest amount of exposure. This morning, however, she'd been thinking of Peter and their night together.

"I think it was bright yellow with red lettering. It was for one of those cigarette brands. I don't remember which."

Serena didn't do any ads that had cigarettes in them. She devoutly disapproved of smoking. Her father had died of lung cancer. As a result, the agency had no ash trays and was completely smoke-free.

"What was on the other side?"

"Chase, where is this going?" She was getting frustrated.

"It may not be too late." Chase spoke more to herself than Serena. She rushed to the window and looked out. "They're there," she said as if she'd discovered something. Serena couldn't think of what. The ground was thirty floors down. What could she possibly see?

"Come on. You've got to see this for yourself." Chase grabbed Serena's arm and her coat. Propelled by her friend, she was pulled from her office. Serena resisted, stopping in the middle of the outer office.

"Serena, have you—"

"Quiet!" Chase ordered.

Serena turned and stared at her vice president. She'd never heard Chase use that tone with one of the secretaries.

"Just humor me, Serena."

Together the two women went toward the elevator. Chase shushed everyone who tried to speak to Serena. When the two of them exited the building Serena saw nothing out of the ordinary. New York traffic darted up the Avenue of the Americas, a broad boulevard that funneled over ten thousand cars a day. Serena looked across the street. The office building that housed hundreds of companies stood in place as she'd left it several days ago. Blue and white police cars patrolled in the slow morning snarl.

"Chase—" she stopped. She'd seen it. That must be what Chase and every other person who'd come into S. M. Coleman & Associates wanted to ask her about. Her mouth dropped open. Shock sliced through her. On the tops of cabs, the sides of buses, and she was sure in the subways were ads saying *Marry Me, Serena.* They were large with white backgrounds and red, twelve-inch letters that looked like Peter had printed them in his own hand. Under the message lay a red rose she knew had been fashioned from a linen napkin.

"That . . . that's not me," she stammered. "Serena isn't that uncommon a name."

Chase folded her arms and lowered her chin, looking at Serena with eyes wide. "And I'm going to be the next President of the United States."

Serena saw a bus go by with the same ad. This one was almost twice as big as the one on the taxi. She closed her eyes and shook her head. She remembered something Peter had said about hiring an advertising agency. It was almost laughable, except that she knew what was going to happen and it wasn't going to be funny at all.

Another bus passed and several taxis. All of them had the same ad. She'd be willing to bet there were at least a thousand taxis in Manhattan alone. If they were all carrying that sign . . . she didn't want to think about that.

Serena turned and reentered the building. She went straight to her office, refusing to stop and answer any of the questions that were thrown at her as she passed. Picking up the phone she called home. Peter didn't answer. She got the answering machine, heard her own voice and hung up. Then she dialed WNYC and asked them to locate him. He wasn't in the building so she got Eddie Davis on the line.

"Eddie, this is Serena." She wanted to scream at Peter and had to hold her tongue when she heard Eddie's voice.

"Hey, pretty lady. Long time, no talk to."

Serena usually smiled when she talked to Eddie. She knew that hiding behind his street-wise jargon was a man who noticed everything, saw everything and recorded it in his trap-like memory.

"Eddie, I'm trying to find Peter. I thought he might be here with you."

"Nope. I haven't seen him today."

Serena was bitterly disappointed. "Doesn't he have some commercials to finish?"

"We did those," Eddie told her. "Most of the ones we needed were done weeks ago. The ones with Peter in them were done last week."

Serena's hopes of finding Peter were dashed. Eddie and Peter had been friends since Peter went to WNYC. If Peter's secretary didn't know where he was and Eddie hadn't seen him, he couldn't be in the WNYC offices. Eddie and Peter had coffee together each morning and he was one of the people Peter spent a lot of time with. The two of them had been known to spend the night arguing over one political news point or another, over the methods of solving

some world crisis, then get up and play basketball like two
long-time team members who knew each other's moves
and complemented each other's playing ability. "If he
comes by, please ask him to call me."

"No problem, pretty lady."

Serena replaced the receiver and flopped into her chair.
Where was he? He knew she'd hate this and he'd purposely
disappeared. "The coward," she said aloud.

"Who's a coward?"

Bill DuBois lounged in the doorway. His arms were
folded across his chest and his shoulder leaned against the
door jamb.

"Bill, what are you doing here?" He was the last person
she expected to find in her office. Serena got up and went
toward him as he came forward with outstretched arms.
She kissed his cheek. "Sit down." The two of them sat in
the chairs in front of her desk. "I thought you had to be
back in Los Angeles days ago."

"I did and I was."

"What brought you back?" Serena was sorry the moment
she asked the question. She remembered her conversation
with Athena. Bill obviously was here to see her. Maybe he
even thought Athena had an appointment with her today.
"Athena tells me you two are an item."

"Athena reads a lot of fiction."

She isn't the only one, Serena thought to herself.

"So tell me what all these ads are about?"

Bill looked over his shoulder as if he were looking for
someone. Serena glanced toward the open door. No one
stood there and her secretary's desk was empty.

"You've seen them, too."

He nodded. "I've also seen the television commercials."

"Wha . . . at." Serena rolled her eyes to the ceiling.
"This can't be happening." She got up and went back to
her desk. "Excuse me, Bill. I have got to call Peter."

"It's all right. I think I can talk to that beautiful vice
president of yours. Chase?"

Serena stared after him. Had she heard a strange catch in his throat when he mentioned Chase? She shook her head, ignoring the imposed thought. She dialed the number to their house. The phone rang in her ear, then continued to ring until the answering machine clicked on. She slammed the phone down.

"It's on, Serena!" Her secretary rushed into her office. She went straight to the television and pushed the power button. She changed the station to WNYC and stood in front of the desk while the screen came to life.

A shot of the Manhattan skyline filled the nineteen-diagonal-inch screen. Overlaid on the World Trade Center was the same logo she'd seen on the taxis and buses. Then the camera moved up the New York Skyscrapers until only the sky remained and the words *Marry Me, Serena*. The rose was there, too. It flew around the words and settled under them before the full screen faded to black.

"You should have seen the whole thing, Serena. It was beautiful," Annette rushed on. "The music begins and you see several different places, Paris, Washington, D.C., someplace in the mountains with a waterfall running, and finally New York. Then the words appear over the city and—"

"I saw that part," Serena stopped the enthusiastic woman. She recognized the places. They were the cities where the two of them had been together, either on vacation or Serena visiting Peter on assignment.

"Isn't it the most romantic thing you've ever seen? If someone did that for me, I'd marry him in a minute."

Serena didn't want to say what she planned to do to Peter. She looked at her secretary. Annette Robinson was in love with love. Serena had been like that, too, when she was in her twenties.

"You are going to marry him, aren't you?" Annette's question brought her back to reality. "Of course, you are." She answered her own question. "How could anyone not marry him after this. Other than being the gorgeous hunk

of a man that millions of women drool over during the
evening news, it's like being asked on national television.
You just can't refuse."

Annette left the office and closed the door, plunging
Serena into a darkness that had nothing to do with how
much light flowed through the multi-windowed room.

Eddie Davis and Bill DuBois came into the gym at the
same time. Both wore shorts and T-shirts. Peter let the ball
he'd shot go. It hit the rim and rolled through the net,
then bounced to the floor unchecked. Eddie stared at
Peter Lawrence. His expression said it all. Peter knew how
he felt about lying to anyone, but to Serena, he hated it.
The two had a history, a mutual respect and Peter knew
he'd compromised it.

"How is she," he addressed Bill.

"She's a strong woman. Most of her office doesn't notice
any change. They think it's romantic and are envious. Only
Chase could see the strain. She's not taking it well," Bill
said.

"Hey, you guys gonna play or is this a conference?" Jack
Murray from Research came in. Jack was a practical joker
and always in a good frame of mind. Bill raised his hands
for the ball and the four of them spread out to play. Jack
and Eddie against Peter and Bill.

Jack passed the ball Peter had been using to practice
free throws and Bill grabbed it. He danced around Eddie
and shot it toward the goal. It went through with a swish.
"Nothing but net," he said.

Chapter 6

Serena continued to call the station and her house trying to find Peter to no avail. After an hour, she could stand it no longer. She dropped the phone in the cradle and resisted the effort to throw it across the room.

How could Peter subject her to this? She swung around to find her name plastered across the television screen, which was still on. Grabbing the remote control, she turned the sound up.

". . . *exactly who is Serena?*" the newscaster was saying. "*That's the question on most New Yorker's minds this afternoon as airwaves, billboards, buses, and taxicabs all ask the same question.*"

Footage of a bus with the sign on its side rolled across the screen, followed by a taxi. Serena hit the power button on the remote control and the screen went dark. She went to the window and looked out on the city. He was out there somewhere. And he was asking her to marry him. What was her answer? Should she marry him? They were compatible on every level, she told herself, remembering last night's lovemaking. Her body warmed with the glow of thought. Could anyone else give her this feeling even when he wasn't in the same room, wasn't touching her? Could anyone else seduce her with only the thought of him? She didn't think so.

Serena mentally gave Peter the advantage on that score. What about other things? They had been separated for years, not really living together except for short periods. Could their relationship withstand time and space together? She didn't know. She wanted to tell herself it could, that being with Peter was the most important thing in the world, that she knew his faults and could accept them and that he knew and accepted hers. The last few days, after her accident, had been wonderful, almost like a honeymoon. He was always there. They talked, laughed, made love. She could find no fault in what they were to each other.

The staggering divorce rate was by far the disadvantage of getting married. She thought of all the weddings she'd been in or attended. She could count the number of couples who were still together and they were few. They hated each other now and some wouldn't appear in the same room with the other.

Serena knew they had begun just as she and Peter had, loving each other, wanting to spend their lives together, but somewhere along the line something had happened. One of them or both of them had changed. Had that already happened to them? Peter had traveled extensively and she had only visited him on some of his assignments.

She didn't want things to change for the worse and marriage seemed to make that happen. Chase had been married to a wonderful guy. Yet with all the love between them their marriage had disintegrated. Her own parents had the same thing. Then her father died and although his death certificate said lung cancer, she knew the downfall of his marriage had contributed to his will to live.

No, she decided, even with the television and billboards screaming her name, she thought it better not to marry.

* * *

He had to be there, Serena told herself. She couldn't stand being in her office any longer with her secretary thinking this was the most romantic thing in the world and everyone coming to tell her when the next commercial was on. Ten minutes ago she'd grabbed her purse and coat and headed for WNYC. The weather was calm and sunny for the end of January but it could have been a tornado outside and Serena wouldn't have noticed it.

By the time she arrived she'd worked herself into a burning headache and had enough tension to detonate a nuclear bomb. At the end of the building an ambulance startled her by suddenly turning on its siren. Serena stopped and took a deep breath, holding her heart to control its beating. She waited a moment, not wanting to go in looking angry. She let her heart return to a normal beat then approached the door. Smiling and signing the visitors register she passed the receptionist who thankfully did not mention the ads. At Peter's office she found his secretary who told her he was in the gym.

Serena yanked the door open several minutes later. She was ready to do battle. Peter had set her up and left her. She wouldn't take that lying down. He had some explaining to do and it better be good. Stepping inside she found the room lighted but empty. It was quiet with the unmistakable smell of recent use. Her anger returned in force. Where was he?

She turned around. Eddie Davis opened the door before she reached it. "Thank God I found you," he said.

Something about the way he said it made her afraid. "What's wrong, Eddie?"

He was wearing gym shorts and a shirt. Usually he dressed like a derelict, but he never sat at his desk at this time of year wearing shorts.

"Peter's been taken to the hospital. He's had an accident."

Serena gripped her throat. She reached for support and
Eddie took her hand, then her shoulder. "Sit down," he
said, leading her to a chair at the edge of the floor. "You're
not gonna faint on me, pretty lady." Serena looked up at
Eddie's warm brown eyes. "He's going to be all right. I'm
sure of it."

"Where did they take him?" She tried to get up.

"Don't move," Eddie told her. "I'll get us a cab."

Twenty minutes later Serena and Eddie walked through
the doors of the emergency room. Bill DuBois met them
coming in.

"Where is he?" Serena asked.

"They've put him in one of the rooms."

"Has the doctor seen him yet?" she asked.

"I think they need you."

Serena rushed to the nurses' station and identified herself. Several nurses sat behind the desk. Others walked
back and forth to the curtained cubicles carrying trays with
medicines and syringes. The room was busy and everyone
seemed to be needed somewhere. Serena felt a little in
the way.

"Are you related to Mr. Lawrence?"

The nurse started to hand her a clip board with forms
attached to it.

"I'm his fiancée." Serena reached for the forms, but
they were pulled back.

"I need a blood relative or a spouse."

"We're engaged," she said. Bill came to stand next to
her. He laid a hand on her shoulder for support.

"I'm sorry, but the law states we can only have authorization from a next of kin, legal guardian, or spouse."

"Does that mean he isn't getting any medical care? That
you're letting him lay there in pain?" Horrible images of
Peter, bleeding and suffering went through her head.

"No," the nurse said emphatically. "There is only so
much we are allowed to do without authorization."

"But—"

"Ms. Coleman," she said calmly. "Your arguments won't change the law. What they will do is delay him getting additional care. If you know his next of kin, please call them and ask them to get here as soon as possible." She paused and looked compassionately at Serena. "We'll do the best we can until they arrive."

"Can I see him?"

She nodded. "He's in number four."

Serena turned to Bill. He steadied her for a moment. "Do you have phone numbers for Peter's brothers?"

"Yes . . . no," she said. "I mean I don't have them with me."

"I'll call the office and have them look up the numbers," Eddie said.

"They're not there, not on his insurance forms. My name is there."

"I'll call his secretary and ask her to look in his Rolodex."

"No," she stopped him. "Peter's Rolodex is still at home. Call my secretary. They're in my office."

Bill led Serena to the room where Peter lay. Ironically, he was in the same bed she'd been in only a few weeks ago. He was asleep, pale looking, with an IV dripping in his arm. Bill held onto her as if he expected her to faint. She went to the bed and took his hand. He didn't move.

"What happened?" she asked, keeping her attention on Peter.

"We were playing ball and he got knocked down. His head hit the floor and he was out for a few minutes. He said he was all right when he came to but when he stood up he passed out again. We called 911."

It couldn't be more than a concussion, Serena thought. She looked at his pillow for any signs of blood. She found none.

Eddie came in then. "I reached his brother, Michael, in Philadelphia. He's on his way."

"Thank you, Eddie," Serena said. Philadelphia was

almost three hours away. If they drove, even if they flew it
would take hours to get through the traffic at La Guardia.
All the while all she'd be able to do was sit here and wait.
She didn't know Bill and Eddie had left her alone. She
only knew that Peter had not stirred at all. She sat with him,
checking her watch every few seconds. Watching minute by
minute as time moved on its slow path.

When would Michael arrive and what would he do? She
knew Peter better than anyone alive. She knew how he'd
felt about organ donation, catastrophic injury, and life
support. She knew what he did and didn't eat, what medicines he'd developed an allergy to. His family knew nothing
of this. She'd had more contact with him than any other
person, yet she was helpless under the system. If they were
married, she could have signed the papers, filled out the
forms, and he would at this moment be getting the treatment he needed. Yet here they both were in some limbo
waiting room where everything moved in slow motion. She
waited here, alone and scared, until Michael Lawrence
could get here.

"Serena." She turned at the sound of her name. Bill
DuBois stood beside her.

"Is Michael here yet?" she asked.

He shook his head. "I've brought you something to eat
and drink. You should come out and eat it, then you can
come back."

Serena didn't argue with him. She stood up, knowing
Bill had done that to get her to move. She'd been sitting
in the same position so long her back ached. Eddie was
still in the waiting area when she came out. The three of
them sat in virtual silence, eating sandwiches that tasted
like sawdust and drinking coffee that was oily and bitter.
Several nurses came in and out, seeing to their comfort.
Serena thought they should be giving as much attention
to Peter as they were to her. Then she remembered Bill
DuBois, not the man she knew, but the movie star. They

weren't attending to her as much as they were trying to gain his attention.

Chase was shown in by another nurse a few minutes later. Bill stood up when he saw her. She went to him and took his arm, but looked at Serena. Serena couldn't help looking at the expression on the nurse's face as she backed out the door. Chase left Bill and came to her friend. "He's going to be all right, Serena."

The two of them stared at each other and then Chase took her in her arms and rocked her for a few minutes. She spoke soothing words in her ear, but Serena didn't hear them. She was thinking about Peter. She had to go back to him. Just being close to him was enough. Maybe he could feel her love through the curtain that kept him from her. She pushed Chase back.

"I'm all right, Chase." Serena worked at keeping her voice calm. "I'm going back now. Please let me know when Michael arrives."

Chase started after her but Bill stopped her. "She needs to be there," she heard him say as she walked back down the hall. Serena resumed her seat and took Peter's hand. His coloring didn't look any better. His skin tone was grayish, not at all the golden brown she knew it to be. Where was that happy smile that could turn her blood to fire and have her crawling all over him with his touch?

She questioned her decision to marry him. She'd been on her way to tell him she wouldn't marry him and now he lay helpless in this bed, not even knowing she was here.

"Please, Peter," she prayed. "Wake up." She rocked back and forth, holding onto his hand, talking to him, praying to herself. Hours seemed to pass, yet it was only minutes when she looked at her watch. Serena looked at the curtain, hoping Michael would walk through it, hoping he would arrive and help would be given to Peter.

Several minutes later Serena checked her watch again. She heard the commotion before the curtain was pulled aside. Erika Lawrence stood there for a second, then rushed to her. The two women hugged. They hadn't seen each other since her wedding to Peter's brother.

"It's going to be all right," she whispered. Serena was crying. She was so glad, so relieved they were finally here, she felt her knees weaken. "Michael is talking to the doctor now. Everything is going to be all right."

"Erika, thank you," Serena said through her tears. "I'm so glad you're here."

Michael Lawrence came to the room. He put his hand on Serena's and she looked up at him. Serena grabbed his hand and squeezed it, sandwiching Erika between them. For a long moment he stared at Peter. Then he moved around them and went to stand by the bed. Serena turned to watch him. Neither of them said anything.

"We need you," Michael finally broke the silence. He turned to face her. "There are some questions that need answering."

Serena sniffed and wiped her eyes with her fingertips. She knew more answers than anyone about Peter's medical history. For fourteen years she'd been his contact, she'd been everything to him, and now they'd waited nearly an hour to get her to answer questions she could have provided earlier. She checked her anger and followed Michael out of the room.

Doctors and nurses steadily filed in and out of the area the moment she and Michael answered all the questions and he signed the forms. They all waited, Bill and Chase, Eddie, Erika and Michael. Several people from WNYC came down making the room appear small and crowded.

Serena could see the curtain around his room move constantly with a flow of people and equipment going in and out. The more people who joined the group the more afraid she became. She continued to check the time. How long would it take to find out he was all right? How come they were sending so many people inside? What was all that equipment needed for?

"Serena," Eddie whispered. He stepped in front of her,

obstructing her view. "They know what they're doing. He's going to be all right."

Serena nodded. She was incapable of speaking. She knew if she opened her mouth, she'd babble and if she started she wouldn't be able to stop herself. Peter had to be all right. He had to recover. She had to be able to tell him she loved him one more time. This couldn't be the end of their life together.

Around Eddie, Serena saw the white coat approaching. She quickly stood up and went to the door. Eddie turned, following and Michael and Erika came up behind her.

"I'm Dr. Weiss," he said when he stopped. "Mr. Lawrence is going to be all right," the doctor said. Serena's hand went out again and this time Eddie caught it. She felt his free hand push into the small of her back helping to support her. He must have known her legs would give. She'd been living on adrenalin for the last few hours and the sudden drop in levels would have put her on the floor, but for Eddie and his insight.

"Can I see him?"

"We're having him moved to a room. We want to keep him under observation for twenty-four hours. If nothing changes . . . and I don't expect it will," he stopped Serena's question. "He'll be released tomorrow." He paused and looked at her directly. "As soon as he's settled in I'll have the nurses take you to him."

He smiled and left her. Eddie still supported her back. Five minutes later the nurse came to take her to see him. Erika and Michael went, too, while the others said good night and they would call the next day.

"Do you need anything?" Chase asked, standing next to Bill.

For the first time memories of Chase and Bill seemed to congeal in Serena's mind. Bill showing up in her office. He wasn't there to see her, he'd come to see Chase. She didn't say anything, but shook her head.

"Call me if you do," she said. "I'll be at home." Chase hugged her, Bill kissed her cheek.

She watched them leave before turning to go to Peter's room. Entering it this time with less trepidation than when she'd arrived several hours earlier.

"The nurse said he probably won't wake up before morning," Michael told her. Serena looked at Peter. He looked different. The light was soft and he looked like he was sleeping comfortably. Michael and Erika left the room without her hearing them. Serena leaned over the side of the bed and stroked his face. She stared at him as if he were her child and she wanted him to feel better. Then she sat down and took Peter's hand. It was warm and strong and tomorrow he would be fully awake and know that someone was there, that she loved him and would always love him.

As darkness became night, Serena thought about Peter's question. It was only last night he'd asked her to marry him and today she'd decided not to. She no longer felt that way. She wanted to tie her life to his. She knew that losing him would kill her. She also knew that her feelings for Peter couldn't be compared with any other marriage; not Chase's, not their friends', and not her parents'. Marriage between herself and Peter would be totally different. It would survive, not because they loved each other, but because they would work at it. They would keep their love alive and that's what would make it last forever.

Chapter 7

The phone rang all morning with well wishers and people concerned about Peter's condition. Erika took over fielding the calls and Serena let her do it. Unless it was Peter or the hospital, Serena was unavailable to everyone except Chase, Bill, and Eddie. She checked the window looking for Michael's car. He'd gone to bring Peter home when the hospital released him. By her watch they should be back any moment now.

She saw the taxi the moment it turned on her street. "They're here," she called, jumping up from the sofa and running toward the door. Erika followed her with a coat. She pushed it around Serena.

"Put this on," she said when they were standing on the street. "We don't want you to get sick, too."

The cab stopped and Peter threw the door open. He had nothing on his head. Serena thought he'd have a bandage. He got out and hugged her. "I missed you."

"Peter, I've never been so scared in my life." She shuddered in his arms, closing her eyes and thanking God he was all right and had been returned to her.

Erika hustled them inside. It was freezing outdoors and neither of them appeared to notice it.

If Michael and Erika hadn't been there, she would have shipped him off to bed, the same as he'd done to her after her mishap. But Peter settled onto the sofa and Erika came in with a tray. She poured coffee and tea into cups and passed around platters of sandwiches. Peter ate hungrily.

"Erika and I can leave now without any regard for your health," Michael teased. "Anyone with an appetite like yours has got to be all right."

"It was just a bump on the head. Let's not make a big deal of it."

"Peter!" Serena said. "You were close to comatose yesterday."

Peter took her hand. "I was just trying to get some needed sleep."

Michael laughed. Erika and Serena didn't see the humor. For an hour they talked about accidents, Peter travels, their families, and finally Michael suggested they leave.

"Well, now that you're back on the road to recovery, Erika and I have to head for home. We know we're leaving you in capable hands."

Serena liked Michael and Erika. She enjoyed spending time with them, but right now she wanted Peter to herself. She was glad they had decided to leave.

On the steps, they said goodbye and Serena thanked them for coming so promptly. Serena invited them back anytime. Erika got in the car while Michael shook hands with his brother. Then he hugged Serena and joined his wife.

Erika drove away while Peter and Serena waved goodbye. They were finally alone. If the phone rang, she would ignore it. All she wanted was to spend time with Peter.

"How do you feel?" she asked when they were inside.

"I'm fine."

Peter took her arm and led her back to the sofa. They

sat down. He kept her close to him, putting his arm around her and cradling her in his embrace.

"You know, when I knew I was falling and that I was going to hit my head I thought of you."

Serena smiled and reached up and kissed him.

"I don't mean I just thought of you. I thought of losing you, of life without you."

"That's exactly what I thought while I sat in that hospital waiting for Michael and Erika. I felt helpless. If we had been married I could have signed the papers and you wouldn't have had to lay there for hours before a doctor saw you."

"It's okay. Everything worked out for the best."

"I kept thinking, if only we were married, then these things wouldn't have to be this way."

"Serena," Peter spoke very quietly. "Are you saying you'll marry me."

"Not because hospital bureaucracy reared up and slapped me in the face." She got up and sat on the table facing him. "I had a lot of time to think while I waited. I thought of all the good times we'd had together and how I might lose those times. I thought of our children and how I couldn't imagine being without you. I thought of how much my life was entwined with yours, but it wasn't enough."

"I don't understand."

"I need more, Peter. I discovered it sitting in that hospital. I need to be able to declare to the world in whatever place we happened to be, that our lives are together, that we come as a package deal. We will always be one and that we couldn't be one unless we were married and not only in our own eyes, but in the eyes of the world."

Peter stared at her. He didn't say a word. He was quiet so long it made Serena nervous.

"Peter, I'm asking you to marry me."

Peter stared mutely at her.

"Are you going to say something?" Had she waited too

long? Had Peter's stay in the hospital made him change his mind?

Without a word Peter stood up and walked away.

"Peter!"

He went into the bedroom. Tears welled in Serena's eyes. She'd certainly lost him. Then she felt his warmth next to her on the table. He handed her an envelope. Serena pushed her tears aside and pulled the single sheet of paper out. She read it.

"You sent in for this?"

He nodded.

"I'll marry you, Serena, on Valentine's Day and in the Rainbow Room."

Tears seemed to gush from her eyes. "You won?"

"We won," he corrected her. "For fourteen years I've wanted to marry you. Valentine's Day and the Rainbow Room seems perfect."

"What did you write?" she asked.

"I'll tell you at the wedding."

Serena stood outside the doors of the Rainbow Room. Atop a Rockefeller skyscraper, sixty-five floors above the ground, she heard the music as Chase and Erika, her only bridesmaids, went down the aisle. It was her turn now and the doors were closed. She could feel the energy in the room, hear the hushed whispers of their friends waiting for her to appear. Serena was more nervous than she thought she'd ever be. She was sure of what she was doing, marrying Peter was the right decision. She loved him more than anything else in the world. She knew it in her heart.

It was all the fanfare that was getting to her. The *Marry Me, Serena* commercials and ads had complicated her life. The press found out who she was and they'd pounced on her. Then the fact that she agreed to marry Peter added to their frenzy for more information. Chase loved it. It

brought business into the firm. They were hiring new staff members to handle the increasing workload.

Michael took her arm and slipped it through his. "Ready?" he asked.

She nodded and the doors opened. Roses! The smell filled the room, turning it into a garden. Serena knew there were twenty dozen of them. They represented their years together, the years apart, all the special times of their lives. And they fulfilled a promise—to fill the room with roses.

The "Wedding March" began and Serena and Michael took a step toward the aisle. She saw Peter, standing with Bill and Eddie. Her smile was spontaneous. Eddie'd been hiding behind the street clothes and dreads. He cut a handsome figure dressed in white tie and tails.

At the altar, Michael kissed her on the forehead and Serena passed her basket of linen roses to Chase. The minister stood in front of them. He performed most of the ceremony, then said, "Today we're here to witness the nuptials of Ms. Serena Coleman and Mr. Peter Lawrence. Please listen while Mr. Lawrence recites his vows."

Peter turned and looked into Serena's eyes. They were bright with happiness. He could find no doubt or uncertainty reflected there. She was truly his and today they would begin building the rest of their lives together. Peter remembered the words he'd written on the contest entry form and he began to recite them for Serena.

"We all want our lives to be rainbows. The day we met the first rainbow piece fell into place. As our love grew other pieces, some bright some dull, fell into our hands. We used them, placed them into our personal rainbow, giving them a place in our lives. A lifetime ago I pledged my love to you. Today I pledge it again for now and always. A love that began with a single flash of light. One that did not have many colors, but one which required we build it day by day. Today, in this room, the Rainbow Room, I vow that the rainbow we started building, which glows brightly with color, will continue to be built until the colors are blindingly vivid, like the love we share and will always share.''

The minister finished the ceremony, but Serena would remember only the words "I do" spoken by herself and Peter. The rest was lost to her. Her mind whirled with the words Peter had spoken. Tears rolled from her eyes and she looked at him with glistening eyes as he kissed her before God and these witnesses.

Epilogue

Serena stretched across the bed like a lazy cat, the sheet wrapped around her like satin skin. She extended her hand as far as an arm's length, looking at the glittering wedding ring Peter had put on her third finger six weeks ago today. It was their anniversary. Unfortunately, they'd only had a two-day honeymoon before Peter had to begin anchoring the news.

It had been a glorious two days and every day since had begun and ended as if she were living inside a fairy tale. Serena heard the clock chiming in the hall. Peter would come through the door before the gong ended its hourly count. More a creature of habit than she was, Serena heard the door close in the still morning's quiet exactly as she anticipated.

Then Peter's footsteps sounded on the polished wood flooring. He headed toward the stairs and the bedroom beyond. Serena felt her body warming, arousing in anticipation of him joining her. She sat up, holding the sheet with one hand, as he came through the bedroom door.

As usual he stood a moment gazing at her. Then he pulled his tie free and came to the bed.

Sitting down he didn't say a word. He stared at her in the semi-darkness, his eyes hooded and unreadable, but Serena knew what they looked like. She knew how they darkened, almost melted, with desire. Peter's hand came up and brushed her hair. Serena leaned into it. Then it went to her bare shoulder and slid down her arm taking the sheet along with it.

Her breasts pointed toward him, already puckered, hardening into peaks that waited for his hands and mouth to touch them, bring them to full life, teach them their one true purpose. Peter's gaze stared at her, taking a slow route up her body over her lips to her eyes.

Slipping his arms about her waist, he pulled her toward him. His jacket felt rough next to her bare skin.

"You should be asleep," he whispered.

"I can't sleep without you." Her voice sounded dark, low and sexy as her body felt. "It has something to do with being married. Married people sleep together."

Serena raised her arms around his neck. Peter kissed her, teasing her mouth, biting on her lower lip, but moving out of reach when she tried to deepen the kiss. He tortured her, offering himself, then pulling back as she tried to get more. She loved the torture, and he knew it.

Gasping, Serena threw her head back and looked at Peter. She heard his groan as he yanked her forward and took her mouth in a deeply passionate kiss that joined their mouths in the same measure as they would join their bodies. His hands slipped over her naked frame, burning down her back and over her buttocks, caressing her legs as he moved the white sheet to uncover her wine-dark skin.

Serena thought she'd run out of breath and she didn't care. Peter suffocated her, made her dizzy, light-headed with feeling. She turned in the bed, arching her back and pressing herself into him. Volcanic heat surged through her as she traced his arms and chest, bringing her hands down to feel his hardness.

Suddenly his clothes were a great barrier. Serena wanted to touch him, know the warmth, the dampness of his skin, smell the essence of him, inhale the love that burned when they joined. She opened his belt and tugged his shirt loose.

"Take it off," she whispered.

Peter stood. He unbuttoned the shirt and dropped tie, jacket and shirt in one smooth movement. Serena was already naked in the bed. She sat on her knees watching him. The sheet covered her in places, over one leg, around her hips, teasingly hiding the one place his body desired to be. His erection pointed toward her as the last of his clothing fell to the floor.

Stepping onto the bed, one knee at a time, Peter joined Serena. He'd waited all day for this moment. His hand cupped her face as his body pressed into her. She gasped a pleasing sound as contact surprised and excited her. He kissed her swollen mouth, pushing her head back and holding her against him. His long arms wrapped nearly all the way around her allowing him to fondle the soft flesh of her side breasts. Then he pushed his way down and took her hardened nipple inside his mouth.

It was like having her. Her back arched as she took a deep breath and held it, letting his mouth drive her, race pleasure signals to every nerve ending in her body. He loved this body, this vessel that accommodated him, giving him her unconditional love. Peter shuddered as she reached between them and took him in her hands. His knees turned to water but his nerves pointed and held in an effort to keep him upright. Millions of euphoric senses shot to attention at the way her hands cradled him, stroked him, moved over the tip of his erection with an insanity-producing effect. Peter wanted to howl. He forced it down, until only a groan escaped. Serena was driving him over the edge.

In one lightning movement, he grabbed her arms and

dropped her sideways on the mattress. He swung above her and opened her legs. Sliding inside her he was already crazy with need. Serena wrapped her legs around him, pulling them closer together and starting the rhythm that drove them to the brink of madness. In the weeks since their wedding, their lovemaking had taken them to a higher level.

Her body felt tight around him, clinching him to her, as he pulled and pushed himself into her Garden of Eden. He thrust into her. She accepted all of him, taking him inside, pulling him by some invisible cord that had him blindly dancing like a puppet to music they composed. The tempo changed, increased, forcing him to thrust harder, faster, until the rhythm escalated to fever pitch. Peter didn't know he could move this fast and feel this good at the same time. She made him do it, had him lost in ecstasy, unable to think. He could only feel and he knew he'd die from the rapture that flowed through his blood. It soared through him as fast as light leaving the sun.

Peter grasped Serena's hips and rolled them under him, imprisoning her in his cocoon of nerve endings, working with her until the two of them became a shining burst of light that exploded into a shattering array of diamonds, flung at the walls like bright facets, each one creating its own star-burst as it touched on the walls and faded into the love-heated air.

Peter dropped, deflated, spent to the mattress. He rolled onto his side taking Serena with him. He hugged her tight, burying his face in her hair, keeping her with him, knowing if he let her go the world would break in half.

They lay like that for a long time. Serena had never been so happy, so fulfilled. They'd made love hundreds of times, but it had never been this intense, this complete. Serena thought her feelings would remain the same after she married Peter, but she'd been wrong. She loved him more now, feeling they had grown closer, that they had completed a puzzle she didn't even know she was working on.

"Regretting marrying me?" Peter asked. She could hear the smile in his voice.

Serena looked up at him. She kissed his chin. "I'll never regret that," she told him, putting her finger where her mouth had been.

Peter hugged her closer. She felt the difference in his touch. It was tender, caressing, a touch as light as a feather, yet as strong as human bonding. He often held her like this when emotion overtook him and he couldn't formulate words. She'd been so set against marrying and he equally for it. Now that they were husband and wife she wanted him to know she'd been wrong.

"Marrying you was the one perfect thing I did." She paused. "The only thing that could have been more perfect was a longer honeymoon."

"Don't worry about missing a real honeymoon. We'll do it next year, on our first anniversary."

A grin spread on Serena's face. "I don't think so," she said.

"Why not?"

"Remember that night you told me Michael's final words that would make me marry you?"

Peter frowned. She could see his features change with the shadows.

"He said I should remove all your arguments."

Serena stared at him, waiting for more. "How were you going to do that?" she prompted.

"I was going to tell you . . ." His eyes opened wide. Serena could almost see the light bulb turning on in his head. "I was going to tell you I was pregnant."

"Bingo!"

Peter sat up, almost propelled upward. He tried to speak, but stammered over every word. Serena watched the efficient anchorman, one known for never flubbing his lines, never tripping over a foreign name, or requiring a retake, completely lose his ability to converse in English at the news that he would be a father this time next year.

How could she have ever doubted being married to him? He was exactly what she wanted. Their love would change as time passed. It would grow and thrive and live a long and happy life.

Dear Reader,

Love is always in the air, especially at Valentine's Day. Serena and Peter won the real-life contest sponsored by the Rainbow Room and in addition to candy and flowers they got to have their wedding in the beautiful facility overlooking New York. Peter, you may remember as Michael Lawrence's brother from my book, *Legacy*. Serena came to me from my days of "helping out" in the public relations department of an aerospace company. I enjoyed telling Serena and Peter's story and discovering how great a love they have for each other.

I receive many letters from the women and men who read my books. Thank you for you generous comments and words of encouragement. I love reading your letters as much as I enjoy writing the books.

If you'd like to hear more about upcoming releases or others I've written, send a business size, self-addressed, stamped envelope to me at the following address:

P.O. Box 513
Plainsboro, NJ 08536

Sincerely yours,

Shirley Hailstock

ABOUT THE AUTHORS

Robyn Amos's book PROMISE ME was her debut into Arabesque. She lives in Gaithersburg, Maryland where she is writing her next romance.

Gwynne Forster is the pseudonym for an author who lives in New York City, New York. She is a former demographer for the United Nations and has traveled the world. She is busily working on her next Arabesque title.

Shirley Hailstock is a best-selling and award-winning novelist, who holds a degree in chemistry from Howard University and an MBA from Fairleigh Dickinson University. She is a former adjunct professor of accounting at Rutgers University and currently is a systems manager at Bracco Diagnostics. She lives in New Jersey with her family.

Look for these upcoming Arabesque titles:

March 1998

KEEPING SECRETS by Carmen Green
SILVER LOVE by Layle Giusto
PRIVATE LIES by Robyn Amos
SWEET SURRENDER by Angela Winters

April 1998

A PUBLIC AFFAIR by Margie Walker
OBSESSION by Gwynne Forster
CHERISH by Crystal Wilson Harris
REMEMBRANCE by Marcia King-Gamble

May 1998

LOVE EVERLASTING by Anna Larence
TWIST OF FATE by Loure Bussey
ROSES ARE RED by Sonia Seerani
BOUQUET, An Arabesque Mother's Day Collection